Girl v. Boy

Yvonne Collins & Sandy Rideout

HYPERION · DBG
New York

All rights reserved. Published by Disney•Hyperion Books, an imprint of Disney Book Group. No part of this book may be reproduced or transmitted in any form or by any means, electronic or mechanical, including photocopying, recording, or by any information storage and retrieval system, without written permission from the publisher. For information address Disney•Hyperion Books, 114 Fifth Avenue, New York, New York 10011-5690.

First Disney•Hyperion paperback edition, 2009
1 3 5 7 9 10 8 6 4 2
V475-2873-0-09288
Printed in the United States of America
Library of Congress Cataloging-in-Publication Data on file.
ISBN 978-1-4231-0161-1

Visit www.hyperionteens.com

For our mothers,
Maria Collins and Bea Rideout

Chapter 1

I glance around the auditorium, trying to take everything in without looking like I'm remotely interested. "You'd think they'd at least hose the place down over the summer," I say.

"What good would it do?" Izzy asks, leading Rachel and me into our usual row. She stoops to inspect the rainbow of dried chewing gum on the underside of a folding seat before pushing it down with the stenciled tip of one long fingernail. "They should knock the building down and start over."

"It'd be a wreck again in a month," Rachel says, settling into the seat beside Izzy. "No one cares enough to keep it nice."

The evidence supports her claim. Graffiti covers most of the seats, paint hangs from the walls in strips, and one of the curtains framing the stage has a large, reddish stain in the shape of a human body. Mrs. Alvarez—more commonly known as Principal Buzzkill—probably leaves it there to remind us what could happen if we screw up. That's what school assemblies are all about.

"Welcome back to Dumpfield," I say. Everyone uses the nickname, although the tarnished lettering over the stage reads Colonel *Dun*field High School.

Climbing over my friends' legs, I take the seat beside Izzy and plunk my backpack into the one beyond that. I always reserve an empty seat beside me during school assemblies for my FB (future boyfriend). I haven't met him yet, but if he shows up at the end of our row, I'm ready to wave him into position like an air traffic controller bringing in a plane.

At the moment I don't have a CB (current boyfriend), or even an EB (ex-boyfriend). In fact, the letter B appears to be missing from my personal alphabet. I'd be more alarmed about that if Izzy and Rachel weren't victims of the same curse. In a school with a population of just over three thousand there must some cute, normal guys, but we never seem to meet any.

Still, I try to keep the faith, and for a few moments at the start of each assembly, I wait for my Dumpfield prince to arrive. It's about the only fun I have at school.

That and counting the hours until it's over. "Only seventy-four days till we're out of here for winter break," I announce.

Rachel groans. "Please tell me it's less than that. Did you subtract Thanksgiving?"

"Of course. And professional development days. Plus a sick day. We can count on one cold each term, I figure."

"I feel sick already," Rachel says, winding her dark,

curly hair into a tight bun and securing it with a pencil. "If you're trying to depress us, Lu, it's working."

Izzy reaches over and pulls a few strands from Rachel's bun. I've seen this move dozens of times, and it always makes me smile. Izzy's parents own Ortega's House of Beauty, and she's a born stylist.

"If I were trying to depress you, I'd have pointed out that it's one hundred and eighty-six days till summer vacation," I say. "Not to mention nearly six hundred until we graduate."

Rachel turns to check out the stream of students filing into the auditorium. "On the bright side, that's six hundred days to meet the guys who are trapped in this dump with us."

"We didn't meet any last year," Izzy says. She's usually the optimist of our trio, but I can't blame her for being a little down. Our freshman year was bleak, both socially and academically, and this one probably won't be any different.

"Heads up," Rachel says. "The queen is in the house."

I generally use a different five letter word to describe Mariah Mendes, who is striking a pose at the double doors of the auditorium, but I'm in the minority. As she lifts her shades to scan the room, sophomore hands fly up all around us. Most of them belong to guys who are eager to wave Air Mendes in for a safe landing beside them. This has less to do with her future girlfriend potential than her blatant defiance of the school dress code. She's wearing stiletto boots, Lycra warm-up pants, a short tank top, and a trucker hat, brim turned to the left. The ensemble breaks three rules: tops are required to meet bottoms, and both hats and sunglasses are prohibited inside.

Mariah has been above rules since she arrived in kindergarten wearing a pink tutu and bragging about being a ballerina. By fifth grade, she realized she needed backup and imported two friends from her dance classes. I call them the Understudies, because they're ready to step into Mariah's shoes at a moment's notice.

It doesn't seem possible (or remotely fair), but Mariah has gotten even better looking over the summer. Her tawny hair, golden skin, and amber eyes seem to glow. Her ego is probably bigger than ever, too. Last spring, Mariah made it onto a dance show called *The Right Moves*, one of twenty finalists out of the thousands who auditioned. That she was the first to get voted off the show hasn't fazed her in the slightest.

"She actually looks happy to be here," Izzy says.

"That's because she'll have a captive audience, five days a week," I say, as people around us call out to Mariah.

"Imagine what it would be like to have hundreds of people know your name," Izzy muses.

"I wonder what it would be like to have *ten* people know my name," I say.

"Ten people do know your name," Rachel says, smiling. "Ten people *have* your name."

She's referring to the nine other sophomores who share the name Luisa Perez. It's impossible to stand out when people have to scroll through a mental list of identical names to place you. Which Luisa Perez? The one with brown hair and eyes? Oh, right, that's all of us. The Luisa Perez who plays flute? The math whiz? Or the one who runs track? None of the above. I have no distinguishing talent of any kind.

"Eleven," Izzy corrects. "There's a new transfer in my homeroom."

"Great," I say. "I'm officially invisible."

Izzy sits up a little straighter in her seat and says, "Maybe not. Mac Landis is trying to get your attention."

I snort. Mac—short for MacEwan—Landis never wastes a second glance on me, despite the fact that he, like Mariah, attended my elementary and middle schools. Back then Mac was an average kid, but the God of Puberty was kind, and now he's Dunfield's answer to David Beckham, all blond good looks and athletic wizardry. Because of Mac, Dunfield made it into the basketball semifinals last year for the first time ever. More than four hundred students packed the stands to watch the last game. That might not be a big deal for some Chicago schools, but for Dunfield, known far and wide for its complete lack of school spirit, it's nothing short of a miracle.

"Izzy's right, he *is* checking you out," Rachel confirms. "Maybe Mac's the FB who's finally come to claim his throne."

"Or not," I say, more relieved than disappointed as Mac and his pals file into the row behind us.

"He's probably too cool to sit right beside a girl he likes," Izzy says, still hopeful.

Mac folds his six-foot-plus frame into a seat behind mine, and I turn to steal a look at him.

"Hey," he says.

To me. Mac Landis said "Hey" to *me*. I must have changed more than I thought over the summer. Sure, my

5

hair's a little longer and I've started wearing eyeliner, but I wouldn't have dreamed I'd ascended to Mac's league.

Rachel pulls the pencil from her hair and prods me into responding.

"Hey, Mac," I say. It's not much, but it's the closest we've come to a conversation since third grade, when he realized he was too cool for me.

I suppose it's possible that Mac became a nicer guy over the summer. Things like that happen sometimes, say, after a serious illness or accident. If Mac has experienced either one, however, it doesn't show. His face is still flawless.

One of Mac's pals points an index finger at me. "Can you move?"

"Move?" I ask. "Why?"

"Duh. Figure it out."

The guy looks to Mac for approval, but Mac simply smiles at me and says, "Sorry, the juice makes him edgy."

I'm too stunned to process what he's saying, let alone reply. There are popping noises in my head, possibly triggered by the brilliance of his teeth.

Mac's pal flexes his arm. "You're the one on 'roids, dude. This is all natural."

A cloud of perfume closes in, and I look up to see Mariah standing over me, her belly ring twinkling at eye level. "Move, Coconut," she says. "You're in my seat."

She calls me that because she thinks the quality Puerto Rican genes I inherited from my father have been smothered by those of my Irish American mother, who raised me alone. Mariah is a full-fledged Latina, thanks to two proud Puerto Rican parents, and Spanish is her first language. I barely knew a word of Spanish when I started class last year, but I've already picked up enough to know that what she's saying about me to the Understudies right now isn't flattering. There are so many dimensions to Mariah's bullying that I never tire of studying her—preferably from a distance.

"Not so fast," Mariah calls as I scramble after Izzy and Rachel. "I want to hear all about your summer, Coconut. Still slinging hash at the grease pit?"

Dan's Diner *is* a bit of a pit, but Dan himself is the nicest guy in the world. "Yeah," I say, taking a seat in the row ahead. "I like my job."

"Good, because you'll probably be there for life," Mariah says. "Just like your loser sister."

Grace isn't a loser, but she quit school three years ago and works at Dan's full-time. Although we're not exactly close, I feel obliged to defend her. "She's—"

Izzy squeezes my arm. "Don't."

I take her advice and let it go. Mariah has been known to turn the entire student body against someone with a single e-mail. It's one of many techniques she uses to bring insurgents in line. Normally I'm too far beneath her in the school hierarchy to warrant such attention, but better safe than sorry.

Mariah waits a moment and tries again. "Want me to sign a photo for the diner wall? You could pretend we're friends."

I'd love to point out that her fifteen minutes of fame expired when the reality show dumped her, but instead I smile sweetly. "That'd be great. We can put it beside Solana G.'s." As an up-and-coming R & B singer,

Solana is one of the few people Mariah admires.

"Solana comes to Dan's?" Mariah asks skeptically.

"All the time." Once, actually, but I served her.

"She's had her nails done at my parents' place, too," Izzy offers.

"Quiet," Rachel whispers. "Unless you want Mariah hanging around all the time."

"What are you saying about me, Klienberg?" Mariah demands.

Principal Alvarez saves us by clearing her throat at the microphone. As always, she's wearing a sharp suit, and her hair, with its distinctive slice of gray, is swept into an elegant bun. She dresses to intimidate, but underneath the starch and hair spray there's an attractive woman.

"Welcome back to Colonel Dunfield, sophomores," she says in the commanding voice that strikes fear into the hearts of all students—and many parents. "Let us begin by reviewing our code of conduct."

She directs a laser pointer at the screen and walks us through dozens of rules. But just before everyone completely tunes her out, Mrs. Alvarez switches gears.

"I have some exciting news," she says. "The mayor's office and the public school board are staging a citywide contest to see which school can raise the most money for literacy. The victor will be released for winter break two weeks early."

There's a long silence, broken at last by Mac Landis. "You mean we'd get a full month off?"

"Correct, MacEwan," Mrs. Alvarez says. The auditorium erupts into cheers, and she waits for the noise to subside before explaining that we still have to cover all of the same material in our classes, only faster.

"A full month?" Mac repeats, to be sure there's no mistake.

The principal sighs. "Only if Dunfield wins, MacEwan. The competition will be very stiff, I'm afraid. More than a hundred schools are participating."

Mariah elects herself spokesqueen. "We'll win, Principal Alvarez, I promise."

I notice that Mariah's hat and sunglasses have vanished, although her belly ring twinkles on.

"Glad to hear it, Maria," Mrs. Alvarez says, dropping the H in her name. Our principal is less impressed with reality dance shows than she is with sports trophies she can display in the empty glass case outside her office. "Especially since Colonel Dunfield has a rather poor record for extracurricular participation."

There's another cheer, and Principal Buzzkill cuts it short. "That's nothing to be proud of, people. With that attitude, Turnbull Academy will walk away with the prize."

Turnbull is located in one of Chicago's best neighborhoods, where students could probably raise big bucks just by hitting up their parents for donations. On the other hand, the prize might be a bigger incentive for Dunfield's students; Turnbull is so nice I bet no one even wants a vacation.

Mrs. Alvarez ups the ante a little more. "I want the girls to organize half of the fund-raising events, and boys the other half. Let's make it a battle of the sexes."

At the word "sexes," wolf whistles ring out.

"Oh, grow up!" Mariah shouts, and the girls back her in a shrill chorus. "We'll wipe the floor with you guys."

"Bring it on," Mac calls, and the whistles get louder.

Mrs. Alvarez cuts in. "Elect your own leaders. And if Dunfield wins, I'll give the team that impresses me most an extra three days' vacation for spring break."

Mrs. Alvarez is still talking, but no one can hear her over the applause.

English is the only class Rachel, Izzy, and I have in common this year, so we arrive early to stake out adjacent desks at the back of the room.

Rachel caresses the seat ahead of her. "Jason can sit right here."

She's had it bad for Jason Baca since seventh grade, but her parents will only let her date Jewish guys.

"Have your parents given in?" Izzy asks, applying a fresh coat of lip gloss.

Rachel shakes her head. "They'll never give in because the whole 'Jewish boy' thing is just a cover for the fact that they don't want me dating period. Why else would they send me here, where eighty percent of the population is Hispanic? They want to keep me a virgin forever."

"If they want Jewish grandkids, they'll have to relent someday," I say. "Maybe that's why they sent you to work at your uncle's lodge this summer—to meet the right kind of guys."

"Please. The only male counselor was gay. It was the worst summer job ever."

Izzy rolls her eyes. "You spent the summer far from

your controlling parents, whereas I had to work *for* my controlling parents."

Although Izzy complains about her parents' salon, I notice she hangs out there even when she's not scheduled to work. She certainly enjoys the perks: free color, cuts, and manicures. No one has seen her natural, mousy brown hair for years.

"At least you came home from work looking—and smelling—better than when you went in," I say. "I stank of stale coffee and french fries."

And my perfume isn't likely to change anytime soon, because I work at Dan's Diner year-round. Rachel and Izzy aren't allowed to work during the school term because they have to focus on their studies. With Dunfield leading the district only in the area of dropout rates, a lot of parents worry. Rachel's mom does more than that. She reviews Rachel's homework daily, sweeps her bedroom for drugs weekly, meets with her teachers monthly, and performs irregular—and unannounced—locker checks. It's pretty embarrassing for Rachel, but at least her mother cares.

My mother cares about me, but she's not interested in my schoolwork, or education in general. She dropped out of Dunfield herself after tenth grade when she got pregnant with Grace. Now she's a nursing assistant at Cook County Hospital, working mostly nights for the higher wage.

Even with all the extra shifts Mom picks up, we don't live in luxury. There's always food in the fridge, and I never have to scrimp on school supplies or class trips, but Mom's paycheck doesn't stretch much farther than that. I need my job if I want to have a cell phone and decent jeans. Plus, if Mom's feeling the pinch at the end of the month, I have to help out with the bills.

Mr. Sparling steps into the classroom and drops two boxes on his desk with a thud. "Oh, good," he says. "Volunteers."

We complain for effect as we distribute the textbooks, but Mr. Sparling taught us last year as well, and we actually like him. He's the only teacher I've ever had who bothers to try to make his lessons interesting. I didn't even mind the homework, and that translated into my first B plus ever. I was planning to aim even higher this year, but with a natural sedative like Greek mythology on the program, it could be tough.

The classroom fills up, and Mr. Sparling starts talking about how Zeus and his siblings defeated the almighty Kronos and divided the universe. Poseidon got the seas, Hades the underworld, and Zeus the heavens and the earth.

After a while my mind and my pen start to wander. What would happen at Colonel Dunfield if Izzy, Rachel, and I dared to revolt against the almighty Mariah?

The battle raged for days. Hair clips flew, mascara ran, and Lycra pants burst at the seams. The Dancers spent so much time posing for each other and the Jocks that they underestimated their opponents and missed the fatal ambush.

When the dust finally cleared, the Dancers had surrendered to the Mighty Trio. Medusa agreed to turn the Dancers to stone, freezing them for all

eternity in the hamstring stretch. The Mighty Trio
sentenced Mac and the Jocks to a perpetual game of
basketball, in which the hoops are smaller than the
balls.

Their enemies thus neutralized, the Mighty Trio
divided their territory according to their interests:

- *Rachel became the Goddess of Fitness and*
  Nutrition, ruling over Dunfield's athletic
  facilities and cafeteria.
- *Izzy became Goddess of Beauty and Drama,*
  ruling over the girls' locker room, restrooms,
  and auditorium.
- *Lu became Goddess of Uniqueness, granting*
  each student a special trait of his or her own.

The Mighty Trio ruled for years with gentle
grace, allowing the males of the kingdom to compete
for their favor. They selected only the fairest and
most decent as their consorts.

It was a peaceful time, in which gold ran like
water from the fountains and—

"Ms. Perez?"

I look up from my notebook to find Mr. Sparling
standing over me. My classmates lift their heads from their
mythology textbooks to watch.

"I stopped talking five minutes ago," he continues.
"Unless you want me to read your diary aloud, you'd better close it and start reading."

I scramble to put my notebook away and open the
textbook, as Rachel and Izzy stifle nervous giggles.

Mr. Sparling walks back to his desk. "I'll have a word with you after class, Ms. Perez."

Rachel pounces as the classroom door closes behind me. "Tell me he didn't give you detention for writing in class?"

"No detention," I say. "He wants me to write a column for the *Dunfield Bulletin*."

"The what?" Izzy asks.

"The school paper," I say.

"Since when does Dunfield have a school paper?" Rachel asks.

"It was news to me too, but apparently it comes out every Friday. Mr. Sparling has taken over as editor, and he wants to run an anonymous column about the literacy fund-raisers."

The girls assume their regular positions on either side of me so that they can talk over my head if they feel like it. They both have five inches on me, and Izzy is taller still with heels and backcombing.

"Why anonymous?" she asks.

"Because we can be more honest if no one knows who we are. Buzzkill thinks the column will help encourage the 'battle of the sexes.'"

"We?" Rachel says.

"A guy is going to have a column, too. I'll write one week, he'll write the next."

Izzy stops walking to look at me. "You said yes?"

I understand why she sounds so surprised. Avoiding extracurricular activities is a point of pride for us. "Sparling really turned the screws."

14

It's not true, but for some reason it's easier to lie than admit he said my essays from last year showed a unique voice. I have no idea what that means, but it's the first time anyone's used the word "unique" in relation to *this* Luisa Perez. The whole Goddess of Uniqueness thing doesn't seem quite so farfetched anymore.

"I guess he couldn't find anyone else," I conclude.

"You're perfect for the job," Rachel declares. "Your e-mails kept me laughing all summer. The 'Notes on a Greasy Napkin' series was hilarious."

I'd forgotten that I made up stories about Dan's customers and sent them to Rachel. Maybe Mr. Sparling isn't totally off base.

"You'll do great," Izzy agrees. "But I don't see how you'll get to many events, with your schedule."

"I'm going to need help being in three places at once." I give them an ingratiating smile.

"I am not taking your shifts at Dan's," Izzy says. "I'd break my nails."

"Iz, she wants us to be her moles at the fund-raisers."

"But we have a policy against any display of school spirit," Izzy argues.

"I'm sorry to let down the cause of apathy, but I'll make it up to you, I promise."

"Free fries throughout the contest?" Rachel asks.

"Done," I say. Dan usually comps their tab anyway.

Izzy starts walking again. "Maybe this is how other girls meet guys. You know, by getting involved."

Rachel looks at me and says, "Nah."

"Not the right kind of guys, anyway," I say.

15

Chapter 2

I burst out of the elevator and jog down the hall to our apartment. The last time I was this excited to talk to my mother about school was in sixth grade, when Mariah showed up with a half ring of cold sores around her mouth, and Danny Cruz had the matching half around his.

My key is in the lock when I hear Grace's voice. "I don't see why Paz can't help out more. It's his kid, too. He thinks he's off the hook because he earns more money than I do."

Inside, Grace is trailing after my mother while my niece, Keira, sleeps on the couch, dark curls plastered to her rosy cheeks.

"Hi," I say, dropping my backpack on the floor.

Grace raises a finger to her lips. "You'll wake the baby."

"If she can sleep through your whining, she can sleep through anything."

I love my niece, but I'm not a natural around kids. Izzy, on the other hand, dissolves into baby talk the moment she sees Keira, and Grace has started asking her to babysit if Mom and I are working. She even pays Izzy. Money is never on offer when *I'm* the one changing diapers.

"So, let me guess," I continue at a whisper. "I'm spending the night on the sofa because you and Paz had another fight."

My mother throws me a warning look as she slips the top of her blue scrubs over a white T-shirt. "Lu, don't start."

She looks even more exhausted than usual, having followed her week of nights with two extra day shifts last weekend. Mom's trying to put a little money aside for some of the endless things Keira seems to need, like a bigger stroller. The long hours are taking a toll, because Mom looks a lot older than her thirty-four years.

Happily, I can give her a little good news today. "Mom, something cool happened at school."

"Already?" she asks, heading into the kitchen to take her lunch out of the refrigerator. "That's great, honey. The meat loaf will be ready in ten minutes, okay?"

"Dunfield's participating in a fund-raising competition to raise money for literacy."

Grace's face clouds over. She struggled with reading but covered it up so well for so long that no one realized what was happening until she reached Dunfield. By then she refused the remedial help the school offered, insisting that she didn't need it. Not long afterward, she dropped out.

Mom is already jamming her feet in the shoes she keeps permanently laced, so I spit out my news: "Mr.

Sparling asked me to write a column about the competition for the school paper."

"Sparling's an idiot," Grace says, tossing her caramel-colored hair.

I know she's only saying that because Mr. Sparling is the one who realized she had trouble reading and sounded the alarm; but it hurts anyway.

"Grace," Mom says.

"Well, why would he want *her* to write a column?"

"*Grace.*" Mom would say a lot more if she weren't in such a hurry. Instead she slings an arm around my shoulders for a nanosecond. "Congratulations, honey."

I fill her in on the details while she rifles through her purse. "The best part is that the column is going to be anonymous."

"Then you're perfect for the part," Grace says, smirking. "But what's the point of doing it if no one knows it's you?"

"I'll know. And Mr. Sparling and Principal Alvarez will know. If I decide to go to college it'll look good on my application." Before now I hadn't given much thought to going to college, let alone how I'd afford it, but suddenly it feels like a possibility. "Right, Mom?"

"Definitely," Mom says. "Has anyone seen my bus pass?"

And thus ends the celebration of Lu's big break.

I walk into Mom's bedroom and extricate the bus pass from the detritus on her dresser.

"You're a lifesaver," she says, snatching her keys from the table. "Grace, there are fresh sheets on the bed, but you'll have to help Lu move her things. See you at breakfast, girls." She drops a butterfly kiss on Keira's cheek and slips out the door.

I turn to Grace. "Why are we moving my things?"

"So you don't disturb Keira if you need something."

A bad feeling percolates in my stomach. "I'll manage for one night."

"It isn't for one night," Grace says, confirming my fears. "I left Paz. For good this time."

Grace and I may have shared a small room for thirteen years, but we have nothing in common except genes, and even that's debatable. She's tall and big-boned and has the personality to match. In fact, Grace used to solve every dispute with her fists, including some of mine if she felt the family honor was at stake. I sometimes wonder if the reason Mariah Mendes hasn't bullied me as much as some other girls is that she's still traumatized from the day we stepped out of our third grade classroom to find a circle of kids yelling, "Fight! Fight! Fight!" In the middle was Grace, and she was pounding the crap out of Mariah's older brother, Hector, because he'd called her stupid in front of her boyfriend. When she was finished pounding Hector, Grace also punched her boyfriend for not defending her himself.

I was always scared of Grace's temper, and I still am. She has a talent for shriveling people with a single glance. Some of that power comes from multiple eyebrow studs, although she's allowed the lip and tongue piercings to seal over. In fact, since Keira was born she's toned her look down a lot. She can't undo the full sleeve of tattoos on her left arm, but I notice she hasn't gotten any fresh ones. She also cut back on profanity after Keira started mimicking her. But Grace still takes crap from no one, with the possible exception of Paz.

I, on the other hand, take crap from a lot of people, especially Grace. She hates my taste in music, clothing, and television, and never hesitates to tell me so. My theory is that she blames me for driving our father out, since he left when I was still really young. The only photo we have of him shows him holding Grace the day she was born. He was about eighteen years old, and to me he looks terrified, bewildered, and maybe a little awed. I guess having a baby can do that to you.

No wonder Grace's edge has softened. To others the change might be imperceptible, but the very fact that she now likes my friend Izzy—someone she formerly considered lame—is a giveaway. She continues to assume people are idiots until she's proven wrong, but she'll backtrack if someone is nice to Keira.

"The room looks good," Grace calls from the bedroom.

Mom recently redecorated it as a birthday present to me. She's a whiz with a staple gun and paint, and I've always been comfortable having my friends over, even though their homes are far nicer.

Coming to the doorway I see that Grace is already unpacking the first of three suitcases. My bed is strewn with Keira's toys.

"Did you bring everything you own?" I ask.

"I wish I could take all the furniture too. Paz should have to sleep on the floor."

Grace shows up here after every fight, and moves out just as abruptly. It's a revolving door, but Mom never complains. Although she was upset when Grace got pregnant, Mom became really supportive after Keira was born. I guess that's because Mom never had much support herself when she was in the same predicament. Her parents disowned her, so we ended up living in my dad's parents' basement. Then Dad took off on us and moved to New Mexico to start another family that doesn't terrify him.

"You'll be back with Paz by the weekend," I say. If there's a God.

Grace shakes her head. "Not this time."

She throws clothes into drawers any which way, and when she thinks I've stopped watching her, she wipes her eyes with her sleeve.

Okay, this is serious. As far as I know, Grace didn't even cry when she realized she was pregnant. I feel sorry for her, but I know that any display of sympathy will send her into a blind rage. Better to tiptoe around this grenade. "What did he do?"

It can't be another woman, or Grace would be in jail by now for shooting one—or both—of them. She has always been fiercely jealous of Paz, who is really cute and too flirtatious for his own good. I never got the sense that he'd cheat on her, though, because he says Grace is the best thing that ever happened to him. The more outrageous she gets, the more amusing he finds her. He had "Grace" tattooed on the inside of his right wrist and "Forever" inside the left.

She piles my stuff on the floor as an excuse not to look

at me. "Nothing," she mutters to herself.

"I understand if you don't want to talk about it," I say, sensing she does.

"He just doesn't want to be a family, that's all."

I sit down on my bed to face her. "Did he say that?"

"He didn't have to."

Famous last words in any relationship. I know that even though I haven't had one. "What makes you think so?"

"He hardly spends time with us anymore. When his shift is over, he hangs out with the guys for hours. And when he does look after Keira, he just sticks her in front of the TV and ignores her. He doesn't even read to her. These are the critical years when her brain is developing really fast. The book says—" She stops abruptly.

"What book?"

"Just a book about child development. Never mind." She stands and opens another suitcase. "He doesn't care, that's all."

"Paz loves Keira," I say. I believe it, too. He carries her picture around and shows it off to everyone. But he's a bit selfish and lazy, traits Grace could have easily seen before she moved in with him. Mom and I did.

"I know he does." Her resigned tone worries me more than anything else. It isn't like Grace to give up a fight. "And I'll make sure he gets to see her. But I had to take a stand, Lu. I will not be anyone's doormat. I have to set an example for Keira."

"Maybe he doesn't get it. He is a guy, you know."

She zips the empty suitcases closed and looks at me.

"He has to get it. There are no do-overs with kids."

I stare back at her, amazed at how mature she seems all of a sudden. This is probably the most grown-up conversation we've ever had. She must be seeing me as her equal at last. Maybe this breakup has given us a fresh start.

"Paz will come around," I say. "He'll miss you."

Sighing, she pulls me to my feet. "You'd better grab some dinner and get down to Dan's."

"I don't work Tuesdays. It's your shift."

The eyebrow studs rise. "I can't work tonight. I just left my husband."

"Did I miss a wedding?"

"My point is, Keira needs her mother."

Given the circumstances I should probably let it ride, but I know if I don't set some boundaries quickly, my sister will mow me down like a runaway stroller. "Grace, I have a life. You can't just move back in here and take over."

"Fine," she says, pulling a rumpled, red-and-white gingham dress from a pile on the bed. "I'll work. But I don't have a sitter, so you'll have to watch Keira. She'll be upset when she wakes up and I'm not here."

Working suddenly sounds more appealing. "I'll cover your shift, but I'm not doing it all the time."

"Heaven forbid perfect little Lu gets off her ass to help out the family."

All the reasons I resent Grace start flooding back to me. "Don't even start. I help out all the time. It's not my fault you decided to have a kid."

"It isn't mine, either!"

Grace's mistakes are always someone else's fault.

23

The shouting wakes Keira, and she quickly works up a howl. I snatch my backpack and make my escape.

So much for fresh starts.

No matter how bad a day I've had, it gets better the moment I step off the bus in front of Dan's Diner and breathe in the scent of chocolate. Donner's Chocolate Factory just up the street cloaks the entire neighborhood in a sweet, rich cloud. A few years ago some locals complained about the smell, and the plant added new filters. Fortunately they don't work very well.

I cross the road, watching Shirley, a full-time waitress, through the diner's big front window. She's refilling ketchup bottles at the counter, her bleached blond hair teased, as always, into a beehive. From here she looks quite young, but the illusion shatters at close range. She is sixty-three, and garish makeup pools in the wrinkles on her face. Her lips are lined with fuchsia pencil and filled in with frosty pale pink lipstick.

"What a nice surprise," she says when I walk in. "Grace usually does Tuesdays."

Shirley and Grace aren't fond of each other. Both are brassy and opinionated, and naturally, none of their opinions overlap. When the baby was born, Shirley said the name "Keira" was too trendy for her liking. Grace retaliated by saying Shirley's makeup was too tacky for *her* liking, and they've never really patched things up.

I explain that Grace will cover a shift for me later in the week, which had better be true. With my new column to think about, I can't afford to work many extra hours.

The diner has a capacity of fifty people, and on week-ends we often reach it. Tonight it will be busy for a couple of hours over dinner, but manageable with two servers. The three oversize booths along the front window are already full, as are a few of the stools at the counter.

I head to the restroom to change into my uniform. Mom used to make me wear it on the bus, but I dug my heels in last year after hearing one too many yee-haws.

Dan Kennedy only spent the first ten years of his life in Texas, but the way he works a theme, you'd think he was fresh off the horse. He walks with a permanent, bowlegged swagger, talks with a Texan drawl, and wears a uniform of Wrangler jeans, denim shirts, and cowboy boots. There are chili pepper twinkle lights hanging from faux wood beams and lariats nailed to the walls.

After hanging my stuff on a fake horn hook in the tiny staff office and grabbing a cup of coffee, I join Dan on the stoop outside the back door, where he's enjoying a cigar and reviewing his grocery list.

"That'll stunt your growth," he says, eyeing my mug.

"The damage is already done," I say. "But I'll give it up if you quit smoking."

He grins at me, and our ritual is complete. He will continue to enjoy his nicotine, and I my caffeine.

"Coming, Lu?" Shirley calls from the kitchen. "We've got six minutes."

The first dinner break at Donner's starts at five p.m. and at precisely 5:06, workers arrive at the door.

I gulp my coffee. "On my way."

Dan follows me inside and cuts me a piece of coconut

cream pie. It's my favorite, but it's also popular with the factory crowd, so he never lets me at it until the end of the night.

"What's the occasion?" I ask, digging in before he changes his mind.

"First day of school," he replies. "How did it go?"

I hit the day's high points, and he listens with an enthusiasm Mom couldn't muster. He's delighted at the idea of my writing an anonymous column and insists I bring him copies of each one.

Dan is like a fond, overprotective uncle. I was only ten when Grace started busing tables here, and I had to come with her most of the time. When she dropped out of school, Dan promoted her to serving and gave me her old job. Along with the paycheck, I get plenty of advice, because Dan's afraid I'll follow in my sister's footsteps. He doesn't need to be. First, it would be hard for me to get pregnant, given the scarcity of B in my life. Second, while I dislike school in general and Dumpfield in particular, I intend to stick it out until I graduate. I admire my mother for raising us alone on so little, but I want an easier path if I can find it.

Cowbells ring, signaling the start of the rush, and I head out front at a run. You need to be on your game with shift workers. They know exactly what they want, and they want it fast. If you get them fed and back to work on time, they tip you well.

The first group in the door includes Paz Medina. I chant a silent prayer that he'll sit in Shirley's section, but naturally he chooses mine.

"Swap sections?" I ask Shirley. "I'll give you half my tips."

She shakes her head. "Not a chance. It's your turn, kid."

Paz and five other guys in brown Donner coveralls slide into one of the front booths. As shift lead on the truffle line, Paz is well respected by his crew. Despite his supreme stupidity in getting my sister pregnant, he's actually a smart guy, and if he'd stuck it out at Dunfield one more year, he'd have graduated. After Grace dropped out, he got a chance to go full-time at Donner's and took it, saying he'd finish school part-time. That hasn't happened, and it probably won't now that he's making good money.

His Donner posse varies, but aside from different coloring and size, they're all pretty much the same. Each is a smart-ass dropout just like Paz. They surf in here on a wave of testosterone and laugh so loud at their stupid jokes that non-Donner customers complain. I try hard to ignore them, because if they have an audience they get worse.

Be nice, I tell myself as I walk over to their table. *Do not let them get to you.*

"Hey, Shorty," Paz says, as the rest of the guys debate the relative merits of the new burger choices on the menu.

He calls me that because he's height-challenged himself. I have a few nicknames for him too, but in the interest of keeping the peace, I don't use any of them. "Hey, Paz. You guys ready to order?"

"Where's Grace?" he asks, his usually brilliant smile at half-mast.

"Not here. Ready to order?"

"Where is she? It's her night."

The rest of the crew stops talking.

"I took her shift. And I'd love to serve you guys some dinner. How about you, Gordo? The Rodeo Burger, as usual?"

Gordo shuffles his cutlery, unwilling to order without his boss's blessing. Meanwhile, Paz just stares, waiting for me to crack. I won't, because I've already taken enough abuse from Grace tonight. "Look, Paz, what goes on between you and Grace isn't my business, but serving you *is* my business. If you don't want me to do my job, I can get Dan out here to take your order."

He backs off immediately. I guess he's so used to Grace's attitude that it's all he responds to now. "Rodeo Burger," he says.

"Same for me," Gordo says.

And so it goes for the rest of the crew. "Six Rodeo Burgers, hold the fries," I say.

There's an instant clamor: *"I want fries. Fries for me. We need fries."*

Grinning, I drop their order with Dan and move on to the next table. A few minutes later, Paz corners me behind the counter and mumbles an apology.

"It's okay," I say. He's not such a bad guy, and he is Keira's father. "Call Grace."

He leans in, in case anyone is eavesdropping. "She *left*. She took Keira and left."

"Like last time and the time before. Just call her."

"This time is different," he says.

His tone changes quickly when Gordo joins us. "She'll be back," he says, puffing out his chest. "I give her a week tops. Grace can't live without me."

Twenty minutes later, the guys are teasing Paz when I deliver the bill to their table.

"So is Grace really crying her eyes out like he says?" Gordo asks.

"Actually, she was heading out with some friends when I left," I say. "She looked pretty happy."

"Whoo-hoo!" the guys taunt Paz. "Better watch your back, man!"

"Who's with Keira?" Paz asks.

I shrug. "Not my business, remember?"

One of the guys tries to change the subject. "Hey, check out the shirts Paz gave us."

The name "Joey" is stitched on his overalls, but he must be new, because I don't recognize him. Unzipping to his waist, he reveals a T-shirt in the brown-and-yellow Donner colors. It features a chocolate truffle decorated with the words "Paz's Crew."

"Nice," I say. "I suppose tattoos are next?"

"Hope not," Joey says, grinning. "Ink is forever. Shift leads, not so much."

"You're smart not to count on anything permanent where Paz is concerned," I say.

Paz flips me off, but as he's already paid—and tipped—I feel free to flip back before walking away.

"You look fat in that uniform, Shorty," he calls after me.

"And you look short in that body, Paz," I call back.

Chapter 3

Mr. Sparling releases the class five minutes early so we can attend the first girls' literacy fund-raiser—a bake sale.

"Save me a cupcake," he says, winking at me as I pass.

I wait until we're out of earshot to ask Izzy and Rachel, "Do you really think I can do this?"

"Write the column? Definitely," Rachel says, craning to see if Jason Baca is still ahead of us. "Getting cold feet?"

"I guess so. My mother and Grace weren't very enthusiastic about it."

Rachel frowns. "When was the last time Grace was enthusiastic about anything?"

"She's enthusiastic about Keira," Izzy says.

Dissing my sister was more satisfying before Izzy started babysitting for her and misplaced her loyalties.

Rachel revises her previous comment. "Okay, when was the last time Grace was enthusiastic about anything related to *Dumpfield*?"

"You mean, besides the guys?"

Izzy and Rachel laugh. Unlike us, my sister always had boyfriends. None were destined to become nuclear physicists, but they were all cute and treated her well. There are two elaborate dragon tattoos on her shoulders that conceal the names of Paz's immediate predecessors. If he doesn't get his act together soon, something colorful will happen to the "Paz" and "Forever" tattoos on her wrists.

"Grace's grades weren't great, and it might be hard for her to see you starting to distinguish yourself," Rachel says.

"Maybe," I say. "But I'm worried that Mr. Sparling gave me the job because he feels bad about what happened with Grace. Or maybe he thinks he can save me from following in her footsteps."

"Or maybe you're a good writer," Izzy says, redeeming herself. "Unlike some people."

We follow her gaze to the hand-painted sign over the gymnasium door that reads, PIG OUT FOR LITIRACY.

"Remind me again why Mariah is in charge of this campaign," I say.

"Because everyone wants a nice long winter break," Rachel replies. "And with Mariah leading it, people will actually participate."

I liked it better when we could just hate Mariah without reservation. Now I have to feel invested in her success because I'll get something out of it, too.

"You don't have to be able to spell to be popular," Rachel adds, leading us into the crowded gym. She has to shout to be heard above the blaring hip-hop music and the voices of hundreds of students. "Look at the turnout."

"But Mariah and Mac shouldn't be able to just take

over," I say. "Principal Buzzkill said we should *elect* our leaders."

"It's the natural order," Rachel says. "Some things aren't worth fighting."

"Why do you care, anyway?" Izzy asks. "It's not like you want to lead. This is the first time you've ever attended a school event."

"Hello? Eighth-grade dance?"

"That doesn't count. It was pretty much mandatory."

Mandatory torture. I got sucked into going with Porter Bell because he asked me six months in advance and I couldn't come up with an excuse. Naturally I assumed he'd hit puberty in the meantime. He didn't. To make matters worse, I had to wear Grace's castoff dress, which looked horrible on me. Mariah, on the other hand, wore a tight, gold dress sliced nearly to her navel that was *so* inappropriate for a junior high dance. And I was *so* jealous that she could pull it off.

Today her assets are on display once again in a black satin corset paired with yoga pants. She is in the bleachers, leading her Understudies through a series of Pilates moves.

"What's with the workout?" Rachel asks. "It's a bake sale."

I point to the long line of guys at the table closest to the bleachers. "Mariah is doing more than pushing brownies today. She's selling these poor suckers a dream."

Izzy finds our assigned table and moves plates around to make room for our contributions. She and Rachel actually baked something, but I brought a pie Dan kindly donated. I have enough on my mind without learning how to follow a recipe.

I continue to watch Mariah as one of the Understudies presses a Starbucks cup into her hand. Mariah is said to live on black coffee alone; no one has seen solid food pass her lips for three years.

"I've got an angle for my first column," I say, lowering my voice. "I'll write about the irony of a girl who never eats launching a campaign with a bake sale."

"You'd better keep a lid on how you really feel about Mariah," Rachel cautions. "In case you don't stay anonymous."

I'd planned to exploit my cover to diss Mariah, but I see Rachel's point. "Then I'd better go sniff out another story. Plus, I want to see if I can spot the guy who's writing the competing column."

My column will appear in the first edition of *The Bulletin* under the pen name "Newshound." His will run the following week under "Scoop." Mr. Sparling suggested the names because they remind him of his favorite movies from the 1940s. I doubt he was even alive then, but whatever.

"Did Sparling give you a hint?" Izzy asks.

I shake my head. "He said it's a 'state secret.' Someone's been watching too many crime shows."

One of the Understudies stops at our table and points to the cookies Rachel is holding. "What's that? Looks like dog turds."

"It's rugelach," a male voice replies.

We turn to find Jason, the guy of Rachel's dreams,

standing behind us. He drops a five-dollar bill on the table and pops a cookie into his mouth. "Almost as good as my bubbe's," he pronounces.

"Your grandmother is Jewish?" Rachel asks, her voice spiking a few notches.

They gravitate toward each other, and the Understudy rolls her eyes and walks away. Izzy and I decide to give Rachel some space too and stroll through the crowd in search of something newsworthy. Before long we come upon a group of jocks who are tossing a football around, mainly to hear the girls squeal.

"How about you hang around here and get crowd reactions while I keep mingling," I ask.

"You've got to be kidding," Izzy says.

"You said you'd help, and I already lost Rachel. You don't have to talk to them, just observe. And keep an eye out for a guy taking notes. If I can figure out what the competition's writing about, I may get a few ideas of my own."

A football whizzes by Izzy's left ear, and she flinches. "This is going to cost you more than free fries, Luisa."

The problem with being a columnist as opposed to a regular reporter is that no one assigns you a story idea. You're just supposed to walk around and produce one out of thin air and write four hundred pithy words about it. And the problem with being an *anonymous* columnist is that you can't let on to people that that's what you're doing and interview them properly.

I don't know what I was thinking when I agreed to this. There's a reason I don't attend school events: I don't actually like people. At least, not Dunfield people. I haven't fit in since day one. I'm not like the Mariah acolytes, or the jocks, or the tech geeks, or the brainiacs, or the artists, or the goths, or the rappers, or the small but very vocal group of wannabe debutantes that occasionally has to be squashed by Mariah. I'm not even one of the fierce independent kids who cruises the periphery and seems comfortable there. In a school this size you'd think there'd be a place for average kids like Rachel, Izzy, and me, but if there is, we haven't found it.

Standing at the edge of one of the busiest tables, I try to work up the nerve to chat to some girls about what they made for the sale. There has to be a heart-warming story of how a secret family recipe has been handed down from generation to generation from Brazil, or Mexico, or Malaysia. Great-grandma probably couldn't make this special dish when she arrived because the ingredients weren't available. But now a school bake sale gives us an opportunity to share our family favorites. It's multiculturalism at its finest.

"What's wrong with you?" the girl with the cash box asks. "You're staring."

I back away from the table. Most of the food looks like it comes ready-to-serve from Safeway anyway.

"Whoa," a deep voice says. I spin to find I've almost backed into Mac Landis. He's carrying a full plate in one hand and a burrito in the other. "That could have been messy."

"Sorry," I say.

"No worries." He takes an enormous bite of the

burrito, leaving the last couple of inches, which he jabs in my direction. "Open."

"Pardon me?"

"Try it," he mumbles around the mouthful. "Best burrito I've ever had."

Mac Landis is offering me the last bite of his burrito. Have I stepped into an alternate universe? There's no time to ponder because the burrito is already speeding toward my face. I open.

My eyes start to water immediately. Despite my heritage, I don't do spicy. Even Rachel, a descendent of Russian immigrants, has a higher tolerance for heat. My tongue has caught fire.

"Oops," Mac says as I bolt for the restroom. "Habanera sauce."

I can do it. I can just walk up to someone in this gym and talk to her. Or him, even. I can walk up to a guy. I do it all the time at Dan's Diner. All I'm paid to do there is be polite and take orders, but often there's small talk about the food or the weather, and sometimes it even evolves into real conversation.

I can do this because I've done it before. I just haven't done it within Dunfield's peeling walls or within view of Mariah. But I already have the skills. All I have to do is apply them in this new, albeit hostile, environment.

The key is to approach someone who's alone and might be grateful for company. There's a guy sitting on the bleachers who fits the description. He looks like a regular guy, not supercute or athletic. To be honest, he looks sort of miserable. I could imagine him walking into Dan's wearing Donner overalls and ordering a Rodeo Burger and fries. I'll pretend he's just another guy from Paz's crew.

Crossing the gym I deliver my opening line. "Is anyone sitting here?"

"Uh, no," he says, making a show of looking around. "Not unless it's the Invisible Woman."

With that kind of attitude, I don't even have to imagine the Donner overalls. "Sue Storm?" I ask. "I guess that makes you Mr. Fantastic."

He smiles reluctantly. "You saw *The Fantastic Four*?"

"No, but I've read the original Marvel comic books."

It's true. Mr. O'Brien, one of my regular customers, has a collection of originals, and he actually allowed me to flip through them. He normally keeps them covered in plastic because they're worth about ten grand.

The guy moves over to give me more space to sit down. "I'm Tyler Milano."

I introduce myself and answer all his questions about Mr. O'Brien's collection. Who knew the small talk I've made over cheese omelets would pay off so well?

Tyler takes his glasses out of his pocket and puts them on. The frames are rectangular and dark and give him a bookish appeal.

"Let me guess, Sue Storm doesn't like a guy in glasses?" I say.

He gives me a self-conscious smile. "Superheroes wear contacts."

I look at the empty paper plate beside him and remember why I'm here. "So what did you buy?"

He lists off several items and provides mini-reviews of each. "Avoid the maple fudge," he concludes. "It had maple flavoring instead of real syrup."

"You could tell?"

"Sure," he says. "My parents run a catering business. I knew a shiitake from a chanterelle by the time I was five."

"Impressive." I'm pretty sure he's talking abut mushrooms. "I could barely tell the difference between canned spaghetti and canned ravioli at five."

Tyler laughs, and it sounds genuine.

"My mom isn't known for her cooking," I continue. "Her specialty is meat loaf."

"A good meat loaf is hard to find." Tyler describes the best one he ever tasted in great detail, becoming even more animated.

"My mom uses two secret ingredients," I say. "I'm not supposed to divulge them, but since you're such a foodie . . ."

"Caramelized onions?" he asks eagerly. "Sun-dried tomatoes?"

"Close. Onion soup mix and ketchup."

He laughs again, and I marvel at the fact that this cute, seemingly normal guy is finding me entertaining. That's the real story from this bake sale, as far as I'm concerned. I've spent all this time looking for my FB in assemblies, never thinking to check the bleachers.

"My goal is to be a food critic for the *Tribune* one day," Tyler confides.

Rachel breaks into our conversation before I get a chance to question him more. "Lu, I've been looking everywhere for you. I need to show you something."

After introducing Tyler, I try giving Rachel a look to convey that I'm having too good a conversation to leave. The only problem is that she's never seen that look on my face before and doesn't recognize it.

"Nice to meet you, Tyler," she says, literally pulling me to my feet and hauling me away.

"This had better be important," I say. "I was interviewing that guy."

"You were just flirting with him."

"If you knew that, why did you drag me away?"

"You're here to do a job, and I stopped flirting with a guy to help you. I thought you'd want to know I found the other columnist."

Rachel points to Mac Landis, who's busily taking notes as Mariah holds forth on some undoubtedly fascinating topic.

I tell Rachel the burrito story, my face burning almost as much as my tongue did half an hour ago.

When she's finished laughing, she gives me a strange look. "Why is Mac Landis suddenly paying attention to you?"

"He's not *paying attention* to me," I say. "I nearly bumped into him, that's all."

We ease a little closer, taking cover behind a large stack of gym mats so that we can eavesdrop.

"So why won't you let me sample your goodies?" Mac asks. "I'll pay twice the asking price."

Rachel whispers, "Like he'd have to pay."

"Sorry, sweetie, mine sold out in three minutes," Mariah coos. "But if you're nice, I might give you my VIP number."

Mariah has two cell phones—a regular one for general use, and a hot pink one for VIPs. Her number changes every time she dumps a guy.

"This is the best bake sale I've ever been to," Mac says, as the volume of the music goes up and Mariah starts to bump and grind.

She dances closer to Mac. "Here's my secret: You have to put the *kick* in the campaign." Mariah stops gyrating for a second to do a high kick.

Mac takes her hand and pulls her away. "Let's go somewhere quieter to talk."

"See?" Rachel says as they leave. "There's no way he'd cut short a private dance to talk unless he's the columnist."

I'm still not convinced, but it's worth noting that Mac's sports-god status does give him the inside track on everything.

"Now what?" I say, nudging Rachel. The Dunfield cheerleaders—who had very little to cheer about before Mac arrived—have emerged from the girls' locker room wearing red Santa Claus hats over their purple-and-white uniforms. They click by us on stiletto boots to the side door of the gym. I beckon Rachel to follow.

Out on the football field, students are sprawled on the bleachers, smoking or eating. The cheerleaders take up a position in front of a camera set on a tripod. One of Mac's jock pals is behind the camera, directing them, while another climbs a ladder, carrying a large, cardboard box.

"Okay, dude," the photographer says. "Fire."

The guy on the ladder tips the box and sifts fake snow over the cheerleaders.

"And . . . turn!"

The cheerleaders spin so fast their short skirts swirl.

After a few more snowy butt shots, the photographer looks up from his lens and sees Rachel and me watching. "Sorry, ladies," he says. "You can't audition for The Literacy Challenge Calendar. Mac is handpicking everyone."

The guy on the ladder shouts down, "But if you want to show us what's under your jeans, we might be able to put in a good word for you."

Tyler has disappeared by the time I return to the gym, so I sit down alone in the bleachers to study the crowd.

"Always on the outside looking in, aren't you, Coconut?" Mariah asks, appearing out of nowhere.

Mariah used to lob an insult or two my way if I stumbled into her path, but today I think she actively sought me out. I wonder what I've done to earn this promotion.

"Well, someone has to cheer from the sidelines," I say, forcing a smile. But then my lips move again, seemingly of their own accord. "Love the signage, by the way."

Mariah glances up at the spelling error and mumbles something in Spanish. From the sound of it, one of the Understudies was holding the paintbrush.

"I thought it was a marketing strategy," I say. "To prove we really need the money for literacy."

It's a joke, at least sort of, but Mariah obviously doesn't share my sense of humor. She swears at me in English to be sure I get the point. "If you're so smart, why don't you take over?" she says.

"I couldn't. Not with all my hours at the grease pit." I'm digging myself in deeper and deeper. Regular exposure to Grace is having a bad effect on me.

"But you've still got all the hours other girls spend with guys," Mariah says.

Ouch. "True. I'm surprised you get as much done as you do."

Mariah's eyes bulge. "Are you calling me a slut?"

"Of course not!" I would never call anyone a slut, even if she were. How did this get so out of hand?

Mariah snaps her fingers, and the Understudies instantly materialize at her side. "She called me a slut."

The Understudies advance on me, and I realize that while I may have absorbed some of Grace's attitude, I don't have her fists to back it up. I doubt the girls would risk a dance-limiting injury to beat me up, but they have many enforcers around who needn't be so cautious.

There's only one escape route, and I take it. "That totally came out the wrong way, Mariah, and I'm sorry."

She considers this for a moment. "I'll let you off this time, Coconut, but only because the press is here and I can't afford to get a bad rep."

"The press?"

"The columnists for the *Dunfield Bulletin*."

"You actually read that piece of crap?" I looked at last year's issues, and I speak the truth. There's a reason I didn't know it existed. It's hopelessly dull—something I will have to try to change.

"Look, stories get out, and I have a career to think

about. Some of us don't want to spend our lives serving burgers to dropouts."

She saunters off, trusting the Understudies to deliver a last, contemptuous look.

THE DUNFIELD BULLETIN
THE WORD . . . FROM NEWSHOUND
Good Taste and Bad Taste

Dunfield girls kicked off the Year of Literacy this week with a bake sale that attracted nearly a thousand students and generated a profit of $3,000. Now that's tasty!

Students raved about the event, demanding that the school cafeteria serve food that good every day. They're missing the point. Surviving Dunfield cafeteria food prepares us to face any challenge the real world can offer, and as Mr. Sparling always says, no one has died from it yet.

At any rate, Newshound enjoyed sampling cuisines from around the world and is glad to see that something as wholesome and traditional as an old-fashioned bake sale could be such a hit. Kudos to team leader Mariah Mendes for demonstrating that good taste and fund-raising can work together to great success.

Unfortunately, the guys' team has chosen not to follow her excellent example. Under the leadership of Mac Landis, the men of Dunfield are currently putting together a girlie calendar and soliciting participation from female students. A word to the wise: some call this harassment.

Everyone knows that sex sells, fellas, but couldn't you come up with something a little more tasteful? It's too early in the competition to take the low road, although we figured you'd end up there eventually. There are so many creative ways you could raise money. You may have to work harder to find them, but that's what competition's all about. When we beat you, we want to know you played your best game.

Dunfield girls will probably be the ones enjoying the bonus vacation days at spring break because The Dunfield Bootylicious Calendar is not going to win any extra points for originality from Mrs. Alvarez. You might as well put a stop to this ridiculous and sexist project right now.

And girls, if you're asked to pose, *just say no*. You don't need to prove you're gorgeous by stripping down for the benefit of a bunch of guys who still aren't capable of growing a beard. Send a message that Dunfield women will not be considered sex objects. Yes, we're sexy, but we're also smart and funny and talented. We respect ourselves and we expect to be appreciated for our minds as well as our behinds.

Mac, your team is going to have to come up with a better way to raise cash. According to this Newshound, you're barking up the wrong tree.

Chapter 4

THE DUNFIELD BULLETIN
THE WORD . . . FROM SCOOP
The Stench of Sour Grapes

I may share this space with someone else, but it appears to be the only thing we have in common. Unlike Newshound, Scoop is 110 percent behind the Dunfield Bootylicious Calendar. Mac Landis and his crew deserve props for creating such a useful and attractive fund-raising item.

A famous designer once said: "Have nothing in your house that you do not know to be useful or believe to be beautiful." In my humble opinion, this calendar is both. I plan to refer to it often for information and inspiration.

Fortunately, instead of heeding Newshound's alarmist cries to boycott, the women of Bootylicious listened to their hearts and put their butts on display for this very worthy cause. Ladies, your efforts were not in vain. I, for one, respect you more than ever.

As a media rep, I got an advance copy of Bootylicious and avoided the mob scene after the shipment arrived yesterday. Newshound's early publicity meant that all 600 calendars sold out in minutes. For those of you who hate math as much as I do, that's a whopping six G's, and twice what the girls brought in at the bake sale. Hopefully, Mac's dad can pull some strings for another rush print job.

Newshound called this project unoriginal, yet never in the history of Dunfield has there been such a calendar. Mac also showed ingenuity by covering production costs through auctioning off positions on the crew. Everyone except the models had to pay for the privilege of being involved. Apparently, the photographer blew his entire savings for the honor of shooting our Dunfield beauties and said it was worth every penny.

Only one thing could have improved this work of art: Mrs. Alvarez. Mac offered to make her the model for March in the next print run if she agrees to give the guys the bonus days at spring break. Think about it, Mrs. A.

I don't want to use this space to run down the competition. It's all for a good cause, right? The leader of the girls' team knows this and graciously posed for July, which, in my opinion, has never been hotter. As Ms. Mendes says, "You have to put the kick in the campaign."

Scoop can't help but wonder if there's more behind Newshound's complaints—and her pen name—than she wants us to know. Would she be howling a different tune if she'd been asked to pose?

"He called me a dog," I say, slapping the paper on the

counter in front of Rachel and Izzy. *"He called me a dog!"*

"He didn't call *you* a dog," Rachel says. "He doesn't even know who you are."

The *Bulletin* came out yesterday afternoon, and I've read it at least ten times. My friends have already seen it too, but as soon as they arrive at Dan's, I read it aloud anyway. "He thinks I'm jealous I didn't get asked to be in that sexist piece of junk!"

"He's just trying to get a rise out of you," Izzy says, dunking a marshmallow into her hot chocolate with the tip of a fingernail. She examines the photo of Miss July that appears beside the article. "I suppose it *would* be nice to be asked. I mean, what's Mariah got that I don't?"

As far as I can tell, the only thing Izzy and Mariah have in common is their bra size. Izzy is cute in a quirky way, but what you tend to notice about her are the distractions—the bright makeup, the spiders stenciled on her nails, and her ever-changing hair color. Mariah, on the other hand, is beautiful from every angle, in any light, with or without makeup. And that's what you notice.

"Izzy, do you really think it's an honor to be asked for a butt shot by a bunch of pervy guys?" I ask. "What do you think they're doing with this calendar in the privacy of their own rooms?"

Rachel drops her spoon into her coffee with a clatter. "Gross!"

"What's gross?" Shirley asks, setting a plate of fries in front of each of my friends. She didn't have to ask what they wanted; Izzy and Rachel visit me at work every weekend. They try to come when business is slow so that we can

47

catch up in peace. Dan doesn't mind, as long as I keep my customers happy.

I slide the paper toward Shirley. "Check out the picture."

Shirley gives Mariah the once-over before scanning the article. "I was asked to do a bikini shot once—for an advertisement for snow tires."

"And you said no because you didn't want a bunch of greasy mechanics ogling you all day, right?" I ask.

"Oh, I did the ad."

"But you regretted it?" I ask hopefully.

"Are you kidding? I've got it hanging it in my bedroom to remind me of how good I used to look."

"It's a great shot," Dan says, coming out of the kitchen to join the conversation.

I sincerely hope that Shirley brought it in to show him. Otherwise, Dan has been in her bedroom, and if they're that close, I don't want to know about it.

Dan takes a look at Miss July and whistles. "That gal is practically naked."

Mariah is wearing a short leather skirt, fishnets, and nothing else. She has her back to the camera, but is giving a coy half-turn and arching her back, porno style. Her left breast is partially blocked by a bouquet of red roses.

There's a shout from across the room. "Did I hear the word 'naked'?"

It's Paz, and he's surrounded, as usual, by the Truffle Gang. The factory's staggered work week means that even weekends aren't Donner-proof around here. Happily, the guys landed in Shirley's section today. She waves *The Bulletin* at them, and in seconds we're swarmed.

48

"Whoo-hoo!"

"I'd like to stop and smell those roses!"

"She's hhhhhot."

I snatch the newspaper out of Paz's hand. "Toss me a rag, Dan, there's drool on the counter."

"Oh, come on, Shorty," Paz says. "What does it hurt to look?"

It might hurt Grace that's he's leering openly, but I'm not going to say so in front of all these people. Instead I close the newspaper. "Show's over."

"Luisa must be a feminist," Gordo says. "We don't like the F-word, do we, guys?"

"Why not?" I ask. "Are there too many letters in it for you?"

"See?" Paz shakes his head. "Fembos are harsh. No sense of humor."

Rachel leaps to my defense. "Feminists believe in equal rights for both sexes, that's all."

"They're bitter," Gordo says, "because they can't get a guy."

"Or they don't *like* guys," Joey offers suggestively.

"So tell us, Shorty," Paz says. "*Are* you a fembo?"

I can see where this is going. I'll get all shrill and defensive, and the guys will act like I've proven their point. Better to take a different route. "I hear *you're* a feminist, Paz. You've finally figured out how a washing machine works."

The guys chuckle and shove Paz playfully as they migrate back to their table.

Joey reaches for the paper. "Can I take this?"

I pull it out of his reach. "No."

"Buy the calendar," Shirley says. "It's for a good cause."

"He can't," I say, glaring at Shirley. "It's only available to Dunfield students." I leave the "not dropouts" unsaid, but Joey knows what I mean.

Far from being offended, he grins. "We'll find someone to hook us up. Since it's for a good cause."

He ambles back to the booth, and I start clearing the counter.

"You know, that guy would be cute if you took away the Donner uniform," Rachel says, staring after Joey.

"Maybe," I answer, shrugging. "But you can't take away the Donner attitude. And a cute lost cause is still a lost cause."

"Speaking of which," Izzy says, "any progress between Paz and Grace?"

I shake my head. If anything, Grace is even more entrenched in her position that he's a lazy bum and a lousy father. Unless one of them cracks soon, I might as well kiss my privacy good-bye forever.

Rachel and Izzy start talking about Scoop's column again while I make my rounds with the coffee.

"You know what bugs me the most?" I ask, sliding back into the conversation. "That Mariah participated. She's helping the enemy."

"She'd never pass up a chance for exposure," Izzy says. "I heard she's mailing the calendar out with her demo to music video producers."

Izzy picks up a ton of gossip at her parents' salon. Mariah's mother is a regular customer, as is Mac's.

"The guys' team isn't technically the enemy," Rachel

reminds me. "We all want to win the holiday, so it's in our best interest to cooperate."

"Mac is participating in the girls' date auction," Izzy says. "His mother told my mother that he's hoping Mariah will bid on him."

"It's a long shot," I say. Mac's sports-hero status only goes so far with Mariah. She generally only dates "up"—meaning seniors and occasional juniors if business is slow.

Izzy twists the green streak in her hair thoughtfully. "Rachel might be right—Mac could be Scoop. He gave some good ink to Mariah."

"All the guys like Mariah," I say.

"But he quoted that comment we overheard," Rachel says. "You know, about putting 'kick in the campaign.'"

"She could have said it to a lot of people," I say. "It sounded like a slogan."

"But would Mac be able to quote a designer?" Izzy asks.

I concede that Mac is probably only capable of quoting basketball stats. But another possible suspect comes quickly to mind. "Tyler Milano could probably quote a designer. Plus he said he wants to be a columnist."

"A food critic," Rachel says. "Besides, Tyler's too nice to be Scoop."

"You barely met him," I say.

"Actually, I talked to him for ages last night." She drinks the last of her coffee, a grin appearing around the rim of her mug. I stare at her until she adds, "Tyler and Jason walked me home after school."

Izzy and I squeal so loud that Paz and crew imitate us from their booth.

"Fembos don't squeal, Shorty," Paz calls.

"Ignore him," Izzy says. "We have important business here."

Rachel explains that she happened to bump into Jason at his locker after class.

"How many passes did you have to make?" I ask. I know the technique and I've used it myself.

"Seven," she admits with a laugh. "But it was worth it. I said I was walking home, and Jason said he was heading my way. It was all going perfectly until Tyler came along and joined us. Not that I have anything against Tyler," she adds. "I just wanted to be alone with Jason."

"Did you ask him out?" asks Izzy, who advocates a more direct approach, although she's never used it.

Rachel shakes her head. "But I did mention we'd be here today, and he said he might stop by. Maybe he'll bring Tyler, Lu."

"Tyler might have FB potential, but if he also has Scoop potential, I'm not interested."

"He isn't Scoop," Rachel insists. "I'm sure of it."

I'm not sure, but there's no denying that I'm happy when Tyler walks in with Jason ten minutes later. They're with a third guy, who isn't in a hurry to take off his sunglasses.

The guy in shades trips over the leg of Paz's chair as he passes.

"Watch where you're going," Paz says, mopping up the soda that splashed onto his overalls.

"Shades" stops walking. "Your chair is in the middle of the aisle."

"There's plenty of room to go around," Paz counters.

I feel that flutter of anxiety I always get when testosterone flares in the diner. This isn't the first time Paz's chair
has leaped into the path of a non-Donner guy. The more
affected someone looks, the more likely that chair is to
move. Shades was asking for it.

Dan appears in the kitchen doorway. "Quit it, boys."

"Sorry, sir," Shades says. "Just a misunderstanding."
He waits till Dan is out of earshot and adds, "Maybe if these
morons had stayed in school, they'd have learned the chair
goes *under* the table."

I feel the flutter again, and this time it's accompanied
by defensiveness. It's one thing for me to make jokes about
the Dunfield dropouts who join Donner's "Chocolate
Graduate Program," but it's another for some stranger to
do it. Particularly when one of the dropouts is basically my
brother-in-law.

Joey is the first to return fire. "Staying in school hasn't
done *you* much good. Or don't they cover manners till
college?"

"I guess you'll never know," Shades says.

Tyler tugs on his friend's sleeve. "Leave it, Rico."

Dan reappears from the kitchen, and the posturing
ends instantly. By the time Jason, Tyler, and Rico reach us,
they're smiling and the testosterone is directed where it
should be—at us. Rico finally takes off his sunglasses.

"Nice outfit," Tyler says, smiling as he runs his eyes
over my uniform.

"If I'd known Mr. Fantastic would be here, I'd have
dressed up," I say.

Tyler doesn't get a chance to make a comeback before

Jason and Rico start teasing him. I finally come to the rescue by telling them about my customer's comic book collection.

With Dan watching Rico disapprovingly, I suggest that everyone move to a table.

Tyler is still looking at the menu when I go over to take their order. "It doesn't get any better the longer you look at it," I say. I point out the lassos, Dan's specialty. They're just onion rings, but the Texas allusion gives them some glamour. "Try those."

"Lassos?" he asks, pulling out the empty chair beside him and motioning for me to sit. "Tell me about them."

"The chef starts with the finest onions," I begin, perching on the chair. "He slices them finely and dips them in a batter made from his mother's secret recipe. Then he deep fries them to golden glory in oil that's been around since the diner opened in '73. You can taste the history on your tongue."

"An excellent review," Tyler says, laughing. "Very tempting."

Paz's falsetto rings out across the diner. "Oh, waitress! When you're finished socializing, could you settle our tab? Some of us have to work for a living."

Since Shirley is on break, I meet him at the cash register. "You don't have to embarrass me, Paz."

"I do, Shorty, and you'll thank me later. Those guys are losers."

"You started it."

"You know I hate the smell of Dunfield dweeb," he says. "Besides, it's my job to remind them that school is not their only option: they have choices in life."

I laugh in spite of myself. Paz is wasted on truffles. If he used that brain properly, he'd accomplish great things.

He punches me lightly on the arm. "Give Keira a kiss for me. But don't tell Grace."

"Okay, but I wish you'd tell Grace yourself."

He takes the long way out so that he can clomp heavily past Rico's table in his work boots.

Tyler pulls up in front of my building and cuts the engine on his Honda Civic.

I'm trying not to read too much into the fact that he offered to drive me home before meeting Jason, Rachel, Rico, and Izzy at the movie theater. It was only ten minutes out of his way, after all. He's just a nice guy.

"Are you sure you can't come with us?" he asks, turning the key so we can still hear the music.

"I wish I could, but I have plans." More like orders to babysit, but I'd rather let him think I'm doing something more interesting. "Don't you love this song? I've been playing it so much that my sister hid my CD."

Tyler starts talking about the music, and I wait for a sign that he might be my FB. I could totally see myself with a guy like him; someone with an arty, intellectual edge. Last month I wouldn't have aspired to arty/intellectual, but times have changed. I'm a columnist now.

When he stops talking, I unhook my seat belt and gather my things. I'm not going to ask him out. Izzy says I'm old-fashioned, but I think it works better if guys do the asking. "Thanks for the lift, Tyler. You're going to miss the movie if you don't hurry."

"Maybe we can do this again sometime," he says. "Better yet, we could go for dinner. I know this great Italian place."

Arty FB's always know the best Italian places.

"What about Sue Storm?" I ask. "I can't afford to piss off the Invisible Woman."

He gives me an FB smile. "I should probably do the right thing and break up with her first."

I give him an FG smile. "You'd dump Sue for me?"

The sign from the Chinese restaurant across the street reflects in Tyler's glasses, orange and pink and blue—his own neon rainbow. "Maybe," he says. "Would you mind if I kissed you before I decide?"

"That seems fair. It's a big decision."

Fortunately, the shortage of B in my life doesn't mean I'm a novice kisser. There was Porter Bell, of course, who kissed me at the eighth-grade prom. Shortly after that, I met Blake Wilson, whose family moved into an apartment just down the hall from ours. He kissed me in the elevator once, and I like to think he'd have made first FB status if Grace hadn't been standing in the hall glaring when the doors opened.

Last, and definitely best, there was Anton, the dishwasher Dan hired for the summer before I started at Dumpfield. Three years my senior, Anton was the most gorgeous guy I'd ever seen. I traded shifts all summer so that I could stare at his rippling muscles as he lifted trays of dishes, but I never got the nerve to say much to him before he quit for a new job at an upscale restaurant. When he was punching out for the last time, I walked into the staff office. We sort of circled each other for a second, and then he grabbed me and kissed me. I held on to his belt for dear life and didn't let go until Grace walked in and glowered at us. She just stood there, and filled the tiny office with her attitude until Anton gave up and left with a muttered good-bye. I never saw him again.

That was over a year ago, and I hope I haven't forgotten how it's done. I lean toward Tyler and he leans toward me. Our lips touch for a mere moment before a sudden noise makes us leap apart. Someone is rapping on the windshield. With a sippy cup.

Grace stands over the car, glowering yet again, with Keira on one hip. Her eyebrow studs look like a row of nails drilled right into her head.

"Do you know her?" Tyler asks.

My plan was to avoid mentioning the teenage-mother issue before having the whole B thing locked down. Tyler might think I have similar ambitions. "My sister."

I step out of the car, and Grace is on me instantly. "Do you know what time it is?"

"Yeah, it's a full hour before your shift starts."

"I have to pick up some things on my way in."

"You should have said so earlier. I can't read your mind."

Tyler opens his door and comes around the car to meet Grace, which is pretty brave of him.

"Grace," I say, "This is—"

"I don't care." She thrusts Keira into my arms and walks away. "I've got a bus to catch."

I apologize to Tyler. "I'd like to say she's not usually that rude, but unfortunately she is."

He reaches out to Keira and asks, "Who's this?"

Keira recoils and unleashes an ear-piercing wail. "My niece."

He backs away. "Sorry, sorry. I guess I should get to the movie."

I hope Mr. Fantastic is up to a challenge.

I settle Keira in front of her favorite Barney movie and head into the bedroom to check my e-mail. The phone rings.

"Well?" Rachel asks.

"How come you're not in the movie?" Tiptoeing to the bedroom door, I peek into the living room and confirm that Keira is now sound asleep on the couch. I close my door and settle onto the bed so that my voice doesn't wake her.

"We snuck out for a minute," Rachel says. "So we'll have to talk fast."

"How'd it go with Tyler?" Izzy calls from behind Rachel. "We couldn't get much out of him before the movie started."

"Well, for starters, he asked me out, and then he kissed me." A general squawk of excitement reverberates at the other end. It sounds like eight people. "Where *are* you guys?"

"In the restroom," Rachel says. "So *then* what happened?"

"He's kissing me, and it's great, and then Grace comes out with Keira and bangs on the window."

"Oh, crap," Izzy says.

"I know! He got out of the car to meet her, but you know how Grace is."

Now there's a chorus of dismay. "Grace ruins everything," Rachel says.

My sentiments exactly!

"Well, don't give up," Izzy says. "If Tyler likes you, Grace won't scare him off."

If Grace could scare off Anton, she can scare off Tyler.

Rachel apparently agrees, because she suggests that I call him instead of waiting for *him* to call me. "I think he's worth it, Lu. He's smart and cute. Plus, he's got a car. His parents just bought it for him because they're moving to West Ridge and Tyler wants to finish the year at Dunfield."

West Ridge is a pretty nice neighborhood. His parents' catering business must be taking off.

"Maybe I will," I say, just to get them off the subject. It works, too.

"We'll strategize tomorrow," Izzy says, before they hang up.

After checking on Keira again, I take out my iPod and lie down on the bed for a moment and replay the car scene in my mind the way it *should* have gone. I'd add about two minutes on to the kiss and then make a smooth, casual departure. "Call me," I'd say as I opened the door. "We'll see how fantastic you really are."

Tyler. It's a good name for a boyfriend. I know that he's not my boyfriend yet, but he might be soon. And then I'll be a whole new Lu Perez—the one with the boyfriend who has his own car. The one whose boyfriend lives in West Ridge. The one whose boyfriend wants to be a food critic someday.

Tyler and Lu. It works. It really works. It sounds like an upscale clothing store, or a swanky restaurant. A swanky restaurant that serves food worthy of a critic.

> *We're in New York City at a hip, new restaurant Tyler is reviewing for the* Times. *He orders five or six different dishes to sample.*
> *"Try the paella," he says.*
> *"I can't," I say. "I don't do spicy."*
> *"You do now. You've got to expand your horizons, Lu. A girl cannot live on meat loaf alone."*
> *He extends a forkful of paella. It's an explosion of flavor in my mouth. Hot, but not too hot. "Wow! Amazing!" I say.*
> *"I know," he says. "And so are you."*
> *We gaze at each other across the tiny, candlelit table. The moment is perfect . . .*

Except for that annoying noise in the background.

I yank off my headphones and sit up, realizing that I've been sleeping. And my cell phone is ringing. I fumble for it, hoping it's Tyler. If it is, I want to sound cool and casual.

"Hello?" Just right. I sound almost bored.

"You sound awfully calm," Grace says.

"Why wouldn't I be?"

There's a laugh at her end, but she doesn't sound amused. "You don't even know, do you?"

"Know what?" I ask, suddenly worried.

"How's Keira?"

"Fine," I say, already on my feet. "She's asleep on the—*Oh, no!*"

"Missing something?"

I'm running around the apartment now, opening doors and pulling curtains aside. "Is this a trick, Grace? If it is, it isn't funny."

"No, it isn't funny," she agrees. "Where's my baby, Lu?"

"You must know," I say, getting down on my knees and peering under the couch. "Or you'd be freaking out too."

"But you're the one looking after her."

For a second I wonder if I'm actually having a nightmare right now. Maybe if I just admit the truth I'll wake up. "I don't know where she is, Grace. *I don't know.*"

Grace lets my hysteria rise for a moment before saying, "Mrs. Maneiro found her wandering in the hall."

I try to come up with a good excuse, but there is no good excuse. "I must have dozed off, Grace. Keira was asleep on the couch and I thought she'd be okay."

"You've got to chain the door, Lu. You've got to *watch* her."

"I know. I'm sorry."

It's not enough. Grace is just getting warmed up. "You think you're too good to watch my kid, now, don't you?"

"Of course not. Don't yell." Everyone in the diner is probably staring at her and listening in. My regulars will realize I'm a terrible aunt.

"Ever since you started writing, you're all full of yourself. Well here's a news flash, Lu: you're nothing special. You're no better than the rest of us. In fact, you're worse than the rest of us. You're useless."

Before I can say another word, she slams the phone down, nearly blowing out my eardrum.

Chapter 5

Rachel and I stop and wait for Izzy to catch up. Her stiletto boots keep getting stuck in the grass as we walk across Dunfield's back field toward the bleachers.

"I don't understand why they're holding this outside," Izzy grumbles, scraping dirt off her heels. "It's not a sporting event."

"Don't kid yourself," I say. "This is a competition. Expect a fistfight or two."

"Over Mariah, probably," Izzy says.

The date auction is taking place on a makeshift stage erected in the center of the track because attendance is expected to be so high. Hundreds of students are already milling around, although the auction itself doesn't start for nearly an hour.

"It's all material for Newshound, right, Lu?" Rachel asks.

When I shrug, Izzy asks, "What's wrong?"

I start walking again, and they follow. "I'm thinking of quitting the *Bulletin*."

"But you were so into it last week," Izzy says. "It's not because Scoop called you a dog, is it?"

"No, but thanks for reminding me. There are too many events to attend, that's all."

Izzy rolls her eyes. Unlike Rachel and me, she's adapted quickly and well to being a fully participating Dunfield student. It makes me wonder if we were holding her back last year.

"I'm not saying the events aren't fun," I continue. "But between homework and my job, I don't have much time left over for my family, and they need me right now."

"You need time for yourself, too," Izzy insists. "And you said this column is an opportunity."

"I've had second thoughts. I don't think it'll lead to anything."

"Tons of successful writers launch their careers at a high school paper," Izzy protests. "Right, Rachel?"

Rachel doesn't say anything. She's remained uncharacteristically quiet throughout this discussion.

"Success doesn't exactly run in my family," I say.

"So you'll break the mold," Izzy says. "You have so much going for you."

"Please. I couldn't even keep track of my niece. I'm useless."

"I knew it!" Rachel bursts out. "This is about Grace, isn't it? She said something, didn't she?"

"She said a lot of things. I lost her kid, Rachel."

"It was an accident."

"I wasn't paying attention and it could have been a disaster."

"But it wasn't."

Izzy chimes in. "You made a mistake, Lu, that's all."

"Grace has made plenty of mistakes herself," Rachel says. "Big ones, some of them. She should cut you some slack."

Izzy stops walking again. "Don't be mad at me for saying this, Lu, because you know how much I like Grace. I think she's a good mother, I really do, but I don't think she's always a good sister. I think she's jealous of the fact that you have more options than she does."

That it's Izzy saying this somehow gives it more weight. Still, in this instance I was definitely in the wrong. "It's not just Grace. My mom said I'm spreading myself too thin—that I need to focus."

It's harder for them to argue against my mother, but Rachel takes it on. "Focusing is important, but you need to have dreams, too. The only reason I can drag my butt into this dump every day is that I'll never become a conservationist otherwise."

"A conservationist?" Izzy says. "I thought you wanted to run a lodge."

"A lodge *in the Serengeti*, Izzy," Rachel says. "I want to lead wildlife safaris."

Izzy stares at Rachel as if seeing her for the first time. It's that "how could we be so different and still be friends" look. Whereas Rachel loves communing with nature, Izzy prefers communing with her blow dryer. She always denies it, but Iz fully intends to take over her parents' salon one day. I know she'll expand far beyond its current Mom-and-Pop status, too. She's already pushing them to try new things, but they're satisfied with being an unchanging neighborhood institution.

"My point is, you can't let this thing with Grace hold you back," Rachel says. "Like my father always says, 'If you dream big and work hard, you're sure to succeed.'"

Izzy nods in agreement. "Now, let's go find Newshound a story."

Both girls smile, satisfied that their work is done. Feeling better, I link my arms through theirs and start walking. I may not be able to choose my relatives, but I did a great job of choosing my friends.

If I were a regular reporter instead of an anonymous columnist, I could simply chronicle Izzy's journey through today's auction. She's decided to bid on someone, and we are shopping for the lucky guy now.

"Rico didn't do it for you?" Rachel asks. She'd hoped we could all hang out together with Jason, Tyler, and Rico.

Izzy shakes her head. "First, there was the thing with Paz at the diner. Then he told me about his girlfriend who lives in Mexico. He sees her every summer, but in between they're supposedly allowed to see other people, as long as it's casual.

"You mean he's looking for a friend with benefits?" I ask.

"Correct," Izzy says. "I mean, do I look like that kind of girl?"

She doesn't. Izzy is fond of glitter and trendy clothes, but she doesn't show much skin or flaunt her chest size. And while she believes in taking the initiative with guys if she likes them, she's still a traditional girl underneath.

"I need a guy with some class," Izzy continues. "And I'm hoping forty-eight dollars will buy it."

"That's a lot of money," I say. "Are you sure you want to throw it away on a single date?"

"Quality doesn't come cheap, Lu."

"How will you know you're bidding on quality?" Rachel asks. "You can't always see that from a distance."

Fortunately, Mariah has eliminated some of the guess-work by preparing a complete list of the auction partici-pants, along with a description of the "dream date" each is offering. To raise extra money, she's selling that list half an hour before the auction begins. Meanwhile, everyone on the list will be working the crowd so we can check out the merchandise up close.

"You can tell a lot about a guy from his dream date," Izzy says.

I find it hard to believe that any Dunfield guy has the imagination—or money—to offer a classy date at a charity auction, but Izzy is less cynical than I am.

The crowd parts to reveal Mariah heading for the stage. Her leather jacket is undone, and I can see that in honor of the occasion, she has actually abandoned her usual workout gear in favor of the short leather skirt she wore in the Bootylicious Calendar, heels, and a low-cut tank. She climbs the stairs and turns to face the crowd.

"I know you want this," she says, displaying the pre-auction package teasingly. "But you've got to wait another twenty minutes. In the meantime, start mingling. If you see someone wearing one of these"—she points to the number pinned to her tank top—"talk to them. If you fall in love, you still have time to run to the ATM."

Coming down the stairs, Mariah's eyes light on me. "What, no number, Coconut? I'm pretty sure zero's still available."

"Thanks, but I could never compete with you."

She takes my comment at face value. "So true. We'd have to give money *back* to get someone to take you off our hands."

It's another beauteous day at Dumpfield.

Leaving Rachel and Izzy to study the auction guide, I start circulating. It's not long before I come upon the tech nerds, who have gathered in a conspiratorial clump beside the bleachers. They're emptying their pockets, handing their money to a guy wearing a faded *Star Trek* baseball cap.

"What's the total, Curtis?" a guy with greasy, straw-colored hair asks the Trekkie.

Curtis's lips move as he counts. "We've got one hundred twenty-three dollars and sixty-one cents."

"That should do it," the greasy-haired guy says. "Let's review the strategy. Curtis: you've got to hold off until everyone else has finished bidding, and then shout a last-ditch offer. If you fire too soon, she'll beg someone to outbid you."

I think I've found my story: *Guys pool their money to give nerdy pal shot at a real date with hot girl.* That is so sweet!

"Do not forget your mission," Greasy Hair says. "You won the bet, but you have an obligation to the rest of us. Did you hook up the spy cam?"

Curtis points to his cap. "Operational."

"Okay, you know the drill. Start with cleavage shots.

67

Then stand behind her and ask her to reach for something, because we want thong action. And belly ring. I'm talking extreme close-up. We want to know if that girl waxes or shaves."

Ew. EW. EW!!! I have to report this to a teacher. The pervs must be stopped.

"Are you kidding?" Curtis asks. "Mariah wouldn't shave."

On the other hand, who am I to ruin an underdog's big chance?

Tyler finds me on the bleachers. "I've been looking all over for you," he says.

So Grace hasn't scared him away after all! "You have?"

"I want you to do me a favor," he says. "It'll cost you, but I promise to pay you back. It's for a good cause."

I notice he's holding a folded number in his hand. "You're going on the block?"

He nods sheepishly. "My cousin is on Mariah's planning committee, and she pressured me into it. But I'm afraid no one will bid on me."

"Of course they'll bid on you. You're Mr. Fantastic."

"I've got news for you, Lu: you're the only one who thinks so."

I smile. "Well, I could help you out, but I'd need to know what entertainment's on offer. To quote Izzy, you can tell a lot about a guy from his dream date."

"The Bulls are providing the entertainment," he says, pulling two tickets out of his pocket. "I'm just providing the seats."

I wrinkle my nose. "Basketball? What happened to a nice Italian dinner?"

"The game will be way more fun than fettuccine, I promise. How about it? I'll be humiliated if no one bids on me."

"So it's not so much that you want to go out with me as that you want me to save you from public humiliation."

"Not to mention ugly bidders," he adds.

"Tyler! That's terrible."

He grins. "I'm just saying I'd be proud to leave the stage with you. And as a special thank-you, I'll throw in the nice Italian dinner."

I pretend to think about it. "Including dessert?"

"Three courses. And that's just the beginning."

He reaches over, grabs the zipper on my hoodie, and pulls me toward him. We're surrounded by people, yet I feel quite comfortable kissing my Arty FB because Dunfield is the last place on earth you'd ever find Grace.

When he finally pulls away, Tyler says, "Consider that a sneak preview."

"You think one kiss is going to convince me to bid on you?" I ask.

His smile falters as I climb down from the bleachers. "Where are you going?" he calls.

"To round up some cash."

I collect my purse from my locker and check my wallet. Thirty bucks. That *might* be enough to win Tyler, especially since he's not up till later in the program. By then most of the girls will have blown their budgets on the seniors and the jocks. So few Dunfield girls recognize a superhero in disguise.

Just in case, I decide to make a quick pit stop at Mr. Sparling's office on my way back to the field. He offered me some petty cash to cover my costs at events. I doubt he'll foot the entire bill for a dream date with Tyler, but he said a good journalist dives into the action, so maybe he'll give me a top-up.

I hear Mr. Sparling's voice before I reach the door. "This is not the kind of writing I expect from you," he lectures. "I'm very disappointed."

"Oh, come on," a familiar voice says. "It's funny."

I place the voice: it belongs to Mac Landis. Taking another step, I peer through the crack in the door. Sure enough, there's a blond mop of hair in the chair opposite Mr. Sparling's.

"It's juvenile," Mr. Sparling replies. "You're capable of so much more. That's why I gave you this opportunity."

"But you gave us free rein to share our opinions. That's the purpose."

"No, the purpose is to stretch your mind and your writing skills."

Mac murmurs something I can't quite catch, but it's obviously not apologetic enough for Mr. Sparling, because he says, "Whether you aim low or aim high, you'll reach your target, Mac. Do you want to settle for low?"

The blond head droops. "Okay, I'll rewrite it. Sorry, sir."

"Just do your best. That's all I ask."

I back away before Mac leaves the office. As soon as I

turn the corner, I start to run. If I hurry, I can still make it to the ATM.

Back in the field, Mariah is already on the stage, warming up the crowd with some dance moves as loud music thunders out over the field. I fill Rachel and Izzy in on the details of my scouting mission, ending with Mr. Sparling's conversation. "It looks like you guys were right about Mac being Scoop," I tell Rachel. "Mr. Sparling sounded really disappointed. I'm surprised he expected more of Mac. He must see something we don't."

Finally, the auction begins. Eighty students parade around the stage before lining up. The cheers are almost loud enough to drown out the music.

Griffin Gonzalez has volunteered as auctioneer. He'll be working from his fellow seniors down to the sole freshman who had the nerve to put himself on the block.

Determined to take the plunge, Izzy bids on the very first guy. And the fourth. And the seventh. Each time, she is defeated by girls with deeper pockets. Number seven, who offers a limo ride and theater tickets, pulls in a whopping sixty-eight dollars.

Izzy is down but not out. When number fifteen steps up, she tries again. He's tall and cute but more rugged than her usual type.

Rachel says, "In case you didn't notice, he wearing hiking boots, Izzy."

I consult the auction guide. "This guy's dream date is rock climbing. You're afraid of heights, Iz. And you only wear heels."

"But I like seniors," Izzy says. "And sometimes you have to compromise."

Only one other girl is willing to compromise, and Izzy lands number fifteen for a bargain: twenty-two dollars.

When Mariah's turn comes, she struts to center stage and does a pirouette before settling into a contrived pose. Before the auctioneer even opens the bidding, hands soar. There are a few hoarse shouts—the sound of desperate men with money to blow.

"Opening at thirty dollars for a night of dancing at an all-ages club," the auctioneer says. "Do I hear forty?"

With each new bid, Mariah strikes a new pose. When it crosses the hundred-dollar mark, she does a high kick, which in that short skirt nets another flurry of bids.

A football player bellows, "One twenty. Final offer."

There's laughter followed by a long silence. Finally Griffin says, "I have one twenty. Can anyone do better? *Going . . . going . . .*"

"One twenty-three," Curtis the tech geek calls. "And sixty-one cents."

Mariah is still smiling as she scans the crowd for the voice. Her eyes land on Curtis, and the smile vanishes. She rushes toward the auctioneer, calling, "Wait!"

It's too late. He has closed the bidding at $123.61.

Although successful bidders are supposed to wait till the auction is over to claim their prize, Curtis is already stumbling up the stairs to the stage. Mariah clutches the auctioneer with one hand, while Curtis pulls on her other arm.

"Sorry, Mariah," Griffin says. "He won fair and square. It's for charity, remember?"

Izzy, Rachel, and I laugh hysterically as Curtis half carries Mariah off the stage. This is one of the moments in life that you always, *always* remember.

Mac takes center stage to the sound of whistles and catcalls from Dunfield's female population. A junior I recognize from the Bootylicious cheerleader photo shoot raises her hand. "Twenty dollars."

"I have twenty dollars from Brianna Mills for Mac Landis and his so-called mystery date on Friday," the auctioneer says. "Do I hear thirty?"

"Thirty," I call.

The word is out of my mouth before I can stop it. It's an involuntary reaction, like a sneeze.

"I have thirty from"—Griffin struggles to identify me—"some girl wearing a purple hoodie."

"Thirty-five," Brianna says.

"Forty," I say.

There's a series of other bids, but I've been restrained by Rachel and Izzy. "What are you doing?" Izzy asks. "Have you lost your mind?"

"I want to know if he's Scoop," I say.

Rachel stares at me. "Does this have anything to do with the burrito incident? Tell me you're not into Mac Landis."

"Please. My FB is not a brainless jock."

I can understand why my friends are confused, since I'm a bit confused myself. This Luisa Perez isn't the type to bid on the hottest guy in her year, even in the name of research. I'm not deluding myself that my two recent exchanges with Mac meant anything, especially when he hasn't even said hello to me since. But there was something about Mac's conversation with Mr. Sparling that made me want to talk to him privately. That can't happen in the hallway, where the school hierarchy barely allows him to acknowledge I exist.

Wrenching my wrist out of Izzy's grip, I wave and shout, "Ninety dollars."

"One hundred," Brianna says. She stands on tiptoe to give me a menacing glare.

"One ten," I say. It's muffled because Rachel has her hand over my mouth, but the auctioneer hears it.

"You won't have anything left to bid on Tyler," she says. "You promised."

Rachel is right. In all the excitement, I forgot about Tyler. I drained my bank account earlier, but I only have one twenty in total.

"Brianna says one fifteen," the auctioneer calls. "Do I hear one twenty from the Hoodie?

Rachel pinches my arm and I hesitate.

"Going once . . ."

"You guys can lend me money, right?" I ask. "I'll repay you with petty cash from Mr. Sparling."

"Going twice . . ."

I don't wait for an answer. "One twenty-five!"

Brianna's superior smile collapses, and I know I've won the bid.

My head is spinning as the auctioneer calls, *"Sold to the Hoodie."* Still, I register Mac's incredulous look in my direction as he steps back into the line. I don't blame him. I can't believe it happened either.

* * *

It turns out I seriously underestimated the appeal of the arty type. Although I amassed thirty-seven dollars from Izzy and Rachel, it's nowhere near enough to buy a date with Tyler. After bids from at least five attractive girls, he sold for a very respectable seventy-three.

If the highest bidder had been one of those attractive girls, Tyler might have forgiven me. But it wasn't. It wasn't even an ugly girl. In fact, it wasn't a girl at all. And as a result, he is no longer speaking to me.

I follow him to the student parking lot, pleading, "Come on, Tyler, I bid what I could."

Tyler pauses with his hand on the car door. "You mean you bid what you had left over."

"It's not what you think. I don't *like* Mac or anything."

"You mean his 'mystery date' was that appealing?"

"I *had* to bid on him." I run through a list of possible excuses in my mind, each seeming lamer than the last. "But I can't tell you why."

Tyler opens the car door, shaking his head in disgust. "I thought you were different, but you're just like the other airheads."

"That's not true. I wish I could tell you why, but I can't. I'm really sorry."

"I'm not," he says, climbing into the car. "I'm glad I found out now."

There's a shout behind us, and Tyler's face reddens. It's the guy who won the bid. "Hey, Milano," he shouts. "Just drop the Bulls' tickets in my locker and we'll call it even, okay? Forget about the dinner."

Tyler slams his door in my face, and in a squeal of rubber my Arty FB is gone.

Mariah is perched on a sink in the girls' restroom when I enter. It's the only place Curtis can't follow her.

I consider turning around and leaving again, but I don't want to give her the satisfaction. "Hi," I say, trying to sound breezy.

She stares at me for a moment. "You know this isn't going to happen, right?"

I pull out my lip gloss and apply it. "What isn't?"

"You and Mac Landis. Not. Going. To. Happen."

Arguing would only convince her that I'm interested in Mac, which I'm not, so I take a different tack. "You know that you and Curtis *are* going to happen, right?"

She grips the sides of the sink and mutters something in Spanish. I can't tell which one of us gets the worst of it, Curtis or me.

Hopping off the sink, she waves a threatening finger in my face. "At least I don't have to pay for it, Coconut."

I smile, mainly because I don't have a comeback, but it seems to rile her more. Normally I'd be running already, but I'm less intimidated when it's just the two of us.

Mariah continues, "Mac would NEVER go out with someone like you if it weren't charity."

"I know," I say, backing toward the door. "It's not like you and Curtis. You're going to be *great* together."

Something heavy hits the door behind me as I leave.

Chapter 6

The L train rumbles into Roosevelt/State station. "Where are we going?" I ask. Not for the first time.

Mac silently shrugs his broad shoulders. Also not for the first time. He's barely said a word since we met on a street corner twenty-five minutes ago. He has, however, communicated nonverbally—through grunts, shrugs, and throat clearings—that he'd rather be anywhere else than sharing a day off school with me.

Finally Mac deigns to speak. "It's a *mystery* date."

I'd settle for less mystery and more communication. I've tossed out all sorts of conversation-starters, including a question about basketball, but he won't take the bait. If I don't find Mac's "on" switch soon, I'll never learn whether he's Scoop. And I have to find out, or it will mean I threw away both my Arty FB and a lot of money on nothing. Worse than nothing: to be treated like crap.

"If I tell you where we're going," he adds, "it won't be a mystery."

Another full sentence! Things are picking up.

The train doors open, and Mac steps out without warning. I leap out after him and almost get caught in the closing doors. By this point he's already walking away at such a clip that I have to jog to keep up. If he's trying to shake me, he's going to have to work harder than that.

"Could you slow down?" I say.

He looks at me, and something registers on his face. Maybe he's realizing that as much as he doesn't want to be here, I did pay good money for the pleasure of his company. "You're short," he says.

That wasn't the sort of acknowledgment I'd hoped for, but he does slow down slightly.

"Are we going to Grant Park?"

"Nah, the cops are always on patrol," he replies cryptically.

I've never noticed that. I guess it's only a problem if you're committing crimes. "The aquarium, then? I hear the cop-to-dolphin ratio is pretty low."

He gives me a quick look to see if I'm joking before shaking his head.

I highly doubt the museum is his idea of a great date destination, but I ask anyway.

"Do I look like a loser to you?" he says.

"I guess that rules out the planetarium too."

His blue eyes light up, the first sign of life he's shown so far. "You figured me out," he says. "We're going to the planetarium."

"You just decided that now, didn't you?" I ask. "You

only billed this as a 'mystery date' because you had nothing planned."

If Izzy is right, and you can tell a lot about a guy from his dream date, there isn't anything to know about Mac. He's an attractive, empty shell.

He glares at me and mutters, "No wonder you don't have a boyfriend."

Okay, he's not empty: he's full of venom. Well, I don't have to take this abuse. Ten out of eleven Luisa Perezes might be desperate for Mac's attention, but not this one. "For your information, I *nearly* had a boyfriend. I was supposed to bid on him, but I bid on you instead."

"Tell me something I don't know."

"Because his dream date was tickets to the Bulls," I say. "And I hate football."

"Basketball."

"Whatever," I say. I have more important things on my mind right now than sports. Such as surviving the worst date of my life. Even when it's no longer the *only* date of my life, I'm pretty sure it will still be the worst.

Mac checks his watch and then picks up speed again. When he gets closer to the entrance, he waits for me to catch up. "Just stick close," he says. "And if anyone stops us, let me do the talking."

He opens a heavy glass door and lets it swing shut in my face.

"Can you try to keep up?" he asks, when I join him inside. Grabbing my wrist, he tows me over to a large group of tourists who are speaking what sounds like German.

"Hello," Mac says, directing a brilliant smile at a young couple. "How do you like Chicago?"

As they respond in halting English, we all migrate together through the barriers and into the planetarium. Without paying admission.

Once inside, Mac slips away from the group as easily as he joined them.

"That was stealing, you know," I say.

He responds with more nonverbal communication: a dismissive wave. "The sky theater's this way."

Leading me into the theater, he chooses seats as far from other guests as possible. A few moments later, the lights go down, and the night sky appears overhead.

I settle back in my seat and stare up at the stars. The view is so realistic, it's easy to forget I'm in a theater. The only other time I've seen the stars so clearly was when I went camping with Rachel's family at Starved Rock State Park. I was ten years old, and I remember how small and insignificant I felt under that sky. But I also remember feeling awed and overwhelmed by its beauty.

It's hard to believe that this pleasant flashback comes courtesy of MacEwan Landis, the Venomous Jock. If he likes the planetarium, maybe there really is more to him than it seems.

"I've never been here before," I say. "It's amazing,"

He shushes me, provoking me to offer a few more observations about the sky above. Suddenly my view of the stars is eclipsed by a large shadow, and Mac's mouth is on mine. In fact, his tongue is in my mouth. And his two hands have become ten.

With a lot of effort, I manage to push him off me. "What the hell are you doing?" I ask, wiping venom from my mouth with my sleeve.

"That's what you wanted, isn't it?" he asks.

One of his hands slips under my sweater and travels north faster than the asteroid shooting through space above me. I slap my hand on top of his.

"If you don't stop now I'll *scream*," I say. I put enough emphasis on the last word that the hand immediately reverses course.

"Are you serious?" he asks, throwing himself back in his seat. "Then what did you pay a hundred and twenty-five bucks for?"

"Not to rent a gigolo. Believe it or not, I wanted to talk to you."

"Talk?" he says, sounding incredulous. "I didn't bring you here to talk."

"Then let's look at the stars. It is a planetarium."

"Chicks don't normally like this kind of thing," he grumbles. "I can never get them to pay attention. We always end up—"

"Making out? I suppose that's someone's dream date, but not mine."

"You're the first to complain," he says, and it's probably true.

"How many times have you brought girls here?"

He sidesteps the question. "Do you want to go home?"

I think about it for a moment. Mac is an idiot, but I'd like to stick it out long enough to figure out if he's Scoop.

81

No one else needs to know that our dream date was a total bust. On the contrary, over time, people might even forget that I had to pay for it. One day as I walk across the stage to collect my high school diploma, someone will whisper, *"Isn't she the Luisa Perez who dated Mac Landis?"*

"We might as well watch the show," I say. "Since you went to so much trouble to get us in."

There's a sound like a snort beside me. With anyone else it might signify amusement, but I'm not sure whether Mac even has a sense of humor.

I point to the ceiling. "There's the Big Dipper."

"That's Pegasus," he corrects me, using the contemptuous tone generally reserved for parents and morons.

"Are you sure?" I'd believe anything he said about sports, but I've never sensed any hidden gifts in the science arena. "It doesn't look like a winged horse to me."

Mac lifts his hand and traces out a figure. "It's upside down. The square is the body and the two lines coming out of it are the legs."

"Really?"

"Yes, really." He sounds annoyed. "Do you want me to bring in an astronomer to verify it?"

"No, I believe you." Sort of.

"The constellations don't always take an obvious shape," he acknowledges. He shows me how a few stars form the hero Hercules, poised with a club. I would never have seen this on my own, either.

"I read about Hercules in English," I say. "I never thought I'd like mythology, but Mr. Sparling manages to make it interesting, doesn't he?"

Mac doesn't respond, so I press on. "He's a good teacher. Did you know he's editor of the school paper?"

"Who cares?" Mac says. "I never read the school paper."

"Not even 'The Word'?"

"What word?" He sounds genuinely confused.

"You know, the column by Scoop?"

"Oh, right," he says. "The guys said it was funny. I should pick it up."

Well, I'm not making much progress here. "What do you think of Mr. Sparling?"

"I think you talk about him a lot. Are you hot for him?"

"Ew! I'm just saying he's all right, for a teacher."

"Sparling and I don't see eye to eye." He points to the ceiling again, effectively cutting off my line of questioning. "See those three bright stars to the far right of Pegasus? That's Orion's belt."

"And Orion is . . . ?"

"You're the mythology fan. You tell me."

"As I recall, Orion was the Greek god of fashion and accessorizing."

This time the snort is definitely amusement. Something tells me I might be the only girl he's brought here who's ever accomplished that.

Mac explains that in one version of the myth, Orion was a great hunter who fell in love with Artemis. Her brother, Apollo, didn't like Orion, so one day he put a scorpion in his path, and Orion chased it into the ocean. Then Apollo put a beam of light on Orion's back and dared his sister, a slick archer, to hit it with an arrow. Poor Artemis ended up killing her own lover. When Orion's body washed up on shore, Artemis begged the almighty Zeus to put Orion in the sky for all eternity.

"If you look way down there," he says, pointing again, "there's the scorpion."

"I can see it," I say. "That's so cool. How do you know so much about this stuff?"

"My grandfather used to bring me here all the time."

"But now you've ditched him to bring girls instead?"

There's a pause and then, "He died a few months ago."

Oops. "I'm sorry."

He sits in silence for so long that I figure we've reverted back to the grunt-and-shrug phase, but eventually he speaks again. "My grandfather wouldn't have minded about the girls, actually. But he would have been pissed about my not paying admission."

I laugh. "You're lucky you had a relationship with your grandfather. I don't really know my grandparents. My parents were young when they had my sister, and no one was very happy about it."

There's something about a dark room and stars over-head that makes it easier to share things with people you normally wouldn't trust.

"That sucks," he says, and unless it's my imagination, his tone verges on sympathetic.

"Sometimes it does," I admit. "But mostly it's okay."

Mac starts telling me more about his grandparents, but when the lights come up, his voice trails off. It's like he remembers that he's Mac Landis and I'm just one of Dunfield's many Luisa Perezes.

He stands and slips into his jacket. "I guess that's it."

"I guess so." I take my time putting on my coat before saying, "Are we going for coffee?"

He turns and appraises me. "I could use a coffee."

As he leads me out of the theater, he says, "So this guy you were supposed to bid on . . . It was Tyler Milano, right?"

"How'd you know?"

"Bulls tickets are something you notice. He's not your type anyway."

"Oh? What *is* my type?"

"Not him."

Paz is always making similar pronouncements; I sense he won't think anyone is ever my type.

Mac adds, "He's a loser."

"Tyler's a nice guy," I say, secretly flattered that Mac now believes I deserve better than a loser. "He was even going to take me for dinner after the game."

"Are you implying I didn't give you your money's worth?" he asks, grinning.

"Now that you mention it, you haven't spent a dime," I say. "I'll have to tell that cheerleader—Brianna, right?—how cheap you are."

"Then I'll have to tell Tyler you put out," he counters.

"You'd better not!"

"Kidding," he says. "I guess I could buy you a burger."

"For a hundred-and-twenty-five bucks, it had better be the best burger I've ever tasted."

He bows and opens the planetarium's front door for me with a flourish.

THE WORD . . . FROM NEWSHOUND
Out Front Where We Belong

The girls' fund-raising team is back in the lead where it belongs, thanks to its wildly successful Date Auction. The guys attempted a comeback with Casino Night, but couldn't compete with romance when the chips were down. Although nearly 500 students gambled the night away on Saturday, an astounding 1,500 converged in the school's backfield earlier in the week to bid on 80 of Dunfield's finest men and women. Kudos to those brave enough to step onto the block.

Newshound fully endorsed this creative fundraising event, unlike the Bootylicious Calendar. Dating for dollars is not the same thing as stripping for them. You can fend a guy off if he's drooling all over you in person, but you can't control what he's doing with your photograph in the privacy of his bedroom. Still, Newshound understands that the Bootylicious calendar may be as close as some guys (columnists included) ever get to a pretty girl.

Rumors have reached Newshound's ear that some Dunfield men are buying into Scoop's chauvinistic crap. You're making a mistake, guys. Cavemen are only interesting in the history books, so you may as well drop the act. It's boring, and it makes you boring. Everyone knows that evolution doesn't happen overnight, but how about speeding it up a little?

Dunfield women would find you much more interesting if you'd stop pretending to be so tough all the time. And stop assuming we'll have sex with you when you can't even bother to talk to us. Nonverbal communication only works for lesser primates. Either learn the art of conversation or find yourself a chimp who can walk in heels.

Believe it or not, women want to know what you're thinking. You don't have to share your deepest, darkest secrets (although we'd love it if you would, at least eventually). Mainly, we're interested in hearing about your family, your interests, and your hopes for the future. If you're hard up for topics, try movies, books, or current events. All it takes is picking up a newspaper now and then.

It would be nice if you'd show some interest in our lives, too. Ask a few questions. It really isn't that hard.

In fact, here's a little tip from the Newshound on how to seduce a girl: get to know her.

Maybe if you gave a little more, you'd get a little more.

Izzy hoists her oversized, studded hobo bag onto her desk and gropes around inside it. She pulls out a variety of makeup and other necessities of life before finally locating her mythology text and a notebook. I've tried to convince her that a backpack makes more sense, but Izzy is too fashion conscious for that. Passing the bag to Rachel to hold open at the edge of the desk, Izzy sweeps everything back into it, leaving only her books, a pen, and an emery board. That's when I notice her torn and ragged nails.

"Rock climbing," Rachel says in response to my shocked expression.

"You've already had your date?" I ask. "Why didn't you call me?"

"I left you a voice mail on your cell," Izzy says.

I wonder what else I missed. Grace commandeered my phone on the weekend because hers died. Naturally, having a child trumps my need to communicate. I bet she won't pay a dime of my bill, either.

"Was he worth it?" I ask, gesturing to the destroyed manicure.

"Absolutely. He's a senior, he's cute, he's smart, he's funny, and his parents are from the same town in Mexico as mine." She stops filing to add, "Did I mention he's a senior?"

I laugh. "You did, yeah."

"Does this mean you're turning into sporty girl?" Rachel asks.

Izzy rolls her eyes. "Never. You can't have nails like this and work in the beauty industry. But I'm willing to cheer my man on from the sidelines if I have to."

I have a sudden vision of myself in the bleachers cheering Mac on, and give my head a hard shake to dispel it. "Did the rock-climbing senior ask you out again?"

Izzy's fuchsia ponytail swishes a negative. "Not yet. But he mentioned that he was going to the dance. So we"—she points to Rachel and me—"are going to the dance. I'll have an entire night to work on him there."

"I'm pretty proud of the fact that I've never attended a Dunfield dance," I say.

Izzy stops filing to fix me with dark eyes. "Newshound owes me."

I hold my finger to my lips and look around, only to find Mr. Sparling standing beside me. "Cut the chitchat and the manicures, ladies," he says. "Class has officially begun."

He walks to the front of the class and writes something on the board. Rachel uses the opportunity to slip me a note that contains only one word: *Mac?*

I shake my head. It's not like I expected him to call me after our "date," even though we hung out for two full hours before he left for Casino Night. But I did think he'd acknowledge me in the halls. Maybe he will if I ever run into him. Normally he's everywhere, moving in the center of a gorgeous pack, but lately he's nowhere to be found.

I write one word on my notebook and hold it up: *Sick?*

Rachel shrugs and writes back: *Let's stake out his locker later.*

I nod just as Mr. Sparling turns. "Luisa," he says. "I see I'm boring you already. That must mean you've read ahead in your text."

Mr. Sparling has been supportive of my work for "The Word," but if I had any notion that our editor/columnist relationship might extend to the classroom, it's clear from his expression that it does not. If anything, I feel worse being caught socializing than I normally would.

"So," Mr. Sparling says, and I know what's coming next. He'll use that time-honored teacher technique of throwing out a question to prove that I wasn't paying attention. And since I have not read ahead, I'm probably going down. All I can do is try to minimize the damage.

"Tell the class what you know about Apollo's sister," he says.

Having Googled Artemis after my date with Mac, I'm able to provide so many details that Mr. Sparling finally interrupts. "Thank you. That will do. Now, moving on . . ."

Rachel winks, and I smile back. It felt good to know the answer and deliver it on command, something that hasn't happened often before.

As we file out of the classroom, Rachel resumes our conversation. "So you're sure Mac isn't Scoop?"

"Pretty sure," I say, although the jury is still out. Mac may not have fallen into the traps I set for Scoop, but he's not totally in the clear yet.

"We could check out basketball practice," Izzy suggests. Since Mac has shown his good side, my friends are all for my hanging out with him.

I shake my head. "Too obvious. Besides, it wouldn't do any good. Guys like Mac are never interested in girls like me." A Sporty FB is not my destiny.

"Think positively," Izzy says. "I'm going after my rock climber and I'm hardly in his league. Who knows, maybe *he'll* think I am."

"Your guy sounds nice," I say. "And while Mac may be nicer than I thought, he's still a caveman."

"Caveman?" a voice echoes behind us. We turn to see a girl wearing a sweater that's a couple of sizes too small. "Are you talking about that column in the school paper?"

"Well, uh, yeah," I say. "*Newshound*, I think?"

The girl nods and snaps her gum. "This week's

column is so on the money. My boyfriend didn't even know my last name until, like, the third time I slept with him. But I'm sick of how he treats me, so I told him to give me more respect or he's done."

"You told him that because of the column?" Rachel asks.

The girl nods. "It just got me thinking, you know?"

Izzy nods. "That's what the best columnists do."

The girl starts walking away, but turns back to ask, "You don't think Newshound's a lesbian, do you?"

Rachel manages only a strangled choking sound, so Izzy says, "No, why?"

"Well, my boyfriend said she sounded gay."

"Typical guy cop-out," Rachel says. "You hold your ground with him."

"I will," she says, disappearing around the corner.

The girls give me high fives.

"See?" Izzy says. "You're changing Dunfield one person at a time."

"Just another few thousand to go."

Chapter 7

Dan is doing paperwork when I walk into the office to punch my time card.

"What are you doing here?" he asks, scowling.

I've seen that scowl before, but it's never been directed at me. "I'm working tonight."

He taps on the calculator. "It isn't your shift."

"I know." It's Grace's shift, but I don't see why it's a big deal. We've traded shifts a hundred times, and he's never complained before. "Is there a problem?"

Dan uses his pencil to tip his hat back so he can look me in the eye. "You tell me."

"Grace wanted a night off, and I could use the extra cash. I've put a big dent in my savings lately."

"Have y'all put a big dent in your homework? You've got a math test on Monday."

Dan's interest in my education has its downside. Mom never remembers when I have a test.

To placate him, I promise to study all day Saturday, even

though it means canceling a trip to the mall with Rachel.

He smiles at last. "Atta girl. You want to keep that column, don't you?"

"I guess so," I say, sighing.

It was obviously a mistake to tell Dan that Mr. Sparling threatened to give Newshound the ax if my overall average ever drops below a C plus. It's a totally unreasonable condition, because my grade in English should be all that counts. My brain only processes numbers efficiently when there's a tip involved.

"What do you mean, 'you guess so'? Of course you do." Dan pats the binder on his desk that contains my first two columns. He wanted to hang them over the cash register, but I nixed that idea in a hurry. Plenty of current—and former—Dunfield students come in here; one question from any of them and Dan would start bragging and blow my anonymity.

As I put on an apron I tell Dan about the girl at school who said she liked my column.

"I'm not surprised, sugar. I bet you have hundreds of fans," he says. "Your family must be so proud of you."

If they are, no one's let me in on the secret. My mother took the *Bulletin* to work to read on her break and never said a word afterward. With everything on her mind these days, I guess she forgot.

Grace is another story. I left copies on the coffee table, but if she's read them, she hasn't bothered to diss them. I know she's still mad at me over the babysitting incident, but it isn't like her to deprive herself of the pleasure of running me down.

"I don't think they've read them," I say, straightening my apron as an excuse not to look at Dan.

"They must have," Dan insists. "Grace knows this is important to you."

Dan naively believes that brothers and sisters are always loving and supportive. He's also fond of Grace, even if she causes more trouble than I do.

"Don't say anything to her," I warn him. If Dan takes my side, it will just become an issue, and I don't need any more issues at home. "You know how she is."

Fortunately, noisy singing prevents Dan from arguing with me. I poke my head out of the office to see Shirley standing on one of the old wooden tables, surrounded by Paz's crew. They're belting out an old Beatles song in different keys and tempos:

Will you still need me
Will you still feed me
WHEN I'M SIXTY-FOUR

"Get me down, you morons!" Shirley shouts as the song ends.

"Is that any way to treat your favorite customers?" Paz asks, as Joey and Gordo help her off the table. "We made you a special birthday gift, you know."

He lifts the lid off a box containing the numerals six and four made out of white chocolate, Shirley's favorite.

Shirley purses her lips. "Maybe I'd treat you boys better if you didn't advertise my age to the entire planet." Her tone may be harsh, but I can tell she's thrilled they're making a fuss.

She brings an empty coffee cup down on the number

six to smash it, and the guys scramble to grab pieces. It says a lot about the quality of Donner's chocolate that they still enjoy it after working with it all day.

Joey beckons to me. "Have some. There's plenty to go around."

"Thanks," I say. "I love white chocolate."

He selects a large chunk and passes it to me. "Made with my own two hands."

"In other words," Gordo says, "watch for fingernails."

"Shut up," Joey says. "I was wearing gloves."

"Plus a hairnet," Gordo adds.

"Nice," I say. "Girls love guys in hairnets."

Joey runs a hand through his dark hair, as if fearing he might have left the net on by mistake. "It's a regulation, not a fashion statement."

"Then how come I have to remind you to take it off?" Gordo asks.

"You're just jealous because I look better in it than you do," Joey says.

Gordo reaches into his pocket. "Let's put them on now and get Lu to judge who's hotter."

"Go for it," I say. I already know who I'm going to choose, and it isn't Gordo. The poor guy is the least attractive of all the Donner guys. Not that I'm looking.

Joey shakes his head, grinning. "Only our team should have to see that."

"Guys," Paz says, cutting in, "Lu's busy."

"My shift hasn't started yet," I say.

"We need a round of coffee, and Shirley can't serve at her own birthday party." He snatches the last bite of chocolate off my napkin and pops it into his own mouth.

"Hey!"

"You can't afford the calories."

Shirley gives Paz a gentle kick in the butt. "Why are you so mean to your sister-in-law?"

"She's not my sister-in-law," Paz says. "Grace and I aren't married."

"Where I come from, a baby says you're married," Shirley says. "Anyway, don't call Luisa fat."

"Why not? She calls me short."

"You call me Shorty all the time," I point out.

"It's different for girls," he says seriously. "It doesn't matter if you're short."

It occurs to me that Paz has been my main window on the male world for so long that my perspective could be permanently skewed. "Look on the bright side," I say. "I could be calling you Baldy."

The guys start snickering behind Paz.

"Luisa," Shirley says reprovingly, "a lady never draws attention to a man's receding hairline."

"It's not receding!" Paz says.

"Of course it's not," Shirley says, flustered. "Have some more chocolate. And Luisa, would you mind getting the coffee?"

"Seven coffees, coming up," I say. "Six regular, one with Rogaine."

Shirley steps between Paz and me, arms outstretched.

The cowbells ring, and I turn to see Mac Landis standing at the door. There's something commanding about his presence that pulls all eyes toward him. His success as an athlete seems to have infused him with confidence. Until last Saturday, I would have said arrogance.

Okay, it *is* arrogance. But any guy who can admit he adored his grandfather can't be *all* bad.

Mac smiles and waves, and all eyes turn from him to me. Paz opens his mouth to say something, but Shirley distracts him by asking for help with the jukebox.

Mac joins me at the counter. "Did I interrupt a private party?"

"No, just the usual mayhem," I say, gesturing to a stool. "Have a seat." I pour coffee into a mug and slide it toward him.

He appraises me over the rim of his cup. "Nice outfit."

"It's fire retardant," I say, giving a half spin so that the skirt swirls. "Didn't some designer say everything should be both beautiful and useful?"

If Mac recognizes the quote, he doesn't let on. "Wish I'd asked you to be in the Bootylicious Calendar. Although there's not much booty showing."

The weight of Mac Landis's eyes on my crinolined backside makes me so jumpy that I forget to share my views on that sexist piece of crap.

At last he turns his eyes to the Donner guys. "Don't some of them go to Dunfield?"

"Past tense," I say. "They're Cocoa grads now."

Since Shirley is keeping the guys distracted, I offer Mac a menu. I assume he's here because I bragged to him about Dan's burgers.

"On the house?" he asks, grinning hopefully.

"Just the coffee, cheapo," I say. "The burger's on you."

I place Mac's order and stall for a moment, assailed by doubts. Maybe he wants to be alone while he waits. Why would he want me hanging around?

"Can't you sit down for a few minutes?" he asks.

Mac Landis wants me to sit down with him! I realize he's just killing time, but still. Maybe it's because I am such a good listener. It's probably my only advantage over people like Mariah and Brianna the cheerleader.

"I'm on my way to do my grandmother's grocery shopping," Mac says as I perch beside him. "She lives a few blocks from here."

"You do her grocery shopping? That's so nice!"

My voice swoops up at the end, making me sound more like a giddy groupie than the level-headed Lu Perez that Mac apparently enjoyed talking to last week. *That* Lu didn't gush. *That* Lu kept the whole Mac Landis mythos in perspective.

"I owe her," Mac says. "When I was at Lincoln Elementary, she'd make lunch for me every day."

"Lucky," I say. "The cafeteria food there was even worse than Dunfield's."

Mac looks puzzled. "You went to Lincoln?"

I shrink an inch on the spot. "Uh, yeah. I guess all the other Luisa Perezes have you confused."

He has the decency to look embarrassed. "Well, I never paid much attention in class. I guess I only noticed the people sitting right in front of me."

Untrue. He always noticed Mariah, no matter where she sat.

"Wait a second," he says. "I think I remember you from Mrs. Burton's class."

I nod, instantly knowing why. "That was the year you stole my Tamagotchi."

"I stole a lot of Tamagotchis," he admits. "Because it made the girls chase me."

Even at nine he was a dog. "Well, mine *died* under your watch."

I don't intend to say so, but I was devastated at the time. Sure, it was just a stupid pink plastic egg, but I didn't get a lot of toys while they were still popular. Mom would wait until things went on sale (i.e., after they were no longer hot) to get them at a discount—when she could afford them at all.

The year the Tamagotchi took over the classroom, I staged a massive campaign to get Mom to buy me one for my birthday. She didn't cave, because the new coat I needed pretty much consumed her gift budget. The night of my birthday, however, I found a Tamagotchi on my pillow. Grace said she'd found it on the bus, but Mom told me later that she'd emptied out her piggy bank to get it. It was the nicest thing Grace had ever done for me. Make that *has* ever done for me.

I took such good care of my Tamagotchi that it lived long after everyone else's. And then, when it was the only one left to steal, Mac snatched it off my desk. By the time I'd recovered it in the school yard, it was dead.

Mac grabs my hand and gazes at me through wide blue eyes. "I'm so sorry I killed your toy. Can you ever forgive me?"

I know a hundred girls have forgiven Mac for similar crimes just because he looked at them that way, and I fall for it anyway. "You could have at least come to the funeral."

Business picks up, and I have to leave Mac to eat by himself. When I deliver the bill, he makes a big show of leaving me a tip—fifteen percent of the pre-tax amount, calculated to the penny.

"I'd better get going," he says. "My grandmother's expecting me."

"Okay, see you at school," I say, pleased with my own nonchalance.

He walks toward the door, and I summon my nerve to call after him, "Are you going to Mariah's fund-raising dance next week?"

He turns to reply, but Paz beats him to the punch. "Yeah, All-star. You going to the dance or what?"

I turn to Paz and find six Donner guys watching us. They're all wearing hairnets. "Shut up, Paz," I say.

"Oooh, Shorty must like him," Paz says, in a singsong voice. "What do you think, guys?"

"Yup, she's hot for him," Gordo says. "She's not usually that red."

"When's the last time Lu sounded all girly?" asks Ace, another guy on Paz's crew.

"Never," Paz says. "I didn't think she *was* a real girl."

I look at Mac, expecting to see contempt on his face. Instead he's standing in the doorway, grinning at me.

Izzy's mom welcomes me into the living room of their small but immaculate bungalow. She's wearing surgical gloves and holding a paintbrush covered in white goo. Hair clips line the waist of her jeans, and the smell of chemicals fills the air. There's a work in progress around here.

On cue, Izzy's Aunt Alicia appears, her hair in foils. "Hola, Luisa!"

"Hola," I say. "Another transformation?" Alicia's hair had black-and-cherry streaks the last time I saw her. The time before that it was blond with very dark roots.

"I like to keep the boys guessing," she says. Alicia is still happily playing the field at thirty-six, with no signs of settling down.

It's obvious where Izzy learned to like variety, because her mother is the exact opposite—mousy and conservative. The house is mainly a study in beige, although there are splashes of color here and there in the form of gifts from Izzy that her mother feels obliged to display.

I head down the hall to the door with the prominent KEEP OUT sign and I call, "It's me."

Inside, a riot of color assaults the eye, from red curtains, to an orange bedspread, to yellow cushions. Books and makeup and hair accessories are strewn all over the desk, and clothes are piled high on a chair. The top of the dresser is barely visible among the photographs in bright, sparkly frames. Front and center is a picture of the three of us in second grade, wearing matching outfits and long, dark ponytails. As always, I'm in the foreground, the short one even at age seven.

Izzy is lying on her unmade bed, holding up a small mirror and applying blue eye shadow to her lids, while Rachel is sprawled on the floor, sorting through CDs. The wall behind them that used to be terra-cotta has recently become cobalt blue.

"I see you've started matching your hair to your walls," I tell Izzy.

She raises the mirror to admire her locks. "It's my blue period."

Rachel gives me a knowing smile. "You'd better be nice to Izzy."

"Or what?" I ask, noting that she is wearing false eyelashes. Rachel usually rebels against being Izzy's guinea pig, but I guess Jason has weakened her. "She won't glue Astroturf on my eyelids?"

"Or she won't share the new issue of *The Bulletin*," Rachel says.

"But it's only Thursday. How did you get your hands on it a day early, Iz?"

"I waited on the school steps until the delivery truck arrived and flirted with the driver until he gave me one," Izzy says. "Some people *like* blue hair."

"*Everyone* likes blue hair," I assure her, grinning. "So what does Scoop have to say this week?"

Rachel hands me the paper. "We waited for you to read it."

THE WORD . . . FROM SCOOP
Silence Is Golden

Newshound got one thing right last week: the women of Dunfield do belong out front—so that the men can enjoy the view from behind.

Yes, the Date Auction was more successful than Casino

Night, but Scoop feels compelled to comment on Newshound's blatant hypocrisy. After whining that the Bootylicious Calendar was no more than an excuse to sell sex, she fully endorsed an event that had women literally selling themselves to the highest bidder. It was practically prostitution.

Don't get me wrong, I'm all for it—for men and women alike. But don't bill it as romance. Fifteen hundred students didn't swarm the backfield in search of a spiritual connection.

Admit it, Newshound, the calendar's success showed Dunfield women that sex brings in the real coin, and you wanted in on the action. But we don't mind your stealing our ideas if it helps you to stay in the game.

In the meantime, with you up front we can avoid your bellyaching and nonstop chitchat. Newshound stated that men don't communicate enough, but how would you know when you never stop talking yourselves? Concert tickets don't come cheap, and Scoop would have liked to have *heard* The Strokes last week. Unfortunately, the girls around him would not stop talking to each other long enough to enjoy the music. So how about giving those mouths a rest? Unless we're making out, that is.

Newshound claims girls want to know guys from the inside out, but Scoop begs to differ. If you got inside our heads, you'd be shocked at what you found there. You could analyze and spin it for all it's worth, but you still wouldn't be happy. The truth is, you don't actually want us to speak our minds, you want us to follow some script that's in your minds. And when we get our lines wrong, you freak out.

So a word to the wise, men of Dunfield: to keep a girl interested, keep your mouth shut. That way she can tell herself that you're mesmerized by what she's saying instead of thinking about how hot her best friend is and whether they might consider a . . . But no, this is a school paper and I'd better not go there.

If you don't like what I'm saying, ladies, blame it on the Newshound. She's the one who wanted me to express what I'm really thinking.

Izzy, Rachel, and I stare at each other, dazed. Then Rachel's false eyelashes flutter down to rest like wings against her cheek as she shakes her head in silence.

"*Puerco!*" Izzy says.

"Pig," I echo. "He's talking about *threesomes*. In the school newspaper! I cannot believe Mr. Sparling approved that."

Rachel shrugs. "Well, Mr. Sparling is a guy, too. God knows what *he* thinks about when his wife is talking."

We collapse in disgusted laughter at the thought.

"Apparently we haven't got a clue what goes on in guys' heads," Izzy says.

"I'm not sure I want to," I say. "If that's how their minds work, count me out."

Rachel reaches over and puts a CD into the player. "That's just what Scoop *wants* you to think, Newshound. He's trying to throw you off your game."

"On the other hand, reading more into his words is doing exactly what he says we do, right? Maybe we should take it at face value."

"Not all guys are pigs," Rachel says. "At least, Jason isn't. I may not know what goes on in his head, but I'm pretty sure he's not imagining any"—she pauses to collect herself—"three-ways."

I cram the newspaper into my bag. "Because if you thought he *was*, you'd . . . ?"

"Kill him," Rachel says. "Or myself. But according to my mother, men do have more primitive brains than women, and the only way to survive a relationship is to turn a blind eye to some things."

"And what you can't ignore," Izzy picks up, "you try to train out of them. My mom has to tell my dad how to think all the time."

"I see I missed a lot being from an all-girl family," I say.

Izzy starts collecting her makeup and beckons me over. "I've got a new look in mind for the dance next Friday. Let me do a trial run."

"Work your magic," I say. "I want something that will get Mac Landis to forget he ever forgot he knew me."

After I've told them about my encounter with Mac at the diner, Rachel says, "I still think he might be Scoop. There's *puerco* potential in that boy, and you know it. He practically jumped you at the planetarium."

"I know, I know." I'd rather dismiss all the negative things I know about Mac right now, because today he was a nice, normal, gorgeous guy who dropped by the diner to hang out with me. If he oinks now and then, is it really such a big deal? Maybe my standards are too high.

I pull out the column and scan it again. "Aha! Scoop says he went to The Strokes concert, but Mac went to

Casino Night. So they *can't* be the same person."

"Do you notice how happy she looks about that?" Rachel asks Izzy.

"So happy I can't get eye shadow on her," Izzy says, closing my eyelids by force.

Chapter 8

Crossing from one side of Colonel Dunfield High School to the other is like a journey backward through time. The building has been renovated gradually over the decades, turning the interior into an odd patchwork of architectural styles.

As the fire alarm blasts, my history class leaves via a long, beige corridor built in 2003. Principal Buzzkill christened it Senior's Hall and assigned the new lockers to twelfth grade students. Her theory was that seniors would be least likely to deface them, and she's right: it's the dullest stretch in the school.

Giving the rest of my class the slip, I hang a left at the end of the hall and catapult into the 1980s, where terracotta lockers complement the peach-and-turquoise decor of the library.

A sharp right beyond the library takes me to the well-traveled cafeteria expressway. The cafeteria itself dates back to the 1970s, and features orange-and-white floor tiles and purple plastic chairs.

Next comes Frosh Alley, a narrow hall lined with powder blue lockers that have rusted considerably since their installation in the 1950s.

A narrow concrete hallway then connects the "new" wing (if you can call something built in 1944 new) to the old. Apart from ceilings that are a little higher, and windows that stick when the ancient boiler heats classrooms to tropical temperatures, the old building is similar to the new one.

Finally I reach the main foyer, with its worn marble floors and oak paneled walls. On one side is a life-size portrait of Colonel Dunfield himself; on the other, a painfully bright mural painted by the Class of '77 in a weekend raid.

Standing at the top of the wide stone staircase, I scan the crowd of students on the front lawn until I locate Rachel and Izzy by the curb. No matter how far apart we are when a fire alarm sounds, we convene here. It usually takes at least ten minutes for the fire department to determine that it was just another prank, which makes a brisk jog across six decades completely worthwhile.

My friends are hopping up and down in their purple and white gym shorts. "Another fruitless audition for the Understudies?" I ask, joining them.

"Remind me to laugh later, after I've thawed out," Izzy says, jealously eyeing my jeans and thick wool sweater.

"I'm freezing too," I say. "I collided with an iceberg coming over here: Tyler Milano."

"Still avoiding you, huh?" Rachel says. "He hasn't spent much time with Jason and me, either. Do you want me to see if Jason can talk to him?"

I shake my head. "It wouldn't be fair to get him involved. And I doubt it would make any difference. I've tried to talk to Tyler three times, but he just walks away."

"Rude!" Izzy says.

"He's doing me a favor. At first I felt terrible about what happened, but now I'm starting to think I'm better off without him. Besides, it's not like I can really explain."

Izzy gestures toward the student parking lot, where Mac is admiring a motorcycle with his crew. "Who needs Tyler when the most popular guy in school is after you?"

"Mac Landis is *not* after me. The only thing he's said to me this week is hello."

"That doesn't mean anything," Rachel says. "You don't have any classes together, so where would he strike up a conversation?"

"In the cafeteria? Or the hallway? I've seen him half a dozen times, but I don't think he's even noticed me. If someone is interested, they make an effort, right?"

"Girls do," Izzy says dubiously. "I don't know about guys."

"Jason tracks Rachel down all the time, right, Rach?"

"*Now*. But remember, I staked out his locker for weeks."

Izzy starts running on the spot, which attracts the interest of several guys who don't even pretend they're not staring at her chest. "You'd probably make better progress with Mac if you came to more of the fund-raisers," she says.

"Not that we mind covering for you, Lu," Rachel interjects, stepping in front of Izzy to block the pervs' sight line.

"The guys' yard sale was my favorite. Jason bought me the cutest ceramic dog, and Izzy got a lava lamp for her room."

"A lava lamp? Aren't they a little retro?"

"Carson was selling it," Rachel explains.

"Carson, the rock-climbing senior?" I ask.

"He gave me a deep discount," Izzy says, grinning. "Besides, it's blue."

I'm glad they don't mind attending events for me, because I have even less free time than before. Grace is making me take some of her shifts at the diner because she says doesn't trust me to babysit. That wouldn't be so bad if I got to keep all the cash, but lately I've had to pitch more money into the family coffers than usual.

"You're still coming to the dance tonight, though, right?" Rachel asks.

I nod tentatively. Grace is scheduled to work, but until I am actually out the door, I won't fully believe it. This Cinderella's coach could very easily remain a pumpkin.

The bell rings to signal the all clear. Once again, our hopes that the school is actually burning down have been thwarted.

We linger for a last moment on the curb as students begin filing back up the steps.

"I'll be at your place at seven with my gear," Izzy tells me. "Prepare to be transformed."

We're going to pool our favorite clothes and jewelry to create fresh looks for the dance. Izzy and Rachel have more and better stuff than I do, but at least I own a few vintage finds they both covet.

One of the gym teachers blows his whistle in our direction. "Move it, girls!"

As we migrate toward the stairs, Mac Landis jogs over from the parking lot and intercepts us. His posse has dispersed. "Hey, Stargazer," he says. "Pegasus was shining bright on Tuesday night. I stopped by the diner to point it out. Did your sister tell you?"

Uh, no. She must have conveniently forgotten that a gorgeous guy came by asking for me. "Sorry I missed you," I say. "I mean, sorry I missed Pegasus."

"It's not going anywhere," Mac says, before taking the stairs two at a time. He turns at the top. "Next clear night, okay?"

Rachel shoves me playfully after the door closes behind him. "He practically asked you out!"

"We're just pals," I insist.

"That's going to change tonight," Izzy says. "I'm coming over even earlier to make sure you're not just hot, but all-star hot."

"You're burning my scalp," I say. "When you said hot, I didn't think you meant literally."

"Suck it up," Izzy replies, holding the curling iron in place. "Beauty takes effort and sacrifice."

She should know. Two hours ago she left school looking like a funky student. Now she looks like a glamorous movie star, with shiny jet-black hair, smoky eyes, and fake lashes.

Rachel steps out of the bathroom modeling a pair of gray pin-striped pants (Izzy's), with a red satin halter top (my best-ever Chinatown deal). Izzy has already painted Rachel's nails and lips a bright crimson to match the top, and pinned her curls into a low knot adorned with a shiny black chopstick.

"Wow," I say. "You look amazing, Rach."

"Va-va voom!" my mom exclaims, joining us in the living room. She sets a tray holding a bowl of popcorn and three glasses of Coke on the coffee table. "That boyfriend of yours is one lucky fella, Rachel."

My mom loves helping us dress up, and our floundering social life has probably been as disappointing to her as it has been to us. I assume that's why she's here tonight instead of taking an extra shift, but I haven't asked. It's enough that she's smiling and happy.

Izzy finishes my hair and starts on my face. "No peeking till we're done," she says, leading me into my former bedroom to put on the outfit she's selected for me.

I emerge from the bedroom to applause from Rachel and my mother.

"I don't think I like my daughter looking that sexy," Mom says with mock disapproval.

Sexy? Me? Is it possible that I've become a sexy Lu Perez with all-star appeal?

I stare into the full-length mirror Izzy has propped against the wall. My eyes look huge, my cheekbones chiseled, and my hair is double its usual volume. Izzy's high-heeled boots and skinny jeans give my legs a boost, and Rachel's long, scoop-necked sweater hugs curves I never knew I had.

"Izzy . . ." I start, but words fail me.

"I know," she says, beaming. "You're gorgeous."

I turn to check out the rear view as the doors open and Grace comes in, with Keira on one hip.

"Oh my God," she says, stepping into the living room. "It looks like a bomb went off in Barbie's playhouse."

Izzy clears a place for her on the couch. "Do you want a makeover, too?"

Grace snorts and jerks her thumb at me. "Not if I'd come out looking like *that*."

I pat my hair anxiously. "Does it look stupid?"

"It doesn't look like *you*," Grace says. "What if you meet some guy who thinks this is what you actually look like? Monday morning he'll catch sight of the real you and freak."

"Grace!" my mother says, and for once there's an edge to her voice. "Lu always looks nice." She pulls my hand away from my hair. "Leave it. You're bootylicious."

As this is not a word she's likely to use in any context, I ask, "Did you read my columns?"

Grace prevents my mother from answering by shoving Keira into her arms. "I need someone to babysit so that I can meet Paz for coffee."

"I thought you were working," I say.

"I thought meeting my ex was more important," she says.

I resist asking if she found someone to cover at Dan's. This is not my problem.

"I'll watch Keira," Mom says. She doesn't sound surprised. Maybe the reason she turned down work was to make sure Grace didn't prevent me from going to the ball.

"Are you and Paz getting back together?" Izzy asks.

"He should be so lucky," Grace says, throwing herself onto the couch and picking up the remote. She turns on the TV to end the conversation and helps herself to our popcorn. "You guys had better hurry. The losers are always the first to arrive."

The music is thumping and the dance floor is packed by the time we arrive. Obviously we didn't need to kill an hour at Starbucks, but after what Grace said, we weren't taking any chances.

The gym is barely recognizable. Long, flowing white curtains hide the bleachers, and banks of colored lights bounce off half a dozen twirling disco balls. If it weren't for the sign overhead that reads *The Dunfield Groove*, and teachers circulating with crossed arms, it would feel like a nightclub.

As we ease our way into the crowd, something strange happens: heads start to turn in our direction. I glance over my shoulder to see if Mariah has come through the door behind us, but I can see only guys. Guys who are looking at us.

"Have you noticed—" I begin.

"That guys are staring at us?" Izzy finishes, linking arms with Rachel and me. "Of course they are, Lulu. We're all-star hot."

A DJ is grooving on a platform in front of a movie screen on which Mariah's two seconds of fame on *The Right Moves* are playing in a continuous loop. In front of the screen, the real thing is gyrating through a series of choreographed moves with the Understudies. Down below, her fans try to follow along.

Like her namesake, Mariah is wearing short shorts, high heels, and a top that would qualify as a bra in my wardrobe. The Understudies are equally underdressed. Either the Dunfield dress code doesn't apply after hours, or the teachers have decided to turn a blind eye because Mariah's team is raking in so much money for the cause. Although Mariah delegates most of the work to her legions of fans, you have to give her credit for scoring one hit after another.

Jason is waiting for us by the locker room door, as promised. "You look amazing," he tells Rachel, kissing her cheek. "And you guys, too. Very hot."

My eyes meet Rachel's, and she gives me a strained smile. We're both thinking about what Scoop said about how guys' minds work. Jason's smile seems so sincere that I can't believe he's imagining anything tasteless.

I hope Jason turns out to be as nice as he seems, because Rachel is head over heels. The only hitch is that her parents still don't know about him. While she's hinted that she likes someone, they automatically assumed he's Jewish, and so far she hasn't enlightened them. Jason's grandmother is only half Jewish, but Rach is banking on a few drops of the right blood being enough to win over her parents.

After Jason and Rachel leave to dance, Izzy and I circulate, pushing through the crowd.

"There are too many people here," she complains. "We'll never find Carson and Mac."

"I already saw Mac. He was at the drinks table with his friends."

Izzy looks at me as if my curls have gone limp. "And you didn't say hi?"

"I don't think he noticed me. I didn't want to disturb him."

"Uh, news flash: Every guy in this room is hoping to be disturbed by a cute girl. Let's go back and see if he's still there."

"Later," I say, but Izzy's already changing course like a missile locking on target.

"Mac liked you as of this afternoon, but some cheerleader is probably sweeping him off his feet tonight. We don't have forever to find the right guy, Lu. The pool will dry up in ten years, tops."

"Ten? That's crazy. Look at your aunt Alicia. She's still dating."

"Yeah, one jerk after another. And how about your mom? When's the last time she had a date?"

Before she married my father, as far as I can tell.

Izzy takes my silence as victory. "All you have to do is ask him to dance."

Like that's a total breeze. "Why can't I sort of lurk until he asks me?"

"Ten years, that's why. Carp diem."

"That's car-*pay* diem. A carp is a fish."

"You're the writer, not me."

Mac is still at the drinks table surrounded by seven or eight of his jock friends when we get there. Izzy gives me a little shove, but my feet are rooted to the floor.

"I can't do it," I whisper. "What if he says no?"

"He's not going to say no. It's just one dance."

"One dance with Mac Landis," I remind her. "Dunfield all-star."

"The same guy who practically asked you out this afternoon."

At this moment, Mac's eyes happen to light on me. There's a brief flicker of what appears to be admiration on his face, but the fact that he doesn't crack a smile isn't encouraging.

"If he's interested he'll walk over here and ask me," I say.

"He's probably saying the same thing to his friends right now. Maybe he's shy. Just because he's popular doesn't mean it's easy being Mac Landis."

Easier than being one of the many Luisa Perezes, I'm sure. "He's not shy. Look at how he behaves around Mariah."

"That's because he doesn't respect her. You earned his respect by fighting him off at the planetarium and now he's intimidated."

I laugh. "You're really stretching."

"All I'm saying is, sometimes you have to help the process along."

As she speaks she's easing me ever closer to Mac. Giving me one last push, she whispers, "Good luck," and races toward Carson, who has just arrived.

I'm practically standing among Mac's posse, but no one acknowledges me. If I want to be noticed I am going to have to speak up. The question is, do I want to step out of the faceless ranks of the Luisa Perezes and put my pride on the line?

I should just ask Mac to dance. Yes, it's a risk, but not a huge one. The guy showed up at my workplace twice in the space of a week. I've already spent hours talking to him. Besides, he's just a guy, and if I'm even starting to consider a career in journalism I'll have to get used to putting myself in uncomfortable situations.

It's moments like these that define a person. I can complain about being invisible forever, or I can ask to be seen and perhaps change the course of my high school life.

Pulling my shoulders back, I straighten to my full, nearly normal height (thanks to Izzy's heels), and do what any self-respecting, modern, intelligent woman would do.

I order a drink.

In the time it takes for the kid behind the table to hand me a soda and count out my change, the posse breaks apart, leaving Mac with just one other guy. Unfortunately, the guy is Morgan McGee—or Morgan the Moron, as he was known at Lincoln Elementary. Like Mac, Morgan eventually grew into sports prowess, and although his IQ didn't change, the term Moron fell into disuse. I've never had much to do with him, but the deadly combination of size and stupidity makes me nervous.

Still, I am determined to make my move. Covering the few steps that separate Mac and me, I say, "Hi."

Morgan is describing a move on the basketball court and doesn't even pause.

"Hi," I repeat, much louder.

Morgan turns to stare down at me. "What?"

I direct my full attention to Mac and ask,

"Doyouwanttodance?" The words tumble out so fast they run together.

Morgan frowns. "Do we know her?"

With an almost imperceptible nod, Mac says, "The auction."

"She must have got her money's worth if she's back for more," Morgan says.

An explosion in my head prevents me from responding.

Mac says, "Look, uh . . . I don't dance," he says, his voice completely and utterly flat. "Ever."

"Oh. Okay. No problem." I'm surprised to see that he already appears farther away when I didn't feel my feet move.

"You got your date," Morgan calls after me. "Don't be greedy."

I turn to make my getaway, and someone sideswipes me.

"Watch where you're going, Coconut," Mariah says. She pushes past me to slide her arm around Mac's waist. "I need you."

He drops his arm over her shoulder. "What's wrong?"

"It's that geek from the auction," she says, pouting. "He won't leave me alone."

Morgan points to me. "Mac's having the same problem."

"You've got to be kidding me, Coconut," Mariah says. You can't possibly think—"

Mac cuts her off. "Where's the geek?"

Behind us, someone calls her name. It's Curtis, and he's wearing the baseball cap with the hidden camera. "You owe me a dance," he reminds Mariah. "I rigged up the sound system like you asked and dubbed fifty copies of your demo reel."

Mariah gives him a strained smile. "I appreciated your support, Kermit, but remember, it's not personal. It's all for the Literacy Challenge."

"You said you'd dance with me," he repeats stubbornly.

"And I will," she says. "But Mac asked me first, so I'll have to catch up with you later."

Mac follows her to the dance floor, and the guy who doesn't dance—*ever*—is soon draped over her with his hands on her butt.

Now I know what happens when you ask to be noticed: humiliation. No wonder Mac seeks me out at the diner instead of just chatting with me at Dunfield: he's ashamed to be seen with me. Among his people, he needs to be with the right type of girl, and I clearly don't qualify. I feel like crying, but I won't. Not now, anyway.

"Would you like to dance?" Curtis asks, peering at me through dirty glasses.

"No thank you," I say. "I'm actually leaving as soon as I find my friends."

"You have time for one dance," he says, obviously less deterred by rejection than I am. Without waiting for a response, he starts jerking spasmodically on the spot. His arms are white and rubbery, and his eyes half closed as he blisses out on the music.

We are not on the dance floor. We are yards from the dance floor. We are surrounded by a crowd—a crowd that is parting to watch the show.

"I'm sorry," I say, starting to walk away. "I really have to go."

In a flash, Curtis circles me and starts flailing again. "Just one dance."

I dart the other way, but he cuts me off. He is dancing *at* me. It's a weird sort of assault. All I can do is stand there and watch, speechless with embarrassment. Taking this as encouragement, Curtis bucks his hips in my direction.

All eyes are on us. In the distance, Mariah is leaning on Mac, laughing as she watches the show. Beside me, Morgan's guffaw shakes the drinks table.

Tears well up in my eyes, and I vow to myself that if I make it out of this with a shred of dignity, I will never again ask to be noticed.

Someone takes my hand and squeezes. "Dance with me?"

I glance up to find Tyler Milano at my side. Even as I'm choking out a "Yes," he is towing me onto the dance floor, away from the writhing Curtis. Once the crowd closes behind us, he turns.

"Thank you *so* much," I say. "You really are a superhero."

"It's okay," he says. "I like to dance."

He's good at it, too. Much better than I am, especially when hobbled by humiliation and footwear a size too large. "I owe you, Tyler."

"You do," he agrees. "Because of you, half the Dunfield population is under the impression that I date guys."

"Untrue. The guy who won your tickets sent out a news release confirming his heterosexuality."

"You know how it goes: the more you protest, the guiltier you look. Not that there's anything wrong with dating guys. If you actually like guys."

"I know how to make it up to you," I say. "I'll set you up with a nice girl."

"Not just a nice girl—a *hot* girl."

I laugh. "Okay, a hot girl."

"Given how humiliated I was, I think you're going to have to make that *two* hot girls—at the same time."

"Dream on," I say. "I will set up a date with *one* hot girl and make sure she gets the word out about how great you are."

"Deal," Tyler says. "On one condition: the hot girl has to be you."

I spin happily under the disco ball, relieved to have gotten my priorities in order before it's too late. The all-star has nothing on Mr. Fantastic.

Rachel, Izzy, and I debrief on the way home, wedged in the back of Izzy's dad's old hatchback. He likes to have his tool-box beside him on the passenger seat at all times since the car breaks down often.

I act out all the parts of Mac, Curtis, and Tyler, to a mixed reaction of sympathy, disgust, and satisfaction.

"I'm so glad you've got another chance with Tyler," Rachel says, her hopes of double-dating reigniting.

"I am too, but I still worry he might be Scoop." Lowering my voice, I describe how he mentioned an interest in a threesome. "Plus, he was wearing a Strokes T-shirt. He was at the concert last week."

"Tyler and thousands of other people," Rachel says.

"He's too nice to be Scoop," Izzy says.

I turn to glare at the side of her head. "Your opinions on guys aren't very reliable."

She sighs. "I'm sorry about encouraging you to ask Mac to dance. I honestly thought he'd say yes. But at least it saved you from wasting another thought on him. Tyler's the better man."

"Not if he's Scoop."

"Every guy you meet can't be Scoop," Rachel says. "Anyway, it's just a column. Scoop is trying to get a rise out of readers."

"Just like you are," Izzy adds slyly.

"I am not! I believe what I write."

"Your views are more extreme in print, though," Rachel says. "You're pretty critical of guys."

"What's happened to you?" I ask. "You totally backed me before."

"We love your column," Rachel says. "I'm just saying it's possible that Scoop is exaggerating his views to create a persona."

Since when is Rachel the type to drop terms like "persona" into casual conversation? She doesn't even like English. Obviously she has allowed herself to be swayed by Jason's views. And Izzy, who ended up dancing for a full hour with Carson, is no better. They have succumbed to pheromones.

One day, when their heads have cleared, they'll look

back on my columns and realize I was more than fair to the guys at this school.

In the meantime, I give them the silent treatment to punish them for their lack of support. They're so busy comparing notes about their guys, however, that they don't even notice.

Chapter 9

THE WORD . . . FROM NEWSHOUND
Dunfield Dogs Take Heart

If you're one of the few students who didn't make it to the Dunfield Groove last Friday night, you missed the event of the Literacy Season to date. The dance put the girls' team so far in front of the guys' that they'll need binoculars to enjoy what Scoop so eloquently called "the view from behind."

Although the guys' performance has been lackluster of late, the girls have more than compensated, and as a result, school board officials just announced that Colonel Dunfield has reached the number four position in the Literacy Challenge. (If exclamation marks weren't the crutch of the amateur, I'd add a row of them here.)

This marks the first time Dunfield has ranked in the fourth place citywide for anything other than arrests and false fire alarms. Oh, right, and one basketball tournament.

There's no time to rest on our laurels, though, because we're still lagging behind Turnbull Academy and Warwick Central. As anyone who watches the local news knows, Warwick's fund skyrocketed last week after a group of renegade cheerleaders kidnapped the principal and staged a fund-raising treasure hunt to locate him. That's the sort of creativity that wins competitions. (Note to Buzzkill: better watch your back.)

Here at Dunfield, we need to unite. If you want to sleep till noon when every other Chicago high school student is in class next January, you need to get involved and stay involved. That means supporting every event—even if the guys' attempts are woefully unoriginal.

In Newshound's humble opinion, the success of the girls' events has everything to do with communication—the very thing Scoop dismisses. If I learned one thing in biology last year, it's that communication defines us as a species. Yet Scoop is advising his Dunfield brethren to ignore thousands of years of evolutionary progress and stop talking now. Obviously it takes a certain amount of effort and brain power to communicate effectively. Maybe Scoop doesn't think guys are up to the challenge?

They certainly don't appear to be up to the challenge of making their fund-raisers appealing to the entire student population. While Golfing for Greenbacks raised some good coin, the guys could do better if they organized events that appealed to more than half the school's population.

When it comes right down to it, Dunfield guys are only interested in impressing each other. They pretend to be interested in us, but the only opinion they really value is that of their buddies. Guys crushing on guys, that's the story.

The Literacy Challenge has been a real eye-opener for a lot of women in this school. We've discovered that the top-ranking primates in Dunfield's male hierarchy are too scared of losing status to step out of their comfort zones.

Get a spine, guys, and you may just get a life.

Mr. Sparling looks up from my draft and stares at me. "Are you sure you want to say that all guys are spineless?"

"I didn't say they're *all* spineless."

"Just Dunfield guys." He leans back in his chair. "That might make Newshound rather unpopular."

No more unpopular than Lu Perez, a girl who guys like Mac Landis are too ashamed to acknowledge within the walls of Dunfield. As I see it, I don't have much to lose.

"It's not a popularity contest, right?" I ask. Over the past few weeks I've become more comfortable speaking my mind to Mr. Sparling—the editor, if not the teacher. "A columnist can't afford to worry about what people think of her. That's why you wanted us to be anonymous."

"I didn't tell you to alienate a whole gender."

His gender. I bet he isn't complaining to Scoop, whose words are even more inflammatory. "You wanted us to feel free to express our feelings, so I am. I can't believe you're going to start censoring me now."

Mr. Sparling's eyes narrow behind his glasses. I suppose no English teacher wants to be accused of squelching free speech, but columnists have to push buttons sometimes—it's part of the game. I know this because I've been researching some of the columnists he recommended. Whether they're writing humor pieces, or about sports, or politics, they all seem to push buttons. They have strong opinions. They say what other people would say if they only had the guts. Writers don't get offered a prime chunk of newspaper real estate for being wishy-washy.

"No one is censoring your opinions," he says. "But Mrs. Alvarez is concerned that 'The Word' is drifting from the Literacy Challenge."

"The whole column's about the Literacy Challenge," I insist. "Besides, *she's* the one who pitted the guys against the girls. She *wanted* to create sparks."

Mr. Sparling ponders this for a moment before nodding. "True enough."

"So you'll run the column as it is?" I ask, convinced there's a hitch.

"It's a little long," he says. "I told you to keep it to four hundred words."

"But I had a lot to say this week, especially with reporting the school board results. Doesn't that deserve a few extra words?"

"I guess so," he says. "This time." He picks up his red pencil and scratches something out before sliding it toward me. The word "Buzzkill" has been replaced by "Alvarez."

"She knows we call her that," I say.

"She also knows who's behind the Newshound disguise."

"I'm willing to take risks to speak for the people."

He sighs. "Pick your battles, Lu."

I push the copy back to him. "Okay. You win."

"Your editor is not the enemy. But he does have to keep the publisher happy, or she'll take away your platform."

I check to see if he's joking. "You mean Mrs. A could cancel the column?" The thought worries me more than I expect.

"She could, but she probably won't," he says. "Since 'The Word' first appeared in the *Bulletin*, we've quadrupled our initial print run, and we're still running out of copies. I don't think Principal Alvarez will want to mess with something that has actually gotten Dunfield students reading."

He smiles, obviously pleased that this is working out so well.

As I stand to leave, Mr. Sparling stops me. "Today's fund-raiser doesn't start for an hour, right?"

I was going to catch up with Rachel and Izzy in the cafeteria, but if my editor wants me to stick around and debate the freedom of the press, who am I to say no? "Right," I confirm.

"Good. Spend some time in the library. Your last homework assignment was a little slapdash."

And just like that, my cool editor morphs back into my English teacher.

As I step out of the office, Mac Landis almost walks into me. "Oh, hi," he says, obviously taken aback.

I make a show of looking in all directions before answering. "Are you speaking to me? Here in a hallway, where anyone could see you? What about your rep?"

He examines his Nikes. "You're mad about the other night."

"I'm not mad," I say. "Okay I *am* mad—at myself for

falling for your nice-guy act. I thought I was a better judge of character."

His blue eyes bounce up. "You don't know what it's like to—"

"To be Mac Landis, basketball star? I can't even imagine the pressure you're under."

Mr. Sparling's voice drifts out of the office. "Mac, do you want help with that asssignment or not?"

Mac's scowls. "Sparling's been on my case for weeks, and my coach says I'm off the team if I don't pass English."

Obviously Mac isn't Scoop. From the sounds of it he's a lousy writer, and Scoop, for all his flaws, is not.

As I turn to go, Mac calls after me: "You won't tell anyone, will you, Stargazer?"

"Don't call me that," I say. "And you should be a little nicer to people if you want them to do you favors."

After the way he treated me, I see no need to put Mac's mind at ease. But I won't tell anyone his secret. If I can help it, I'll never mention his name again.

I stand under the enormous PIMP MY CHAIR banner, waiting for Izzy and Rachel. I texted them to meet me here, knowing the event would be nearly over by the time we found each other in this crowd.

Nearly half the student body has assembled for the guys' latest testosterone fest. The student parking lot has been converted into a racecourse shaped like a figure eight, complete with portable bleachers. There are banners advertising local businesses, and food and drink vendors are scattered everywhere. From the clips I've seen on the sports news, this looks pretty authentic.

Teams have been working for weeks to rig small engines to different kinds of chairs, and today they'll be competing in time trials. The guys have raised money by selling tickets to the event itself, and each team also had to find sponsors to pledge donations based on the number and speed of laps the chairs complete.

It seems stupid to me, but it could be good for a laugh. I assume that's what all the other girls milling around me think, too. Either that or they're here to meet guys, which is more likely.

"There you are," Rachel says as the girls come up behind me. "I was afraid you were going to miss the whole thing."

I'm happy to see they're both alone. Although it hasn't been that long since Jason and Carson arrived on the scene, somehow I already miss my friends. It's weird, because we've spent more time together than ever since the Literacy Challenge started.

"Anything good so far?" I ask.

Around us, the crowd cheers as a purple desk chair whizzes past and crashes into orange pylons. A guy in a purple jacket dusts himself off and raises a hand to signal he's okay. Meanwhile, his "pit crew" carries the demolished chair off the track.

"A couple of spectacular wipeouts, but no major injuries," Izzy says. "Carson's up next."

Three guys in silver jackets push an aluminum chair to the starting position. One of them is wearing a silver helmet, and he turns to wave in our general direction.

Izzy stands on tiptoes to wave back excitedly.

"Ah," I say, examining the broad streaks of silver that have appeared in Izzy's hair. "That explains a lot."

Carson straps himself into the chair as his team fires up the tiny engine. At the sound of the starter pistol, the chair takes off like a shot. Using the joysticks rigged to the arms of the chair, Carson maneuvers his machine around the first bank of pylons. He shoots down the straightaway, but on the second curve the chair swings out wide.

Izzy clutches my arm. "He's going too fast!"

Regaining control of the chair, Carson makes the turn safely, and after that it's smooth sailing for twelve laps until the engine sputters to a stop, out of gas. Amid the cheers, Carson pulls off his helmet and blows Izzy a kiss. She's already running toward him, silvery ponytail swinging. It's a total *Top Gun* moment.

The crowd's cheer grows as Mac Landis settles into a leather chair at the starting line. His pit crew is prancing around him wearing skintight, black vinyl jumpsuits. It's Mariah and the Understudies, and the word *MacNificent* is emblazoned across their chests in red letters.

Rachel laughs at my expression. "To think that could have been you," she says.

Mariah kisses Mac with enough suction to take the chair along with it.

"That would *never* have been me," I say. "I don't do vinyl."

"I don't think they're a couple," Rachel says, reading my mind. "It's just a show for the cameras." She points to the crew from the local television station.

"I don't care if they *are* a couple," I say. "I'm just surprised Mariah is putting pit duty before dancing."

Jason comes up behind us to watch the race with Rachel, and they become so absorbed that they don't see me slip away. I have no interest in watching Mac's ride. My time would be better spent trying to bump into Tyler "accidentally." I expected him to call after the dance, but he hasn't. In fact, I haven't run into him once in a full week, and I don't know what to make of it. Maybe Mr. Fantastic has reunited with Sue Storm.

I haven't gone far when a large wing chair rolls directly into my path.

"Chairs have the right of way," says the guy pushing it.

"Show me the bylaw," I say. I'm not really in the mood to meet new guys, but if I were, this one would be worth meeting. Even with helmet head and engine grease smeared across his cheek, he's cute. I'm not sure what to think about the grown-out blond highlights, but I definitely like his hazel eyes.

"I wouldn't argue with Full Tilt Plaid if I were you." He pats the back of a bulky and battered old chair that is covered in the ugliest green plaid imaginable. "This baby's a certified antique."

"*Old* and *antique* aren't the same thing, you know. An antique has value."

"This has value—to my old man. He bought it at a garage sale twenty years ago. First stick of furniture he ever owned."

"And he's letting you drive it around the school yard?"

"Mom let me take it since it's for a good cause. Dad

won't be happy, though." He points to a tear in the upholstery. "It was a wicked ride. Did you catch it?" He gives me a strange look, half hopeful, half sheepish.

"I got here late. But I heard there were some spectacular wipeouts."

His heightened color confirms my suspicions. "Plaid got the worst of it. She ain't built for speed."

"*She*? That thing is not a 'she.'"

Before he can respond, Coach Martin's voice crackles over the loudspeaker. "All Mixed Heat participants to the starting line, please."

Plaid's driver starts pushing. "You coming?" he asks.

"Me? Why would I come?"

"Because this is a two-person job," he says. "Start pushing."

I intend to scoff, but somehow I find my hands on the green upholstery, and we push the chair to the starting line, where dozens of people jockey for the best position. "You're on your own from here, uh . . ."

"Russ," he says, wiping his hand on his jeans before offering it to me. "Russ Davis. But you can't take off now: it's the Mixed Heat."

"Which means?"

"One dude, one chick, one chair." He motions for me to take a seat. "Let's ride."

"You've got to be kidding," I say, backing away. "I'm not getting near that thing."

"But I need a copilot and they don't come more aerodynamic than you. Whaddaya weigh?"

"I am *so* not answering that!"

134

"I give you one-ten tops," he says. "And you're barely five-one."

He advances on me, and I make a run for it.

"Get back here," he says. "Small is beautiful!"

Russ catches up to me and tosses me over his shoulder. I try to scream as he carries me back, but my voice is swallowed by my own scarf.

In a moment we are ensconced on Full Tilt Plaid, and Russ's pit crew appears out of the crowd. One of them hands Russ his helmet and plants a second helmet on my head. It's so big it falls forward and blocks my view. Meanwhile, Russ's other friend starts the engine.

"I don't want to do this," I say, and the words echo inside the helmet.

Russ lifts my visor and says, "Chill. You're gonna love it."

Some girls might like the idea of being squished between a cute guy and the arm of a chair, but given the way this plaid warrior performed earlier, it's not for me. I don't want to be known as the Luisa Perez who perished in a grisly chair crash.

"Positions," Coach Martin announces over the mike.

Russ drops my visor and reaches across me to grab the controls and maneuver the chair between two others. Adjusting my helmet, I check out the line of chairs and see Izzy's streaked ponytail poking under a silver helmet. She is perched on Carson's lap and doesn't appear to be a captive.

"This isn't going to work," Russ says.

Since I'm the one pinned into a plaid corner by his muscular arm, I have to agree. If the chair tries to throw me, there's nowhere to go but up.

Russ pats his lap, and I barely hesitate before climbing aboard. It's my chance to run for it, but for some reason I don't take it.

"Hold on," Russ says.

The plaid upholstery is too worn and shiny to get a proper grip, so I reach down and clutch his pant legs. This is more intimate than I expected to get with anyone today, let alone a guy I just met.

The starting pistol fires, and we lurch forward. Although we probably aren't going all that fast, it sure feels like it. Full Tilt Plaid takes the first curve at such speed that a screech rips out of my mouth: "We're going to die!"

"Trust me!" Russ yells back.

I bet guys always say that before a fatal accident. "Pull over! I want off! Now!"

Our chair pitches violently to one side as another vehicle smashes into us. I turn to get a look at the perpetrator: It's Mac*Nificent* Landis with Mariah astride.

When we straighten out, Mac's leather chair hits us again. It's clearly intentional. I lift my visor and shout, "Back off!"

Mariah flips me the bird and Mac cackles wildly before coming at us again.

I squeeze Russ's leg. "What are you waiting for? Hit it!"

Mariah is still cursing behind us when we cross the finish line after four laps. It's all I can do to not seize the controls and run over her myself.

Full Tilt Plaid takes third place, and Russ offers me the ribbon.

"Give it to your dad," I say, holding on to the chair to stay upright. My legs are weak, either from excitement or an overdose of testosterone. "She belongs to him."

Russ plucks something from the chair and hides it in his fist while he grabs my wrist with his other hand. "Thanks. We make a good team."

He leans down and kisses me on the cheek while placing something in my hand.

It's a plaid-covered button.

Rachel's message appears on the tiny screen of my cell phone:

Mean Girls on MTV 2nite. U watching?

Can't, I type back. Grace hogging TV. Again.

"Are you bitching about me to your little friends?" Grace asks, grabbing the phone out of my hands as she comes into the kitchen.

"I wouldn't bore them to death by talking about you."

"On my dullest day I'm more interesting than you are."

"Maybe to the Donner crew, but not to normal people."

She crushes her empty soda can with one hand. "Are you saying I'm stupid?"

With Grace, all roads lead to one destination. "No, I'm saying they're easily amused."

"Because *they're* stupid?"

"I'm not calling anyone stupid, Grace."

"If you're calling both Paz and me stupid, you must think Keira is stupid, too. You're a snob."

"My niece is *brilliant*," I say, seizing on the easier issue. "Anyone can see that."

This mollifies her. "She knows more words than any kid in this building."

"Yeah, she dropped the F-bomb the other day. Who taught her that?"

"I've heard you use it a few times."

The trill of my telephone, still in Grace's hands, catapults me out of my seat. Russ Davis asked if he could call tonight, and I've been waiting eagerly. Last month I wouldn't have seen myself with a guy who uses words like "wicked" and "dude," but times have changed. Actually, I still don't get the blond highlights, but a columnist must keep an open mind.

"Give me that!" I say.

Detecting the urgency in my voice, Grace instantly holds the phone out of my reach.

We struggle briefly, but I'm no match for her. With the phone over her head, she presses TALK and yells up at it. "Gracie's Escorts. How may I help you?"

"Hello?" It's Russ's voice and he sounds confused. "Hello?"

I jump at the phone but miss by a few inches. "Russ?"

"If you need a date for the evening, you've called the right place," Grace shouts. "We have all kinds of girls."

"I must have the wrong number," he says.

Grace backs away, fending me off with one hand as she lowers the phone to her mouth. She doesn't intend to give up the game so quickly. "I'm sure you have the right number. It's Russ, isn't it?" I can't hear his answer, but Grace says, "Of course I know your name. I make it my business to know my clients' names. But don't worry, discretion is a priority here at Gracie's Escorts. My lips are sealed."

Grace stops grinning long enough to pretend to zip her lips for my benefit.

I make another lunge, and she stops me with a flat hand to the sternum.

"Luisa?" she asks Russ. "We have a couple of Luisa's on call. What's your type? Short, dark, and mouthy?"

This isn't a battle I can fight on Grace's terms. She is bigger, stronger, and meaner. Fortunately I know her Achilles heel.

Ducking into the living room, I pick Keira up off the couch and carry her into the bedroom. My nerve almost fails, but I remind myself that Grace has tried to ruin my chances with every guy who's ever shown the slightest interest in me. It's time I started fighting back, and if it means fighting dirty, so be it.

"Let's play hide-and-seek, sweetie," I whisper to my niece. "You get under the bed, and I'll tell Mommy to look for you. Stay very, very quiet, okay?"

With Keira hidden, I walk to the hall door and open it. "Grace," I call. "Keira's out in the hall again. You left the door unchained."

There's a thud as my phone hits the linoleum and Grace races down the hall.

I pick up the phone and close the door. "Hi, Russ. Sorry about the comic interlude. My sister is an idiot."

"It's okay, so is mine."

He doesn't say anything else, so I ask, "How's it going?"

"Good."

"Did you get your antique home in one piece?"

"Nah. Tossed it into the Dumpster behind the school. Took six of us."

"May Plaid rest in peace."

There's another long silence, and I wait for him to fill it. Since he called me, I figure he'll take the lead.

He doesn't, and when the silence becomes uncomfortable, I jump back in. "So, did you tell your dad about the race?"

"Yeah. He laughed."

"At which part?"

"All of it."

In the long pause that follows, I hear the television in the background on his end.

I have to speed this up. It won't take Grace long to run down to the lobby and back up. I decide to drop a huge ask-me-out hint. "So, listen—"

"Yes!" he interrupts.

Is he a mind reader?

"Buddy just did a flamingo!"

"A flamingo?" What is he talking about?

"Turn your TV to Channel ninety-three. It's a skateboarding competition."

I've just risked my life at my sister's hands for a guy who's watching TV while we talk? "Maybe I should let you focus on the show."

His voice is suddenly alert. "Don't go."

Hearing the distant slam of the stairwell door, I say, "I have to. Grace is coming back."

Keira has come into the living room. "Mommy no find?" she asks.

I nudge her into the middle of the room and back away. As the door to the apartment flies open, I lunge into the bathroom, slam the door, and lock it. This will buy me a couple of minutes while Grace finds something she can use to pick the lock.

"Everything all right?" Russ asks, now paying more attention.

"Fine," I say brightly. "So . . ."

"So, do you want to get together sometime?"

"Sure."

"Great, I'm going to teach you to skateboard."

"Skateboard! I don't know, Russ . . . I'm not very athletic."

There's the rattle of a pick in the lock, and I try to hold the door closed as Grace pushes on the other side.

"You sound like you're working out right now," he says. "With your low center of gravity, you'll be a natural."

I'd be insulted if he hadn't said earlier that small is beautiful. At any rate, I don't have time to quibble.

"Okay, I'll try it," I say, sliding across the floor as Grace shoves the door open. "Gotta go—"

Chapter 10

THE WORD . . . FROM SCOOP
Now Who's Sucking Dust?

Proving once again that Newshound doesn't know her snout from her tail, the guys' latest fund-raiser was a roaring success. Pimp My Chair attracted 3,000 spectators, many of whom don't even attend Dunfield. That's 3,000 people who paid admission, sponsored riders, and pushed the guys' team ahead of the girls' again.

Scoop's sharp eye detected a lot of girls in the crowd—maybe not fifty percent, but close to it. Pimp My Chair had major crossover appeal, and if Newshound can't concede that, it must be because no one asked her to participate in the Mixed Heat. Personally, I've never gotten so much out of eight minutes in a desk chair.

The event offered nonstop entertainment, from Russ Davis's spectacular crash to Carson Cota's even more spectacular win. And who will ever forget the sight of Mr.

Sparling piloting his rickety desk chair around the track with the lovely Principal Alvarez aboard? That little stunt raised $450. A wipeout would have topped a grand, but you can't have everything.

I've been pondering what Newshound said about Dunfield men crushing on each other. Although Scoop can't speak for everyone, he's secure enough in his masculinity (and anonymity) to admit that he's guy-crushing on Carson Cota. That ride was enough to make anyone's heart pound.

Did Carson enter the race simply to impress his friends? Of course not. The guy loves speed. He loves competition. A performance like that comes straight from the heart, and that's what impresses other guys. Pure artistry.

If anything, it's Dunfield's women who live to impress one another. You can't make the simplest decision without taking a poll to see which way the estrogen blows. If your gal pals think you look good in blue, your whole wardrobe transforms. And if they think you should hold out for a guy with better hair, a cooler car, or higher social status, you do that, too. You never have an independent thought. After your friends finally endorse a guy, he discovers he's dating all of you, with none of the fringe benefits.

Once again I wonder if Newshound's attack is motivated by personal experience. If I were a betting man (and after Casino Night, I am), I'd say Newshound got burned at the Dunfield Groove. Maybe no one asked her to dance—at least no one who shows well enough—and now she's down on all guys.

Get over your bitterness, Newshound, and you may just get a date.

I crumple the *Bulletin* and turn up the volume on my iPod. If I weren't sitting on a bus right now, I'd set a match to the paper. Scoop is so far off the mark. I am not bitter, and I am not a snob. It's true that I didn't want to dance with Curtis the tech geek, but that's because he's a pervert, not because he doesn't "show" well. I may not like Curtis, Mac, or Scoop, but that hasn't turned me off all men.

What's more, I absolutely make my own decisions about guys. I do not depend on Rachel and Izzy to endorse my choices, although God knows I need their help to figure out what goes on in the male mind.

Take Tyler Milano, for example. He was so nice to me at the dance that I quickly resurrected the Arty FB dream. But then he didn't call. After a week of fretting, Izzy pressured me into calling him, and I left a casual "just calling to say hi" message. And he *still* didn't call. Izzy says I should have been more specific in my voice mail, but seriously, if a guy is too stupid to take a big hint, it's time to find a new FB.

Which brings us to Russ Davis. He has no trouble picking up the phone, but committing to an actual date is another matter. Worse, he continues to watch TV throughout our one-sided conversations.

Romance is much more complicated than I imagined. I remember when I thought landing a boyfriend was as simple as filling an empty seat beside me at the school assembly. Back then, guys seemed so elusive. Now I know they're easy enough to find and even to talk to, but impossible to understand. They have a mysterious—and sometimes malicious—way of viewing the world.

Someone nudges my backpack on the seat beside me. "Is this seat taken?"

I hear the question over my music but ignore it, keeping my eyes trained on the window. Obviously the seat is taken—by my backpack. That's how I keep losers at bay. There are other free seats.

"Excuse me," the voice repeats. "Could you move your backpack?"

I sigh. My policy is to move the backpack when asked directly. I'm not about to instigate a fight with some guy on a city bus; he could be armed. Pulling the backpack onto my lap, I continue to stare out the window as he slides into the seat beside me.

"What are you listening to?" he asks.

I sigh louder to let him know I'm not open to idle chitchat with strangers. Sulking is taking all my energy.

He tries again. "Carrying that attitude around must be exhausting."

This gets my attention. I turn to see a guy with dark eyes, unruly dark hair, and smooth olive skin. The last time I saw him, he was wearing a hairnet. "Joey, right?"

"Right. You working today?"

I nod, hoping he doesn't plan to talk the whole way. I need time to shake off my mood before I get to the diner; I learned long ago that nobody tips a grumpy waitress. Besides, I have no intention of becoming too friendly with someone on Paz's crew.

"You finished with that?" Joey asks, pointing to the crushed newspaper on my lap.

"Sure, take it," I say. If he reads, he won't talk.

He smoothes out the paper and starts to read Scoop's column.

I replace my earbud, only to yank it out again a second later when he snickers. "That columnist," I say, "is an idiot."

"Well, he's opinionated, that's for sure," Joey replies.

I shrug and look out the window. "*The Bulletin* is lame anyway."

"No argument there." He tosses it back into my lap.

I happen to write for that paper, so I'm the only one who gets to call it lame. "You don't even go to Dunfield," I remind him.

"I can recognize lame when I see it. I think it's universally understood."

I suppress the urge to smile at this. Joey is obviously like Paz—too smart for Donner's but not smart enough to stick it out in school. They probably share the same desperate need to prove their brilliance. It's the hallmark of insecurity.

Joey points to a building as we pass the corner of South La Salle and West Adams. "Did you know that The Rookery is the oldest high-rise in Chicago?"

Just as I thought. Paz is forever dropping useless bits of trivia into a conversation. I've learned that the best response is to sound bored. "Yeah?"

"Finished in 1888 and still standing."

I can tell he's burning to tell me more, and if I were in a good mood I'd let him think he's enriching my world.

But I'm not in a good mood. "I guess Frank Lloyd Wright knew how to build them."

Joey is silent for so long that I start to feel cheap for showing him up. Mom hates that kind of behavior. Turning, I add more kindly, "That's a famous architect."

"I know who Wright is. But he didn't design The Rookery. John Root did."

He sounds convinced of that. "Really?"

"It's a common mistake," he says, "because Wright remodeled the lobby in 1905."

Whatever. So he knows a few facts about architecture. There are information plaques all over town, and anyone who pays attention could pretend to be an expert. I may not pay attention, but I can call a bluff. "You seem to know a lot about buildings," I say. "Name your top five architects."

"That's a tough one," Joey says.

I bet it is, Mr. Fake Smarty-Pants.

"I'd have to go with van der Rohe, Aalto, Gehry, Libeskind and, at number one, Antoni Gaudi."

"Gaudi?" For all I know Joey is passing off a hockey team as architects, but if I keep him talking, cracks in his knowledge will eventually start to appear. "Why?"

"Because his work is so organic," Joey says.

Organic? How does that relate to architecture?

"You know, unrefined," he continues. "Gaudi designed this one apartment building that doesn't have a straight line on it. Even the roof is a work of art. The chimneys look like dozens of little sculptures."

"I've never seen it," I say. "Is it downtown?"

He stares at me. "Well . . . downtown Barcelona, I guess. Gaudi lived in Spain in the late 1800s."

The jig is officially up. "I knew that."

"Sure you did," he says, laughing.

It's more gracious than Paz would have been in the same situation. "So you've been to Spain?"

"Are you kidding? I've never been on a plane. But I took a bus to Florida once."

"Well, that's more than I've done."

Joey tells me that his mother moved to Tampa with his two sisters after his parents split six years ago. He stayed behind with his father, who worked such long hours in construction that Joey has been virtually fending for himself ever since.

"Grace and I had to be pretty independent too," I say, pulling out my other earbud and resigning myself to the conversation.

"At least you stayed in school," he says. "It's hard to be motivated when you've got a lot of freedom."

"How did you become so interested in architecture?"

"My dad used to take me to his construction sites. I got my first hard hat and steel-toe boots when I was six." He grins at the memory. "I loved all of it: the machines, the noise, the blueprints. Imagine how it must feel to design a building that will stand for centuries after you die. Wouldn't it be cool to leave a legacy like that?"

I nod, thinking it's a shame he probably won't be able to achieve that vision. Even with an education, leaving a lasting legacy is a rarity. "Why don't you work in construction instead of at Donner's?"

Joey frowns. "Because I was on my dad's job site the day he got hit by a steel post. He'll never be able to work in construction again."

Now he's the one staring out the window.

"I'm sorry," I say, feeling awkward.

Joey shrugs. "It is what it is. I know you don't have it easy at home either."

My defenses prickle. Joey barely knows me, and if he thinks I have it hard at home, Paz has been talking. "We're fine," I say, plugging my earbuds back in.

Joey backpedals. "I just mean that I know your mom has had to work really hard to raise you guys on her own. Paz says he wants to do as well for Grace and the baby."

"He left them," I point out.

"I heard it was the other way around."

"Well, don't believe what you hear at Donner's." I throw him a warning look, but he doesn't take the hint.

"Paz is going back to school someday, you know. He says if your mom can save for your college education on a tight budget, he can too."

This startles a response out of me. "She's not saving for me."

"That's why she picks up so many extra shifts. At least according to Grace."

My mother has never said a word to me about college, and I highly doubt this virtual stranger knows more about us than I do. It must be a story Grace concocted to make herself feel better about my mother's working so hard for Keira. I certainly wouldn't want to be the one adding lines to her face.

"For your information," I say, "my mother is earning extra money to help Grace with the baby. Not that it's any of your business."

Joey leans back in his seat. "Sorry. I'm just telling you what I heard."

"This is my stop." It's stating the obvious, since Joey gets off at the same one. He stands, and we wait in silence until the door opens.

Outside, he picks up where he left off. "I didn't mean to offend you."

"Then don't talk about my family like you know us."

"Sorry," he repeats, sticking to my side.

I pick up my pace. "Do me a favor? Sit in Shirley's section today."

I needn't have worried, because Paz's crew doesn't show up. Now and then they go up the street for a sub or pizza. I'm sure it has nothing to do with my conversation with Joey.

Dan complains about business being slow, but the downtime gives me a chance to catch up on my homework. He's helping me with a history project on the expansion of the West. By "helping me," I mean he's trying to seize the pen and write it himself. He actually brought in a prize set of antique spurs to inspire me. If we don't end up with a good grade, someone will be very disappointed.

Rachel and Izzy arrive at the diner near the end of my shift. They've been walking the Loop to sell rubber bracelets stamped with the phrase *Support Dunfield, Support Literacy*. It's Mariah's latest fund-raising idea, and although it's unoriginal, it has been effective.

Bypassing her usual stool, Izzy throws herself into a chair, exhausted. "We've sold two hundred and forty-eight bracelets at five bucks a pop," she says.

"It'll be two-fifty after Shirley and Dan buy theirs," Rachel adds.

"I spent twenty dollars on your raffle tickets and didn't win a thing," Shirley says.

Dan protests, too. "I donated a pie for the bake sale and sponsored Lu for the walkathon. That set me back thirty bucks."

In the end, Dan sends me home early with the girls to put a stop to their cajoling.

Although the Saturday shift at Donner's doesn't end for three more hours, I lead Rachel and Izzy in the opposite direction just in case, explaining that there was a creep at my usual bus stop earlier. It's more or less true.

We take the long seat at the rear of the bus and launch into a discussion about guys.

"How's it going with Russ?" Rachel asks.

"It's not. He's called four times and still hasn't set a day to get together. He's obviously not interested."

"Of course he's interested," Izzy says. "He offered to teach you to skateboard."

"Something I'd pay good money to see," Rachel offers, grinning. "Maybe you should charge admission—for literacy."

"Very funny," I say.

"He's probably just shy," Izzy says. "He wouldn't call if he weren't interested."

"It's just something to do when he's watching TV," I say.

Rachel's brow furrows. "Is he watching sports or a regular show?"

"Does it matter? Rude is rude."

"It matters. If he's watching sports, he's just being a guy. If he's watching a show with a story line, he's being a jerk."

"That's ridiculous." I look to Izzy for support. "Isn't it?"

Izzy shakes her head. "Carson was watching hockey when he called the other night, and I still like him."

As I look from one animated face to the other, it occurs to me that I'm doing exactly what Scoop said girls do: taking a poll to decide whether to give Russ another chance.

"So what was it," Rachel presses, "sports or drama?"

"Sports," I concede, relieved in spite of myself. Maybe I am incapable of independent thought, but at the moment I don't care.

The focus turns to Izzy, and she tells us that Carson hasn't formally asked her out either. Although he tracks her down at school all the time, for some reason he hasn't taken his interest off campus.

"Maybe I shouldn't have bid on him at the auction after all," she says. "He must like passive girls."

"Passive is safer," I agree. "Less risk of humiliation."

Izzy knows I'm referring to the call she talked me into making to Tyler and quickly changes the subject. "Do you have a copy of the latest *Bulletin*? They disappeared before I could get one."

I pull the crumpled paper out of my bag and hand it to her. "That's strange. Mr. Sparling said he tripled the print run."

Izzy gathers her things as the bus approaches her stop. "I guess 'The Word' travels fast."

I practically dance into the apartment, wishing I had someone to tell that the *Bulletin* is flying off the newsstand.

"What's up?" Grace asks from the sofa. "Sparling nominate you for Butt-Kisser of the Year?

I notice she's wearing a skirt and has blown out her hair. She hasn't made an effort like that in a long time. "Is that lipstick?" I ask.

She rubs her mouth on her sleeve. "No."

Throwing my backpack onto a chair, I follow the sound of clattering dishes toward the kitchen. "Mom's home?"

It's not my mother putting away the dishes, but Paz. He looks up at me and smiles. "Hey, Shorty."

"Hey. Want me to the put the plates away? I know the shelf's a little high for you."

He snaps the towel at me. "I still got a few inches on you." Motioning toward the fridge, he says, "I made spaghetti if you're hungry."

"I've never known you to lift a finger in the kitchen," I say. "You really have become a feminist."

"I've learned a few tricks since Gracie moved out," he admits. Paz has always been a lot nicer without an audience.

"Am I supposed to be impressed?" I ask.

He hangs the towel on the rack and lifts Keira out of her chair. "Nope. But the person I *am* trying to impress is even harder to please."

I collect the spaghetti from the fridge and take a damp fork out of the dish rack. "Did you blow off a shift tonight?"

He shakes his head. "My crew's down for three days."

"But I bumped into one of your guys on the bus. Joey."

"Carella?"

"I don't know his last name. But apparently you two are so close that you chat about my family."

He doesn't deny it. "Joey and I talk sometimes. He's a good guy and my best worker. Sometimes he picks up extra shifts to help out his dad."

"My point is, I don't want you talking about me to your crew. They're not my friends. I serve burgers, they eat burgers. That's all we have in common."

"Fine," he says, walking into the living room. "You're not that interesting anyway."

I follow, shoveling cold spaghetti into my mouth. "Like you're fascinating."

Paz hands Kiera to Grace. "Little sis has a sharp edge tonight, Gracie. Things tank with the all-star?"

"They did," Grace says. "But now there's Russ."

"Russ?" he says. "Tell Paz all about Russ, Shorty."

Grace saves me the trouble. "He keeps calling but doesn't follow through."

"He's just shy," I say, echoing Izzy's verdict.

"If he has the guts to call, he's not shy," Grace says. "So he must be jerking you around. Right, Paz?"

"Not necessarily." He sits on the couch and pats the seat beside him. "Let's analyze ol' Rusty together. You could probably use a male perspective."

I roll my eyes. "I don't think so. I have homework to do."

I fish my math book out of my backpack and carry it to the bedroom.

"Who said you could study in my bedroom?" Grace calls after me.

"Who said you could entertain in mine?" I reply before slamming the door.

I'm sitting cross-legged on my bed when I hear the distant ring of my cell phone. It's still in my backpack in the living room.

There's another ring, followed by a giggle and rustling. Suddenly I am on my feet, running to the door. "Don't you dare touch my phone!"

"Hi, Russ," Grace says. "It's Grace. Luisa's right here, but her agent wants to speak to you first."

I stand in the doorway and watch as she hands the phone to Paz. There's no point in fighting. It's two against one, and I'm still bruised from taking on the weaker one.

"Hey, Russ," Paz says. "I'm Lu's brother-in-law and I'm worried about her. I hear you keep calling but haven't actually delivered on a date."

I put my face in my hands.

"Don't worry, Lu," Paz says. "It's for your own good. The guy's stringing you along. Aren't you, Rusty?" He listens for a moment and says, "You want to set something up for next Saturday? Let me see if she's available." Paz presses the phone to his chest. "It's a good offer, Shorty. Saturday's a prime night and he's giving you a week's notice."

"So tell him I'm free, already."

"Not so fast," Paz says. He puts the phone to his ear

155

again. "What have you got planned?" More talking on Russ's end. "No. Skateboarding is out, man. Gracie and I cannot afford to have our number-two babysitter sidelined with a concussion." He listens for a moment and guffaws. "She wasn't exaggerating. Total klutz, man."

"Paz!"

He holds up a hand to silence me and continues with Russ. "A movie?" Paz glances at me, and I nod. "I think she can handle that." Paz sits down on the couch again, and his eyes lose focus. "Sounds like you got the game on . . . What's the score?"

"Your family is really, uh, interesting," Russ says, when I get hold of my cell phone and retreat to the bedroom.

"That barely scratches the surface, Russ." There's no point in pretending now. If he bolts I won't even blame him.

"Huh."

I can tell he's not so much stunned as riveted by the football game on TV. To fill the dead air I launch into my usual dance. "So how was your day?"

"Good."

"How was your chem test?" I hope to get him going with this, as he loves all things science. He even belongs to the robotics club. No wonder Full Tilt Plaid outperformed Mac-*not-so*-nificant.

"Sorry?" he asks, as a crowd roars in the background.

I deliver a monologue about my day, but it doesn't take long to run out of material. "Lunch was good," I finish weakly. "The cafeteria fries have improved."

I pause to give him a chance to ask me to the movie.

Paz has already laid the groundwork. How hard could it be? Too hard, apparently. Other than the TV, there's silence on his end.

That's it. I refuse to hang around, hoping, forever. I don't know about the other ten Luisa Perezes, but this one has pride.

"Well, I've got to get going," I say.

"Already?" He sounds disappointed.

"Russ, I've been doing all the talking. You're watching TV."

"I'm not watching TV," he says, and the television is silenced. "It was just on. I'm listening to you."

"Yeah? What did I say?"

He gropes around mentally for a moment. "You like the cafeteria fries."

I sigh. "That is the *least* notable thing I said."

"I'm sorry." It comes across as sincere. "The TV is always on in my room. It doesn't mean I don't find you interesting. I like hearing your voice."

Okay, that's more like it. Obviously I was wrong about guys being hopeless communicators. They just need a girl to identify the issue for them, and they fix it. It almost seems too easy.

Russ and I have a few moments of normal conversation, and then at last he asks me to the movie.

The word "yes" is barely out of my mouth when I hear the faint tapping of fingers on a computer keyboard.

Chapter 11

THE WORD . . . FROM NEWSHOUND
Dawn of the Dunfield Dead

There are plenty of things in life I don't understand—decaf coffee, fuzzy dice, and Ryan Seacrest, for starters. It's becoming obvious that I don't understand guys either. Why, I ask, do they bother to call girls if they're not going to listen?

In an earlier column, Scoop complained about girls talking to each other too much. If we do it's because it's more rewarding than talking to someone who slips into a coma when there's an electronic device in the vicinity.

I'm not bitter, Scoop, I'm just not attracted to zombies. And I'm not the only girl who feels this way. In case you haven't noticed, some of Dunfield's hottest women are taking their search for Mr. Right—or Mr. Conscious—off campus. Two cheerleaders are currently dating Turnbull guys. Scoop will say they're just "dating up," but what about the girls who are dating guys from

Warwick Central? Since that's dating sideways, maybe guys from other schools simply have something Dunfield men don't—like a pulse.

Out of the goodness of her heart, Newshound will offer some advice to help any zombie keep a quality Dunfield girl interested:

1. Don't bother calling us if you'd rather watch TV. Wait until you can offer your undivided attention.
2. Don't say you like girls to take the initiative if it actually freaks you out.
3. Don't treat all girls as if they're identical. We're as unique as snowflakes.
4. Don't keep saying "we should get together" without committing to a date. If you're not interested, don't waste our time.
5. Don't call us when you're out with the guys. Hearing them whooping in the background like a bunch of oversexed hyenas is not a turn-on.
6. Don't pass the phone to the hyenas in the middle of our conversation.
7. Don't answer if your cell rings when we're together, unless it's important.
8. Don't tell your friends where we're going so that they can "accidentally" bump into us. Hanging in a group is fun, but it isn't a date.
9. Don't pretend you've got to get home early if you're actually meeting your friends later.
10. Don't waste so much energy coming up with excuses and evasions that you don't have any left for being interesting.

> And girls, don't give up on the Dunfield zombies. They
> may be lifeless now, but we can resuscitate them. Demand
> the best and I predict you'll get it.

Mariah's voice carries from the next table in the cafeteria. "I *love* this girl! When I find out who she is, I'm going to let her hang out with me."

Izzy glances over at Mariah and then jabs me in the arm with her straw. "She's holding the *Bulletin*. She wants to make you an Understudy!"

"Excuse me while I slip into something more revealing," I say.

"Congratulations," Rachel says. "I'm sorry we can't be friends anymore."

Mariah continues to hold forth. "Mac and I never have a moment to ourselves. He brings Morgan McGee with him everywhere."

This may mark the first time Mariah and I have had something in common. When Russ called me last night, he said he's bringing his pal Carey along on our movie date tomorrow night because poor Carey just got dumped and needs cheering up. I wasn't impressed, but Russ wasn't paying enough attention to pick up on that.

My conversation with Izzy and Rachel about how to handle the situation was pretty similar to the one going on at the next table.

One of the Understudies asks Mariah, "So what are you going to do?"

"Take Newshound's advice," Mariah says. "I'm going to stop putting up with crap from Dunfield guys and hook up with someone from Turnbull."

That's not exactly what I advised, but Mariah doesn't intend to be outdone by cheerleaders.

I risk a glance over my shoulder, and Mariah's topaz eyes light on me immediately. "What do *you* want, Coconut?"

"Just interested in what you're saying about Newshound's column."

"Why? It's about dating—nothing *you* would understand."

The Understudies titter.

"Laugh, puppets, laugh," Izzy says, and their smiles vanish.

Mariah stands. "You mutants had better learn to mind your own business."

Knowing she likes Newshound somehow makes me braver. "Lighten up, Mariah. We're just stunned that you and your friends find time to read when there are so many moves to rehearse."

She doesn't have a chance to respond before Mac and his cronies arrive. He tracks her gaze to me and leans down to kiss her anyway, saying, "Hey, Beautiful."

She raises a hand to block the pass. "Don't."

Mac pulls away. "What's up?"

"Nothing's up."

"If my lips aren't on yours, something's up." Mac grins at his cronies, sparking some shoves of approval.

I roll my eyes at Izzy and Rachel, embarrassed that I was ever interested in a guy who uses lines as lame as that.

"Times have changed," Mariah tells Mac. "If you want a warmer reception, ditch your hyenas."

Chief hyena Morgan McGee steps forward to Mac's side. "You gonna let your girl tell you what to do?"

Mac rises to the challenge. "Drop the act, Mariah."

"Don't talk to her like that," Understudy One says. "Have some manners."

"Yeah," Understudy Two chimes. "Wake up, zombie."

"What's wrong with you guys?" Mac asks, honestly befuddled.

"Nothing," Mariah replies. "Show some respect or we'll find better company."

"Knock yourselves out," Mac says, drifting off with the hyenas.

Rachel turns to me, grinning. "Way to stir it up, Newshound. Couples are probably breaking up all over the school."

"I'm going to be one of them," Izzy says, drooping in her seat. "Carson still hasn't asked me out, so I'm going to have to follow Newshound's advice and demand better."

"Don't give up on him because of me, Izzy. It may be good advice, but let's face it, I haven't had much hands-on experience. Maybe no guy is any better."

"Jason is," Rachel says, although she doesn't look happy about it. "I'm the one who should be dumped."

She explains that Jason has been asking to meet her family for weeks, yet she keeps stalling because he doesn't know about her parents' prejudice against non-Jewish guys. Now he's starting to think she's ashamed of him.

"I'm sure your parents will be fine," Izzy says. "They

know he's been treating you well and getting you home safely. That kind of thing scores big points."

"All they care about is bloodlines," Rachel grumbles, picking apart her Styrofoam cup.

Suddenly a plate of fries coasts along the table in front of Rachel and knocks the cup out of her hand. The plate comes to a stop in front of me, and I look up to see Russ Davis grinning at me, obviously proud of his aim.

He starts to walk toward me, but a piranha in yoga pants intercepts him.

"I know you," Mariah says, yanking her top down a little. "You're the guy with the big . . . plaid chair. Full Throttle something-or-other?"

"Full Tilt Plaid," Russ says, skirting around her to join me. "Hey, Lu."

When Mariah's jaw drops, my annoyance at Russ evaporates instantly. It helps that he looks really hot in his faded jeans and white T-shirt. Plus, he's a senior, and Mariah must know that or she wouldn't be squandering her cleavage on him.

I introduce Russ to my friends, and he tosses a funny remark to each of them. He's a zombie revived.

"Hey, weren't you riding shotgun with Carson in the Mixed Heat?" he asks Izzy. "That is one fierce driver. You should hold on to him."

Izzy blushes, unable to say a word.

I jump in to distract Russ. "Do you want to join us?"

"I can't, I've got a class," he says. "But I don't want to wait another day to hang with you."

"No?" My heart starts to dance.

"Especially now that Carey's crashing tomorrow."

He gets it! He gets it!

"Are you free later?"

Yes YES *YES!*

He writes something down and hands it to me: his locker number. "Meet me right after last class, okay? It's in Senior's Hall."

"Sure," I say, trying to sound nonchalant because I know Mariah is watching.

"Wear your knee pads," he says. "You're going to meet Betty Boop."

"What?" I glance at Izzy and Rachel, who look equally confused.

Laughing, he enlightens me. "I name all my skateboards. Betty's my favorite."

Russ turns and finds his exit blocked by Mariah's thigh. Her foot is resting on a table as she stretches out her hamstrings for Russ's benefit.

"I've been meaning to congratulate you," Mariah tells Russ. She bends, causing her yoga pants to slide even lower and reveal the pointy tip of a tail tattooed near the base of her spine. A scorpion, perhaps? Or Satan?

"Thanks," Russ answers, clearly mesmerized by the tail. He shakes his head as if to dispel the image. "For what?"

"For winning the chair race," she says.

He runs a hand through his hair, leaving it disheveled. "I didn't win."

"Really?" Mariah asks, easing down a little farther.

Russ pulls his eyes away with difficulty. "Carson Cota did."

Her work done, Mariah lowers her leg to let Russ pass. "Well, next time, sweetie," she says. Her eyes flick toward me. "The best person always wins in the end."

We've barely settled into our seats in English when the PA system crackles and Mrs. Alvarez's voice booms into the classroom.

"Attention, students, I have an important announcement. Thanks to the proceeds of the recent motorized chair event and the bracelet campaign, Colonel Dunfield has made the top three in the Literacy Challenge, and unless another school wins a lottery, we will very likely be invited to participate in the mayor's grand finale for the Literacy Challenge."

The classroom explodes into cheers, and then everyone shushes each other to hear the principal explain that the school board is staging an event in mid-December to profile the top three finalists. It will take place in the lobby of the Harold Washington Library Center, and the guest list will include the mayor of Chicago, the media, prominent figures from the community, and student reps from participating schools.

"The winner will be determined at this event," Mrs. Alvarez says. "The mayor's special guests intend to contribute money to the cause on behalf of the school they deem most deserving. Each of the finalists will provide some entertainment."

In other words, we have to put on a bit of a show for

the mayor's moneybags friends by inviting some local celebrities to attend and support us.

"Our literacy columnists will offer some leadership here," Mrs. A continues. "Scoop and Newshound have been distracted by gender politics lately, but I'm quite sure they can come up with something to seal the deal at the gala and earn Dunfield students a nice, long holiday."

From down the hall we hear the bass chant of "Scoop, Scoop, Scoop" and over it the soprano "Newshound, Newshound, Newshound."

Smothering a grin, Mr. Sparling walks over to the door and closes it. "Okay, people," he says. "Can someone remind me where we left off yesterday?"

I raise my hand, volunteering for the first time, perhaps, ever. "I believe we were going to discuss Sisyphus, sir. He was the king who tried to outsmart the gods and was punished by having to push a rock up a hill for all eternity."

Mr. Sparling chuckles. "Very good, Ms. Perez. And what does his punishment symbolize?"

"Vain labor. No matter how hard Sisyphus works, the rock just rolls back down the hill, and she—I mean *he*—has to start all over. It's a thankless job." Just like being a columnist appears to be.

Rachel and Izzy giggle beside me as Mr. Sparling nods. "Correct, Ms. Perez. Because it's never wise to try to outsmart the gods, is it?"

Mr. Sparling catches up to me after class. "A word, Ms. Perez?"

I have more important things to do, like make myself

beautiful for my skateboarding lesson, but I follow him to his office, applying lip gloss as I go.

"It's an informal meeting," he says, settling into the chair behind his desk. "No need to spruce up."

I drop the gloss back into my bag and decide to beat him to the punch. I only have nine minutes to get to Russ's locker, and there's someone only too willing to stand in for me if I'm late. "I'm sorry about my last column, Mr. Sparling. There wasn't much to report about the bracelet campaign, so I sort of filled the void with advice to the guys. But I think it's starting to have an impact."

"I think so too," he says. "There will be mayhem in the halls, and not just Dunfield's."

"What do you mean?"

"I mean 'The Word' is going into syndication."

He waits for a reaction, but I'm not sure what syndication means. "Is that good?"

"Good? It's great. Thanks to the cross-pollination you describe in your column, five other schools have asked to run it in their papers, including *The Turnbull Tattler*. All told, there's a potential readership of nine thousand."

"Wow, that is great," I say. "And scary."

"As long as you cover the Literacy Challenge, just keep doing what you're doing. That's what grabbed everyone's attention."

"No one knows it's me anyway," I say, more to myself than him.

"They will," he says. "Principal Alvarez asked the mayor to let you and Scoop host the final gala."

I'm not so big on *that* idea. It's one thing to write these columns and another to stand up and take the heat for them. Besides, I'd have to be polite to Scoop.

"You've got almost two months to gear up for it," Mr. Sparling says, as I get up to leave. "Well done, Luisa. I'm proud of you."

I barely have time to dump my books in my own locker before jogging over to Senior's Hall. My brain is spinning from all that's happened today. It's hard to believe that just a year ago I found school unbearably dull.

There's no sign of Russ, so I start checking numbers. A familiar dark-haired guy is opening his locker, and I study his profile in disbelief.

Joey Carella looks up and gives me a casual nod, as if bumping into each other at Dunfield happened all the time.

"What are you doing here?" I ask.

"Collecting my things. If that's all right with you."

"Now? How long ago did you drop out?"

"I didn't drop out," he says, stuffing books into his backpack. "You just assumed I did because you think all factory workers are stupid."

"That's not true. You *implied* you dropped out." I scramble to recall his words on the bus last week. "You said it was hard to be motivated."

"It is hard. But I'm still here."

"Then why haven't I seen you before?"

"Because the school's the size of a small town?"

That's certainly true. I rarely bump into Rachel or Izzy unless it's at one of our designated meeting zones, and I'd never seen Russ before the race, either.

Joey isn't meeting my eyes, so I do the right thing. "I'm sorry I jumped to conclusions."

"It's okay," he says, smiling. "I'll still tip you."

For the first time I notice how white his teeth are, especially against his olive skin. "Then I'll make sure you get extra fries."

He waits a couple of beats before saying, "Look, I'm sorry about what I said the other day about your family. You were right, it was none of my business."

"I overreacted," I say. "And *you* were right. I asked my mom, and she said she is saving to send me to college. Apparently, I was the last to know."

He closes his locker door. "You coming?"

"I've got to hang around a while."

"Why?" he asks. "I make a point of not spending one second longer in these halls than I have to. Ask Buzzkill."

Russ is coming down the hall toward us, so I say, "I'm meeting a friend."

"Sorry I'm late," Russ says, squeezing my arm. "Hey, Carella. Skipped chem again, eh?"

Joey shrugs. "I was busy."

"You ditched robotics too," Russ continues, obviously unimpressed. "Cranston's on your case."

Seeing Joey's expression darken, I tug on Russ's sleeve. "Let's go. I can't wait to meet Betty Boop."

Life at Dunfield may be more interesting this year, but that's partly because I've become aware of the land mines buried in its halls.

* * *

"Slow down!" Russ shouts, running after me down the sidewalk.

"I can't!" I scream, careening toward the intersection. It seemed so far off when we started, but a couple of really good kicks and a slight incline have brought me closer very quickly.

"Drag your foot!" Russ yells.

"I can't!" I scream again. I'm barely balanced now. My knees are locked into the bent position Russ showed me when I boarded this rocket. If I move one iota, I'll either veer into traffic or a brick wall. I'd rather take my chances on hitting a green light at the intersection.

A cluster of schoolboys stops at the corner to watch. One reaches out to stop me and misses by a fraction of an inch.

Ahead of us a lady pulls her toddler out of my path. "Sorry," I call.

"Look out!" Russ's voice is fainter now.

As if I can't see the intersection looming thirty—twenty-five—twenty feet before me. "Stay green, stay green, stay green," I chant at the light. Otherwise I'll run full tilt into that city bus as it pulls out.

"Drag your foot!" Russ yells again.

The light turns yellow, and terror brings the feeling back to my legs. I propel myself off the board and continue to run for a few yards. At the crosswalk I grab a pole to slow down and tumble off the curb and into the gutter. Three lanes of traffic are revving for takeoff.

"Oh my God. Oh my God!" Russ is shrieking hysterically.

A taxi swerves to avoid me, and I clamber back

onto the sidewalk on my hands and knees.

"Oh my God!" Russ screams one more time as he arrives at my side.

"It's okay," I say, reaching out to pat his pant leg. I'm touched at how concerned he is, considering we've only known each other a couple of weeks. I'm glad I gave him another chance. "Russ, I'm fine."

He's looking not at me but out into the intersection. "Betty!" he wails, as the bus moves past its splintered remains.

I drop my head onto the sidewalk. "I'm sorry."

"I told you to slow down," he says, jerking his pant cuff out of my hand.

"You sent me down a hill. I didn't know what I was doing."

His voice drops to a whisper. "She was a limited edition Stacy Peralta board. Signed by Stacy himself."

He darts into traffic and grabs a wheel, stroking it with one finger and muttering, "She's irreplaceable."

Something tells me the same cannot be said of me.

My mother looks down at my dirty, torn jeans and asks, "What happened?"

"I tripped off a curb," I say. "You know what a klutz I am." No need to go into details. The woman has enough stress in her life. "What smells so good?"

"Homemade lasagna," Mom says, handing me a stack of plates.

"What's the occasion?"

"That I get to have dinner with both my daughters for

the first time in weeks," she says. "Grace is putting Keira down, so tell me about your day."

"It was pretty good." And it was, aside from a brush with death and the loss of Extreme BF. "My column is being syndicated to five other schools."

Mom stops shredding lettuce to hug me. "That's fantastic, honey, although I can't say I'm surprised. Each one is better than the last."

"So you *have* read them."

"Of course I've read them," she says. "Haven't I— Well, never mind. Let's celebrate." She reaches for a bottle of wine and pours about an inch into two glasses before filling the third. Mom is laid back about a lot of things, but not underage drinking. She hands me a glass and raises her own. "A toast to my very clever daughter."

I clink glasses with her before sitting down. "Mom? What's wrong with guys?"

She laughs and goes back to making the salad. "If I knew that, would I be single?"

"Why *are* you single? You could be dating. Lots of guys have liked you. Mr. Kendricks at the deli, for example."

She takes another sip of wine and considers her answer. "I haven't really had time to worry about that, Lu. Dating is risky when you have two kids."

"But we're grown up now. At least *I* am. You could do the online thing." Knowing she'll protest her cyber ignorance, I add, "I could help."

Fishing celery out of the fridge drawer, she changes the subject. "So how does this syndication work?"

"What syndication?" Grace asks, coming into the kitchen.

"Your sister's column is going to be published in other schools' papers."

"*The Turnbull Tattler*?" Grace says, snickering. "That's the big time, all right."

"Grace," my mother says. "Hold the tongue or forfeit the wine."

Grace examines the glass. "I can barely *see* the wine. Someone forgot to finish pouring."

"Someone forgot to quit while she was ahead," Mom says, reaching for Grace's glass.

That brings Grace around pretty fast. She seizes her glass and sits down opposite me. I tell them about the gala and Mrs. Alvarez's challenge to bring in some high-profile people.

"What about Solana G.?" Grace says. "She could be a celebrity guest. Paz and I saw her perform at Logan Square last year, and she was amazing."

"I was thinking more like a columnist from the *Chicago Tribune*."

"Boring. Who would you rather watch at a gala— a writer or an R&B singer?"

"I doubt Solana would do it," I say. "She's getting really popular. Why would she bother with this sort of event?"

"Because she went to Dunfield?" Grace says.

"Really? When did she graduate?"

"I didn't say she graduated," Grace replies. "She dropped out the year I started."

I don't want to dismiss Grace's idea outright since she's being helpful for a change, but I seriously doubt

Solana G. would support Dunfield for anything.

"She does charity events all the time," Grace says.

"For literacy?"

Grace crosses her arms and glares at me. "You don't want her because she didn't graduate."

"That's not what Lu means," my mother intervenes.

I used to think Grace was just touchy, but with others echoing her view that I'm a snob, I'm starting to wonder if she might be right.

"Actually, I think Solana would be the perfect sponsor," I say. "She's done really well in spite of dropping out, so coming back now to support literacy is practically a stay-in-school message. Mrs. Alvarez will eat it up."

Grace mulls this over for hidden insults and decides to give me a pass. "Let's go look her up online."

By the time Mom has cleared the table and put out dessert, Grace and I have tracked down Solana's agent. With Grace leaning over my shoulder, I type an e-mail about the Literacy Challenge and the upcoming gala. I also tell her about "The Word" and promise to send samples of the column.

"Maybe you should hold off on the samples," Grace says, after I've hit SEND. "She might be put off that you're a man hater."

"So you *do* read my column!"

"How can I avoid it? There are copies in every room."

"Luisa isn't a man hater," my mother says, summoning us back to the table. "That's just her voice for the column. Right, Lu?"

"I don't hate them all," I agree. "Just the ones I know."

Grace rolls her eyes at my mother. "See what I mean?"

"Well, come on, do you see any good role models around here? Deadbeat father. Unreliable brother-in-law."

"Paz has been a lot better lately," Grace says, digging into her chocolate cake. "Maybe he'll turn into a role model yet."

I let this go because it's the first time in a long time that we've spent an evening together without a fight.

My mother raises her glass and says, "If you're really that negative about men, Luisa, I may have to look into cyber romance after all. Someone has to prove to you that there are good ones out there."

Grace gapes at her.

"Mom wants us to help her meet men online," I explain, grinning.

I pick up my glass, this one filled with milk, and clink it against my mother's, who in turn clinks hers against Grace's.

"Here's to finding the good guys," Mom says.

Chapter 12

Rachel is waiting for me outside the old mansion.

"Hey, Rach," I call. "Happy Halloween."

"Lu?" she asks. "You've metamorphosed."

"Arachnids don't metamorphose," I say, flapping eight "legs" at her. "But stick around and I might molt for you."

I study Rachel's costume, but I don't know what to make of the tiny cereal boxes dangling from her jacket. Each has been pierced by a sharp object and daubed with fake blood.

Before I can guess, a familiar hatchback pulls up to the curb, and Princess Leia, in a white robe and coiled hair, climbs out. Izzy waves a light saber at her father as he drives off. "You guys look great. Rachel, you're a cereal killer, right? And Lu . . . a black widow?"

"Tarantula," I say. "Can't you see I'm fuzzy?"

"Well, I make a point of not getting close enough to spiders to know their distinguishing features," she says. "But it's a cute costume."

It is, thanks to my mother's talent with a sewing

machine. I came home with an eight-eyed mask and a couple of black fleece blankets from the dollar store yesterday, and Mom spent half the night stitching two distinct body parts. She even attached three legs to each of my arms with fishing line so that I can move them all.

Jason arrives with a theatrical swish of his magician's cape, and we line up to buy tickets for the haunted house—the Dunfield men's latest fund-raiser. Since Carson is already inside manning the guillotine, I'll soon be the only one without a guy, as usual. For a change, however, I am not unhappy about that. On the contrary, I'm relieved; my recent near misses have chased me back to the sidelines. This Luisa Perez is taking a seat in the stands to watch others get trampled in the arena of love.

Not that there will be much of a show today. Because I have to work at the diner tonight, Rachel and Izzy agreed to visit the haunted house with me at four o'clock on a Saturday afternoon. It's hardly worth suiting up for, especially since I have no faith that the guys' team has enough imagination to make it truly scary. Inside there's probably a chorus line of scantily dressed fairies kicking up their heels for leering goblins.

Jason gallantly precedes us into the darkened house, where we are greeted with recorded screams and echoing, evil laughter. A coffin propped against the wall creaks open just enough to allow a hand to dart out and grab Jason. He screams like a girl and jerks away, causing the rest of us to giggle. So far, so cheesy.

Before I can say as much to the girls, however, unseen hands grab me from behind and push me into a chair. I hold tight to the arms while it spins, determined not to scream. After a few moments my captor disgorges me into something like a sandbox. A red light starts to strobe, and I see that I'm in a mock open grave, and a half-decayed corpse is groping its way toward me.

Scrambling to my feet, I climb out of the grave and stumble forward as the room goes dark again. I feel my way to a doorway and step through it. The strobe flashes again, lighting a long corridor. Ahead, someone in a light-colored costume is disappearing through a doorway. Hoping that it's Izzy's white robe, I scurry after her.

By the time I reach the doorway, my heart is pounding so hard I can't breathe. This is ridiculous. I am in a house in downtown Chicago at four in the afternoon. Ten feet away I can see the faint outline of light leaking around a window frame. Still, at any moment, a Dunfield creep could jump out and maul me in the name of Halloween.

Someone taps on my shoulder and I let out another scream. I start to move forward but the grim reaper has appeared in front of me with his raised sickle. I'll take my chances with whatever is behind me. Leaping back, I flail against something soft. There's a grunt, as if I've winded someone, followed by a thud.

The next flash of the strobe reveals not a terrifying zombie but Mr. Potato Head clambering to his feet. He's wearing a stuffed, beige pillowcase around his torso for the "potato" and a black hat over his entire head. Mr. Potato Head's features are pinned to the front of the pillow case.

"Great costume," I say.

"Thanks, don't wreck it," Mr. Potato Head replies, his voice muffled by the hat.

"Sorry," I say. "Spider reflexes."

"Tarantula?" he asks.

I'm pleased that he could ID my species even in fractured light. "That's right."

"They're carnivorous, right?"

"Totally veggie-free. You're perfectly safe."

"Not safe enough," he says. "I've been attacked by a vampire, an ax-wielding psycho, and a couple of generic ghouls."

"Boo-hoo, Spud. I lost my friends and spent some time in an open grave with a rotting corpse," I say.

The strobe has stopped, and my eyes gradually adjust to the gloom. We're in a grand living room with high ceilings, half a dozen mirrors lining the walls, and a large fireplace. In the center is a large, low, circular object. I nudge Mr. Potato Head. "What's that?"

As if on cue, a couple of spotlights come on to reveal a clear, plastic kids' pool filled with eighteen inches of green fluid.

"Let's take a look," Mr. Potato Head says.

He walks toward the pool, and I clutch at his arm. "Let's not."

"Not so brave now, are you, spider?"

"The black widows got all the guts."

Laughing, he pulls me a few steps closer to the pool until we can see that it's filled with suspicious white globules and long, twisting fibers.

"Just as I thought," he says. "Primordial ooze. It's where we all started."

There's a quick movement behind us, and Mr. Potato Head jerks me aside just in time to avoid the long-nailed clutches of another marauding vampire. I give a shriek that sends the vampire reeling.

"Dial it back a little," Mr. Potato Head says, as the vampire disappears through a doorway. "You nearly blew out my plastic ears."

One of my false arms is snagged on his oversize fedora, and when he bends to give me better access, he knocks my mask askew.

"Hey, Luisa," he says, pulling off his hat. "I thought that was you." It's Joey Carella, rumpled and grinning.

"So you're my spud in shining armor," I say, grinning back at him.

"At your service." He replaces his hat. "You've got a good set of lungs for a spider in distress."

"She sure does," Rachel says, coming into the room with Jason in tow. "Izzy and I could hear her three rooms away."

"You didn't hurry to my rescue," I say.

"We had our hands full," Izzy replies, joining us with a tall, masked executioner.

I introduce Joey to my friends. "And unless I'm much mistaken," I say, "this is Carson Cota."

"Great ride at Pimp My Chair," Joey says, shaking Carson's hand. "How did you build that motor?"

As the guys launch into an animated discussion, Izzy pulls me aside to whisper, "Who's the hot potato? He seems familiar."

"You don't know he's hot," I say.

"I got a look at him before he pulled his hat on,"

Rachel says. "He's hot. And it sounded like you knew him."

"I've served him at the diner," I say. "He's a friend of Paz's."

Rachel frowns. "You mean he's a Cocoa grad?"

For the first time I really understand why Grace gets so defensive about comments like that. We *are* snobs. "No. I mean, yes, he works for Paz, but he also goes to Dunfield."

Izzy cocks her head to one side. "You like him."

"Like him? No. Anyway, I've sworn off guys. After the run I've had, can you blame me?"

"Speaking of which," Rachel says, "Frankenstein over there looks familiar."

Another guy has joined Jason, Joey, and Carson. The green makeup and nerdy wig are a clever disguise, but it's the first time I've ever seen Frankenstein wearing cool glasses. It's Tyler Milano. Having put Arty FB to rest at last, I'm not eager to talk to him now. Fortunately I'm not the one in his sights.

"Carson," Tyler says, wringing his hand. "That ride got my heart rate up, and I wasn't even driving."

"That's pretty much what Scoop said," I murmur to the girls.

"So people are quoting him," Rachel says. "Just like they quote you."

I need some friends who aren't always a step ahead of me. They must sense that I almost *want* Tyler to be Scoop, so I'll have a reason to hate him. It would be easier than wishing he didn't hate me.

A well-built demon with ghastly white makeup and

red-rimmed eyes claps the executioner on the back. "Hey, Carson. Great ride."

It's Mac Landis, and he too is quickly sucked into the discussion of motors and racing. It's like a black hole.

"Carson is a guy magnet," I say. "He's pulled everyone I've ever dated out of the woodwork. This is turning into Lu's Hall of Romantic Horrors."

There's a sudden commotion in the doorway as the Wicked Witch of Dunfield blows in with her entourage.

"Speaking of horrors," Izzy says.

I lower my mask over my face in the hope that Mariah won't recognize me. She's wearing a tall, pointy black hat, but that's her only nod to tradition. In fact, two-thirds of her costume is missing completely. There are black stiletto boots, but the scrap of material that passes for a skirt starts well below her hip bones and ends eight inches later. Her sheer blouse covers only a black lace bra.

"Eek," she says, looking in my direction. "A cockroach! Someone call an exterminator."

"I'm a spider," I say, lifting my mask. "I hope you got a discount for the missing parts of your costume."

"I hope you got yours for free," she says. "Because it sucks."

The big-eared, gray troll glued to her side chuckles. It's a laugh I've heard often, against a background of tele-vised sports. "Russ?" I ask.

He raises a hand, and Mariah smirks. "Oh, that's right. You two know each other."

"Sure," I say. "I think Mac knows Russ, too. Let's ask him."

Mariah casts her eye on the group of guys who are still

so deep in conversation that they haven't noticed the change of scenery. "Mac is dead to me," she says, wrapping an arm around Russ's waist.

"A little louder," I suggest. "I don't think he heard you."

The Understudies, dressed in matching genie outfits, step forward to flank their leader.

"Are you trying to piss me off, Coconut?" Mariah asks.

"Just making an observation. You're as transparent as your costume."

Rachel clutches my stuffed thorax as a signal to cease and desist, but I don't feel like stopping. I may not be into Mac or Russ anymore, but I'm tired of seeing Mariah sweep any guy I've liked off his feet with her broom.

Mariah takes a couple of steps toward me. "You're lucky I'm a literacy leader, Coconut. Because today I'm going to teach you how to spell *dead*."

"Go ahead. You've already taught me how to spell witch with a *B*."

A gasp travels through her entourage—and mine. Mariah takes two quick steps toward me, and I see a flash of her stiletto boot as it lifts off. There's a thump in my sternum as the boot connects, and suddenly I am staggering backward, arms pinwheeling. I hit the side of the pool and topple into it.

The green fluid, as it turns out, is not primordial ooze but partially-set lime Jell-O. I know that because I get a mouthful as I go under. Hands immediately grab my arms and lift me out of the pool. I scrunch my eyes to keep out the ooze while someone pats my face dry. When

I finally open them, Izzy is scraping Jell-O off me with her robe while Rachel glares at Mariah, who is laughing so hard that her false eyelashes have detached. Russ appears to be trying not to laugh, but the same can't be said of Mac.

Tyler and Joey are hovering nearby, and judging by their ooze-covered sleeves, they were the ones who pulled me out of the pool.

Reaching over, Joey plucks a few strands from my costume and says, "Spaghetti." This causes Mac to chortle anew, and Joey adds, "Shut your mouth, Jockstrap." Surprisingly, Mac does.

Mariah is another matter. Her laughter swells until it's all I can hear. A wave of fury rolls over me, and I start toward her. Seizing my arms, Rachel and Izzy drag me away.

Several monsters jump us on the way out, but Izzy wields her light saber with such deadly force that we're on the sidewalk in no time.

Tyler calls after us from the porch. "You guys want to come over to my place? It's not far from here."

"I think Lu wants to go home and shower," Izzy says, knowing I'm too overcome to speak. "Her shift starts in two hours."

"She can shower at my place," he says. "I'll drive her to work later."

Rachel answers for me. "That sounds like a great idea, Tyler. We'd love to."

Mac's head pops over Jason's shoulder. "Watch your seats, man. Jell-O is hell on upholstery."

I don't even want to ask how he knows that.

Tyler turns onto a side street and drives past several large homes with beautiful landscaping.

I'm perched beside him on the blanket Rachel found in Jason's trunk. She sent me on alone with Tyler, to follow with Izzy and Carson in Jason's car. My friends are clearly trying to keep me in the game, but I have never felt less attractive than I do right now. My hair is slick, and the smell of lime fills the car. "Sorry to make you leave early," I say.

"No worries," he says. "I'd had enough horror for one day." He grins at me, and with the green makeup and neck bolts, the effect is somewhat alarming. "Mariah's a treat, isn't she?"

"You have no idea," I say. Still, I'm more annoyed with myself right now. After living with combustible Grace, I know better than to bait people like Mariah. Oddly enough, though, Grace has been mellowing lately, and I seem to be picking up the attitude she's outgrowing. "Thanks for pulling me out."

He swings his Honda into the wide driveway of his house, puts the car in park, and turns to me. "My pleasure."

There's something in his expression that makes me think all prospect of romance might not be gone after all. I don't see how anyone could find me appealing in this condition, but Tyler seems to.

"This is a beautiful house," I say, as an excuse to look away.

Opening his door, he says, "Stay there for a minute."

He jogs around the hood and opens my door for me. It probably has less to do with chivalry than with his not wanting me to touch the car with sticky fingers. But it's nice just the same.

"Let me," he says, and leans across me to release the seat belt. He pauses, his face close to mine. "Can I ask you something?"

"Uh, sure."

"Does green makeup bother you?"

I laugh. "Nope. Does lime Jell-O bother *you*?"

"Lime is my favorite flavor," he says, and kisses me. I'm sort of trapped, but even if I could leave, I wouldn't.

When he pulls away, I ask, "Why didn't you call me back?"

"I didn't think you really wanted me to. I thought you were just grateful that I'd saved you from that loser at the dance."

"I was grateful. But I really wanted you to call."

Tyler kisses me again. I close my eyes and forget about everything for a moment. He may look like Frankenstein on the outside, but he's still Mr. Fantastic on the inside. Maybe I should swear back on to guys and give Arty FB another try. After all, the chances of his being Scoop are slim. Even ruling out freshmen, there must be hundreds of guys who could conceivably write that column. What are my chances of kissing any of them?

Jason has pulled up behind us. "Hey, Tyler," he calls. "Got her resuscitated?"

"She inhaled a lot of Jell-O," Tyler says. "But I think she's going to pull through."

Tyler's bathroom is the nicest I've ever been in. The shower stall alone is bigger than our entire bathroom. It has glass walls and a huge copper showerhead that sprinkles a gentle mist. And the most amazing thing is that it's not the family bathroom, but the en suite attached to Tyler's room. I could totally get used to this. My only complaint is that his products are decidedly masculine. I smell like a cedar forest, but it's better than lime.

After lingering in the shower, I dry myself with a fluffy white towel and pull my gingham work uniform out of my backpack. Rolling up my spider outfit, I stuff it into a plastic bag for later disposal. There's no sign of a blow dryer, so I comb out my hair and hope for the best.

Tyler is gone when I step back into his bedroom. I left him checking his e-mails, but he must be downstairs now with the rest of the gang.

Crossing to the desk, I notice a stack of *Dunfield Bulletins*. Oddly, there are multiple copies of each. I have a stack like that at home. Grace says I'm hoarding them to drag out when I'm old and withered, to relive my glory days.

I can't imagine why Tyler would keep so many, unless he really is Scoop. Maybe a little judicious investigation could put this matter to rest once and for all.

Nudging the computer mouse, I make the screen saver disappear. It's not really snooping if I barely touch it. It's practically an accident.

Another accident takes me to Tyler's e-mail inbox. And that's all I really need to do, because my eyes immediately land on a string of e-mails from Mr. Sparling bearing the subject lines, "The Bulletin," "Revisions," or most damning, "Scoop."

As my hand moves to the mouse for one last accident, Tyler calls, "Lu? Are you all right up there?"

I stand upright so quickly that my head spins. "Coming," I call. And with that, Lu Perez retires to the stands again, determined to keep a safe distance from the arena of love.

Dan's Diner is packed with Halloween revelers. It's always a busy night, and I am always on duty because Grace refuses to work. Halloween is the worst night for tips and manners. When people put on a costume they think it grants them a license to misbehave. I've had my butt grabbed more on Halloween than the whole year put together. In fact, I've learned to wear shorts under my uniform because some guy dressed as an angel or a nun will inevitably flip my crinoline.

"Where's your costume?" Dan asks, leaning into the pass-through as I arrive. "You promised to dress as a spider."

Dan himself has augmented his usual Stetson with chaps, a bandanna, and spurs that jingle when he walks.

"The tarantula came to a bad end," I say, telling him about the haunted house. "I was going to change into my uniform after you saw the costume anyway. I couldn't serve very well with eight arms."

"That Mariah deserves to be lassoed and horse-whipped," Dan says, "If she ever comes in here—"

"I'll cast a spell on her," interrupts Shirley, who is dressed as a real witch in a flowing black dress. A pointy hat sits atop her backcombed hair, tipping perilously to one side, and there's a very realistic wart on her nose.

I mention that we went to Tyler's house, skipping the part about my snooping on his computer. That's something that must stay between my friends and me. Rachel was pretty shocked when I called her after Tyler dropped me off—shocked at what I did, shocked at what I found, and shocked that I was able to hide how I felt while I was still at Tyler's. Obviously I've gained some valuable skills through writing an anonymous column. The old Lu was totally transparent; the new one is a master of obfuscation. Still, I think Tyler suspected something was amiss when he kissed me good-bye. I couldn't quite rise to the enthusiasm I'd shown earlier.

"You take the mermaids and Abe Lincoln," Shirley says, handing me a stack of menus. "I've got Cleopatra, Elvis, and the swamp monster."

The rest of the shift passes in a blur, and at midnight I walk out to the bus stop. Someone has already claimed the old, wooden bench, and when I get closer I see that it's Joey Carella. Like me, he's traded his costume for his uniform.

He doesn't look surprised to see me, which makes me wonder if he's been waiting for me. "You've been de-slimed," he says.

I settle beside him on the bench. "What are you doing here? Didn't your shift end an hour ago?"

He shrugs. "Buses are slow tonight."

It's usually the reverse on Halloween, but I don't say so.

"Plenty of freaks around, too," I say. "At least, there were at the diner."

"How are you feeling?"

"I've had better days. There's a stiletto mark on my chest."

He fights a grin and fails. "I don't suppose you'd care to show it to me?"

"Can't risk exciting the freaks. What did Mariah do after we left?"

"Danced around as usual and gloated. I didn't stay long. Someone was covering for me at work."

There will be even more gloating at school on Monday. "I underestimated Mariah. I didn't really think she'd follow through."

"What are you going to do about it?"

"Either keep a lower profile or bribe Grace to beat her up."

He laughs. "Was this your first fund-raiser event?"

"I've been to a few. But I was surprised to see you there. You don't seem like the school-spirit type."

"I'm not. It's the first year I've participated in any school activities, but it's for a good cause. And a good end: I'd really like the two extra weeks off."

"I bet you'd just take more shifts. Like I would."

This sparks a joint lament about how hard it is to work and go to school. It's a relief to be honest about it for a change. I can't complain much to Izzy and Rachel because I don't want them to feel sorry for me, and it's even harder to talk to my mom.

Joey understands, but I still feel the need to add, "Of course, it could be so much worse. I'm lucky to have what I have."

He nods. "I know. But it would be nice not to worry sometimes, wouldn't it?"

That's it, exactly. I don't mind wearing Grace's castoffs, and I actually like working at Dan's, but it would be nice not to worry—about my mom, our finances, my grades, and everything else.

Joey sees me glance at my worn jacket and reads my mind. "Try wearing your father's hand-me-downs." He explains that his mother used to buy clothes for his father that he never wore. They sat untouched for years, and after Joey hit a growth spurt, the clothes started appearing, gift wrapped, at Christmas and birthdays. "I guess Dad didn't think I'd recognize them," he concludes. "But it's hard to forget an acrylic sweater with a snarling wolf on it."

"Did you wear it?"

"Not that one. A son's love does have its limits. But I've worn some of the other stuff so that he wouldn't feel bad."

Obviously mine isn't the only family where much goes unsaid.

The bus arrives and we take a seat at the back, chatting easily. He doesn't seem in the least interested in me, and it's a huge relief. I can just be myself. After all, he's seen me at my worst—knocked down and slimed by the hottest girl in school.

"Where's your stop?" I ask as we approach mine.

"Three streets back," he says. "But I'm going to a Halloween party. Want to come?"

"I'd better not. It's late."

"We'll only stay an hour. It's close to your place."

"But my costume is in the Dumpster behind Dan's."

"I wouldn't be caught dead at this party dressed as a potato," Joey says. "So we'll go as we are: a waitress and a factory worker."

It would be nice to have a positive end to one of the worst days of my life, so I stand and smooth my crinoline. "Okay. But in case you get any big ideas, I'm wearing shorts under here."

Joey leads me to the door. "Life is full of disappointments."

"Imagine my surprise," Grace says, watching me pull out the sofa and spread my duvet on the bed, "to see my kid sister walk into a party with Joey Carella."

"Imagine *my* surprise to see my sister sitting on the lap of her ex-boyfriend at that same party."

"There were no other seats," she says. "I had to sit somewhere."

"Is that how we ended up with Keira?"

She throws a pillow at me. "If you think so, someone should teach you the facts of life."

"It probably shouldn't be you."

Grace thinks about pursuing this but remembers she has an ax to grind. "What were you doing there with Joey? I thought you hated the Donner guys."

"What were you doing there with Paz? I thought you'd broken up."

"You don't want to go out with Joey Carella."

"We're just friends." And barely that. We spent an hour chatting with some of his coworkers and he walked me home. End of story.

"I hope so, because Joey isn't your type. He's one of Paz's guys."

"Meaning?"

"Meaning he's going nowhere."

"Grace! You're the one who's always accusing me of being a snob. Besides, I'm sure Joey's going somewhere. He's smart."

"So's Paz," she says. "And look where that got us." She comes around the sofa to harass me from closer range. "Of all the guys you could go out with—"

I cut her off. "You don't want me seeing *anyone*." At least, that's how it's starting to seem.

"How about listening to me for a change?" Grace asks, her voice rising.

"How about staying out of my love life?"

"What love life?" another voice asks.

It's my mother, standing in the doorway in her pajamas.

"I don't have one," I say. "Thanks to Grace."

"Can we discuss this tomorrow?" Mom asks. "You'll wake Keira."

"Yeah," Grace says. "You'll wake Keira."

"And, Lu," Mom continues, "that singer called. Solana? She says she'll meet with you."

The news is so exciting that Grace actually squeals—a sound I haven't heard since before her first tattoo.

Chapter 13

Rachel gives my hand a squeeze as we walk toward Letizia's Bakery. "Thanks for letting Izzy and me tag along," she says.

"You're doing me a favor," I say. "It's nice to have some moral support."

"I'm surprised Grace didn't insist on coming."

"She wanted to, but she has to work."

"Huh," Rachel says. "I guess she has changed a lot lately. The old Grace would have made you work her shift and met Solana *for* you."

"Tell me about it," I say. "I haven't had to cover for her at the diner in weeks—or even babysit. Still, it's not like she's completely lost her edge." I spot the sign for Letizia's. "Wish I had a bit of it right now."

"You're worrying too much," Rachel says. "I'm sure Solana's friendly. Otherwise, why would she agree to meet you?"

"She didn't sound that nice on the phone. I bet her agent made her do it."

Stepping inside, we scan the small café for Izzy, not quite sure what to look for, since she planned to update her hair color for the occasion.

The room is cozy, with its wooden tables and exposed brick wall, but it's not the kind of place I expected. Since Solana says she comes here all the time, I thought it would be trendier.

We have nearly an hour before Solana is due to arrive, so Rachel and I choose a table near the back of the café and order a pizza.

"I hope Izzy managed to get the new *Bulletin*," I say.

"I don't see why Sparling won't just give you an advance copy," Rachel says.

"He wants me to 'experience' Scoop's column like everyone else. But I'm the only one whose weekend is ruined because of it. Especially now that I know Tyler is behind the byline."

"You don't know that for sure," Rachel says.

After initially accepting the evidence I found on Tyler's computer, Rachel lapsed into denial. I love that she tries to see the best in people, but how she can ignore the cold hard facts is beyond me.

"I saw the proof with my own eyes, Rach. And I'm glad I did. Now I don't have to waste another second thinking of Tyler as my FB."

Rachel studies me for a long moment and then performs one of those best friend mind-reading feats. "He called you, didn't he?"

There's no point in protesting since she can read me like an open book.

"You didn't even call him back, did you?" Now her tone is accusing. "Lu, that's so mean."

"Do you even need me in this conversation?" I ask, hoping she won't pick up on the fact that there's more. Tyler e-mailed a couple of times, too. "He didn't return my call last month, remember? Besides, it's only Friday. I could still call him." But I won't. That door is closed, locked, and bolted.

Rachel seems more upset about this than she should be, so I do a little mind reading of my own. "Did something happen with Jason?"

Her eyes well up instantly. "We broke up. I didn't want to say anything until after your meeting." She describes how her parents ambushed Jason last night when he dropped her off. "They totally flipped out, and they won't let me see him again."

"Did you tell them about the Jewish blood?"

She wipes her eyes with her sleeve. "It wasn't good enough. Still, if it were just that, I'd find a way to keep seeing him. We've managed this long. But Jason's mad at me, too."

"Why? It's not your fault."

"I didn't tell him the truth about my parents, so it hit him like a tornado. And you know what? He just stood there. He didn't say anything to them."

"Did you?"

She nods, a faint grin appearing on her lips. "Enough that I lost my cell phone and computer privileges for a month. But that was after Jason left. I didn't say much in front of him because we were all standing in the street, and the neighbors already think my parents are weird."

"Have you called him?"

Rachel nods. "From a pay phone this morning. He said he loved me but he can't deal with lies and bigotry. And then he broke up with me."

I seize on the most important point. "He said he loves you? That's fantastic!" Rachel is the first person in our group to hear those words from a guy. It's a landmark.

"*Loved.*" She scrapes her arm over her eyes again. "Past tense."

We notice Izzy, newly blond, standing in the doorway.

Rachel excuses herself to freshen up before Solana arrives. Izzy stares after her, asking, "Is Rach all right?"

I tell her the story and suggest we do something special later to help her get over the breakup—another landmark.

"Guys," Izzy says, exasperated. "Life was easier when none of us dated." She tosses the *Bulletin* to me. "Would you believe I had to stop at Warwick Central to pick this up? There wasn't a single copy left at Dunfield."

"Wow, enemy territory," I say. "That's going above and beyond."

Rachel emerges from the washroom composed, and asks me to read the column aloud to distract her from her troubles.

THE WORD . . . FROM SCOOP
In Defense of the Dunfield Undead

First, I want to solve a mystery for Newshound. If guys are watching TV or checking e-mail while they're on the phone with you, there's a simple explanation: you're boring. I can barely get through your column without nodding off. With all the preaching, nagging, and guy-bashing you do, it's a miracle guys call you at all. You must be hotter than I thought. Why else would someone put up with that attitude?

Take my advice, Newshound: if you want to improve your love life, loosen up. Try finding a role model. The girl Scoop has his eye on is a perfect example. She's interesting, fun, and spontaneous—everything you are not. Obviously she's brilliant too, because she's crazy about me. So much so that I probably won't have to deal with the sticky issue of commitment to get this beauty where I want her. One more blast of the Scoop charm and she'll be begging me to hook up.

Dunfield men, ignore Newshound's Top 10 unless you want to take care of your own needs for the rest of your life. I, on the other hand, will offer some *useful* advice to the ladies:

1. Don't be so sensitive. If a guy calls while he's watching TV or checking his e-mail, it isn't disrespect, it's multitasking.
2. Don't be needy. If you don't demand to hear from your guy every night, he won't have to multitask.
3. Don't hit the snooze button. Say something interesting and you'll increase your chances of being heard. Save the details of your fight with mom for your best friend. Try talking sports.
4. Don't rattle on endlessly. The best conversations are brief.

5. Don't digress. If you jump from your math test to your new shampoo to your dog's ear mites in the space of five minutes, your guy will jump to the TV remote.

6. Don't expect an endless supply of news. If you saw your guy three hours ago, nothing worth telling has happened since.

7. Don't complain about spending time with your guy's friends. It means he's willing to be seen with you. It's a compliment.

8. Don't expect this to last forever. It's high school. What are the chances?

9. Don't hesitate to dump your guy if you lose interest. Make it fast and make it clean. Don't string us along while you look for your next victim.

10. Don't get your friends to do your dirty work. Have some guts.

"Oh my God, he's an idiot," I say. "I can't believe I let him kiss me."

"Famous last words," someone says.

We look up to see Solana G. standing beside our table. She's smaller than she looks on her video, but prettier. With her dark hair in a ponytail and very little makeup, she could be anyone. Only the treble clef tattoo on her neck hints at her occupation.

I stand and offer my hand. "Hello, Ms. Gomez, I'm Luisa Perez, columnist for the *Dunfield Bulletin*. Thank you for meeting with me today."

I expect her to tell me to call her Solana, but she doesn't.

Obviously I was right to adopt a mature and professional manner. Real journalists do not gush like groupies. Better to impress her with my composure.

Taking the seat opposite me, Solana nods at Izzy and Rachel as I introduce them. They smile at her, wordlessly, having been briefed in advance about my mature and professional strategy. They're so worried about saying the wrong thing that they're nearly paralyzed.

Solana's dark eyes lock on mine. "So, what can I do for you?"

I'd planned to lob some getting-to-know-you questions before hitting her up with the literacy pitch, but I'll follow her lead. "Dunfield is in the top three in the citywide literacy fund-raising competition. The winner is going to be chosen at a gala in December, and I was hoping you'd appear on behalf of Dunfield."

Her eyes scan the café continuously as I'm talking and return to me when I stop. "Why me?"

I thought that was obvious. "Because of your connection with Dunfield?"

"More like a *dis*connection. You know they kicked me out?"

"Everything I read said you *dropped* out."

"Promotional materials give things a positive spin. I got the boot."

"From Mrs. Alvarez?" I ask, noticing that my voice doesn't sound calm and professional anymore. Rachel and Izzy exchange nervous glances.

"Mr. Monteiro," she says.

He reigned before my time, but I heard he was

uptight, even by Buzzkill's standards. "Why?" I ask.

She leans back in her chair and crosses her arms. "Attendance, mainly. I had better things to do than show up at Dunfield. I hated that dump. In fact, if the school burned down, I'd throw a barbeque."

This is awful. If she feels this way, why did she agree to see me today? "So you won't come to the gala?" The professionalism is totally gone now. I sound desperate. Mr. Sparling will be so disappointed if I blow this opportunity.

The waiter arrives with a pot of tea for Solana. For him she smiles, but it fades as she turns back to me. "I may not like Dumpfield, but I believe in literacy programs."

Relief surges through me. "That's great. We've raised more than a hundred thousand dollars already, and we still have a month to go."

"But how are they going to *use* the money?"

It's a good question, and I don't really know the answer. I've been so caught up in the competition that I haven't worried about what comes afterward. "I guess it'll go to tutoring."

Solana waits a few moments before responding. "If you can convince me that this money will be spent on programs that actually work, count me in. But if Dunfield is going to hire a couple of tutors and blow the rest of the cash on varsity sports, I'm out."

"I'll look into it right away and get back to you, Ms. Gomez," I say.

She pours her tea in silence, and I notice when her sleeve rides up that she has as many tattoos as Grace, only hers all have a musical theme. It gives me an idea. "If you do the gala—" I begin.

"A big if," she says, stirring her tea.

"—there's a song I hope you'll sing. I've listened to it over and over, and it's so different from everything else on your CD. It's beautiful, but also really sad."

"Which one?" It may be my imagination, but her voice sounds slightly warmer.

"It's called 'Exiled.' The liner notes said you write your own lyrics, and I was wondering what inspired the song."

Solana sips her tea before answering. "Dumpfield, actually. I felt like I didn't belong there."

Izzy finds her voice at last. "We felt like that too."

Solana gives her a withering glance. "I wasn't like you guys. I wasn't popular." She looks us over. We've all worn our best in an effort to impress her, but it's clearly had the opposite effect.

"You think we're popular?" I ask in disbelief.

"I read the columns you sent," she says. "They're all about dances and parties and dating. That's not how it was for me at Dunfield."

I turn to Rachel. "How many dances or parties did we go to last year?"

Rachel joins her thumb and index finger to form a zero.

Turning to Izzy, I ask, "And how many dates did we have last year—collectively?"

Izzy repeats the zero sign and adds, "If it weren't for having to go to the fund-raisers, it would probably still be that way. The column changed everything."

"Okay," Solana says, and now there's a definite thaw. "I got the wrong impression."

"You had to be cooler than we are," I say. "You had music."

"I also had a learning disability," she says. "*Have* a learning disability. You don't outgrow it, you just learn to deal with it."

"Is that how you know which programs work?"

She nods. "You can't just throw money at the problem. I found the right one, and I'll be getting my diploma soon."

"That's great." I'm careful not to overdo the enthusiasm, because it always rubs Grace the wrong way. "And I'm sure Mrs. Alvarez would be glad to talk to you about programs. Mr. Sparling, too. I think they really care about literacy."

"If they want my advice now, that's cool, but no one listened to me when I was there. Dumpfield needs to get its act together so that other kids don't go through that."

I get another idea. "Would you consider giving a talk at the literacy gala to share your experiences? It would be such an inspiration to kids who face the same challenge."

She shakes her head. "It's one thing to talk to you about it and another to share it with the whole city."

I notice she's talking about the event as if it's going to happen. "Okay, I understand. But you'll sing 'Exiled,' right?"

Solana turns to Izzy. "Is she always this persistent?"

"Unfortunately yes," Izzy says. "But at least this time it's for a good cause."

* * *

There's a spring in my step as I carry the coffeepot around the diner. After a rocky start, my meeting with Solana went pretty well. Nothing's definite, but it looks promising, and meeting people like her makes me feel like I'm going places. I'm the Luisa Perez who hangs with celebs in arty neighborhoods.

Paz comes through the door with his posse. Bringing up the rear is Joey, who waves to me.

"Menus, Shorty," Paz calls, choosing a table in my section. "And make it fast. We're on a short turnaround tonight."

His manner would irritate me on another day, but my experience with Solana has convinced me that I won't have to serve burgers to the chocolate-stained masses forever.

Paz takes the menu but doesn't look at it. "I've been meaning to talk to you, Shorty."

"Yeah? About what?"

"About Joey Carella. Grace says you're into him. Is that true?"

As Joey is sitting directly across from Paz, this is obviously meant to be a performance. I try to stay calm. "Grace says you cried through *The Notebook*. Is that true?"

The posse laughs, but Paz doesn't fall for the decoy. "Are you saying you're *not* into Joey?"

He grins across the table, but I don't have the nerve to check on Joey's reaction. It doesn't matter. This is about Paz being a jerk. "Are you going to pretend to check the menu, or order the usual?"

Paz continues as if I haven't spoken. "It's nothing to be ashamed of, Shorty. Women have needs too."

I scratch notes on my order pad. "Six Rodeo Burgers, coming up."

"Joey will have his with a side of Lu," Paz says.

"Paz, just shut up."

He turns to Joey. "She got bitter after the jock dissed her and Russ ran off with some babe. But she's all yours if you want her."

It takes all my strength not to whack him with a menu. "Six Cokes?"

"And one phone number," Paz says. "Call me an ambassador of love."

"You got the 'ass' part right."

"Good one, Lu," Gordo says.

Paz shakes his head. "Do you want me to ask her out for you, Joe?"

Joey speaks for the first time. "No."

There's a long pause in which I find myself writing the word "no" over and over on my order pad.

Then Joey adds, "I can do that myself."

I escape to the counter, my face burning. Paz has embarrassed me times without number, but this is the worst because Joey and I were becoming friends. We had lunch together on Monday after he found me in the stairwell hiding from Mariah. And yesterday he waited at my locker to walk me home because the Understudies were patrolling for me. In other words, he's a good guy and I don't want Paz to make him so uncomfortable that he avoids me.

Sympathetic for once, Shirley agrees to take my section, leaving me to serve people at the counter and muse about how to handle this situation.

Since he works for Paz, Joey might feel obligated to do the honorable thing and ask me out. If he does, I'll have to let him off the hook graciously. He isn't interested in me, and I'm certainly not interested in him. I'm not interested in *anyone*, because I am on the bench. With most guys being such losers, it's the safest place to be.

Even if I wanted to get back in the game, it wouldn't be with Joey. I mean, he's nice and we share a similar background, but I'm looking for someone who will expand my horizons. Someone who will support me in my ambitions while having ambitions of his own. Someone like Tyler, only with integrity.

Joey is cuter than Tyler, though, I will give him that. His hair is unruly, but in a good way. And his eyes are so dark they're nearly opaque. As for his physique—

"I think she's diggin' you, Joe," says Paz.

The shout startles me out of my trance. I've been staring in the guys' direction with a coffeepot suspended over a mug.

Gordo adds, "Either Dan's burning something or I can smell the smolder from here."

After that I retire to the kitchen, leaving Shirley to handle the dinner rush alone. I'll owe her big time, but there's only so much humiliation a girl can take.

I emerge when the coast is clear, only to find Joey coming back into the diner. "I wanted to apologize for the guys," he says. "They get carried away sometimes."

"It's okay," I say, rearranging sugar dispensers on the counter. "It's just Paz."

"Look," he begins.

I know where he's going and cut him off. "You don't have to say anything."

"Yeah, I do. Paz was right: I've wanted to ask you out for a while."

A sugar dispenser drops out of my hand and rolls off the counter to shatter at his feet. "Oh, no!"

"That's not the answer I was hoping for," he says, taking a crunching step backward.

I glance up at him. "I meant the sugar."

He smiles, and I see it's not just his hair and eyes and shoulders that are perfect. It's everything. While I've been searching elsewhere, the Perfect FB has been sitting in my section all along. "So," he says. "Will you?"

When a guy is willing to walk on broken glass for a girl, what is she to do but haul her butt off the bench and get back into the game?

THE WORD . . . FROM NEWSHOUND
No Manners on Planet Ego

Thanks for the tips in your last column, Scoop. Too bad no one's going to take advice from a guy who can't tell the difference between multitasking and being rude. I'm big enough to admit I may have been guilty of guy-bashing in previous columns, but is it any wonder when I have your columns to inspire me?

I'm sure the men of Dunfield were insulted by your last column. Under the guise of giving tips to the ladies, you've actually said that guys have the attention span of gnats, are totally insensitive to women, and care about nothing but sports.

Newshound refuses to believe that. In fact, she's met some smart, considerate guys lately—or one, anyway—and it's enough to restore her faith in mankind.

My advice is meant to bridge the gap between the sexes, whereas Scoop's widens it. But I actually agree with him about one thing: no one should get a friend to do his or her dirty work. It's best to face a problem head-on and leave the grapevine to elementary school.

That's certainly how Newshound intends to handle the ups and downs of her new relationship. Not that I'm anticipating any downs, because the guy I've met is perfect. He listens, he shares his feelings, and he values an intellectual connection more than a physical one. And when he asked me out, there were no games. It was straightforward and romantic—the kind of thing a girl replays in her mind forever.

I wish you luck with your new girl, Scoop, however hard up she must be to date a guy like you. Maybe she'll be able to transform you into a decent human being. I just hope her expectations are low, because otherwise she is going to be very disappointed. A less romantic guy has never graced Dunfield's halls.

Which brings me to an important point . . . While Scoop has been trying to get his needs taken care of, Newshound has been doing something constructive to secure the extra two weeks off we all deserve. I've landed a special guest for the literacy gala: rising star Solana G. After a chat with Mrs. Alvaraz this week, Solana has agreed to perform two songs—one of them my own special request, "Exiled."

So, Scoop, if you're not too busy telling the world how great you are, maybe you could do a little something for your school and find a celebrity guest of your own.

"One more reason to love Fridays," Mariah says, slamming her locker shut with the heel of her boot. "Newshound is my hero!"

"She's brilliant," says Understudy One.

"Beyond brilliant," says Understudy Two.

I think about adding my agreement to the chorus, but while Mariah's boot print has faded from my sternum, it's still very much imprinted on my psyche. Only by giving up all my usual habits have I managed to avoid her until now. And for the moment my locker door is providing adequate cover.

"I've seen Solana's video," Mariah continues, "and she has some pretty good moves." Mariah demonstrates a few of them, causing a three-guy pileup in the hallway. "But I could teach her some new ones." Mariah does a fancy spin and slashes her arms in the air—a kung fu dance combo that would probably leave Solana speechless, but not with admiration.

"What are you going to do?" Understudy One asks.

"Introduce myself at the gala and offer to work with her. I'll give her a few pointers in exchange for a role in her next video. How could she say no?"

Solana is quite capable of putting Mariah in her place, but I still don't want my guest being harassed.

Closing my locker door, I say, "But, Mariah, you were on *The Right Moves*."

"I'm aware of that, Coconut," she says, glaring at me. "*Everyone* is aware of it—probably even Solana."

"A credit like that will only intimidate her. And she's doing us a favor."

Mariah stares at me, deciding which way to go. "Don't waste my time with the nice act, Coconut. I know what lies beneath that hairy shell: Jell-O."

The Understudies laugh up a lung apiece.

"Whatever," I say, wishing I could do better.

"By the way," Mariah calls as she starts down the hall, "Russ is an *incredible* kisser. Too bad you never had a chance to find that out."

"But I thought you said he was a terrible kisser," Understudy One says.

"Shut up and get him on the phone," Mariah commands.

The Understudy pulls out her cell phone and begins to dial. "Do you want me to tell Russ he's history?"

Mariah snatches the phone out of her hand. "We're not in grade school anymore. From here on in, I do my own dirty work."

Chapter 14

THE WORD . . . FROM SCOOP
Rising to the Challenge

I couldn't help noticing that while Newshound has often referred to Scoop as a braggart, she has no trouble tooting her own horn. However, I agree that Solana G. is a good score, and she'll make a nice warm-up act for my guest, Chicago Bulls point guard Jordan Peters.

That's right, Jordan Peters. Not a newcomer, but a bona fide superstar. Sorry to trump you again, Newshound. You can enjoy some humble pie when we meet at the Washington Library Center in six weeks.

In the meantime, I'll just have to take comfort in the admiration of my number-one fan. Scoop's lady is all that he hoped: smart, spunky, gorgeous, and best of all, completely undemanding. Unlike so many girls who take on a guy as a makeover project, this one is satisfied with Scoop as he is. And she is far from hard up. She's had plenty of quality Dunfield guys at her beck and call, but she's proven her genius in choosing me.

As for my co-columnist's "perfect" guy who "values an intellectual connection more than a physical one"? I've got news for you, Newshound: your boyfriend's gay. No straight guy within the walls of this school values the cerebral over the physical when it comes to women. Check your science textbook under "heterosexual" and cross-reference with "teenage male," and you'll come up with a synonym for "excitable" that can't be printed here (I did try).

Don't get me wrong—enlightened guys like Scoop do value a nonphysical relationship, but never more than the physical one. Making our priorities clear can only help to bridge the gender divide.

Something tells me even Newshound doesn't buy her story, because if her gay boyfriend were that perfect, she'd be spilling her guts to him instead of in a newspaper column. We get it, Newshound: you're lonely and misunderstood. What you really need is a diary, where you can let it all out privately, and spare us from your overwrought ramblings.

Fortunately, Scoop doesn't have to settle for fantasy. While you're busy connecting with your so-called boyfriend intellectually, I'm connecting on a much more satisfying level. As predicted, the lady wants a Double Scoop, and since a gentleman always keeps his lady happy, I intend to give it to her.

Meanwhile, you just keep making notes in your diary, Newshound. It'll make a great romance novel someday.

The *Bulletin* hits the wall and drops behind the couch. I

was an idiot to let Tyler's glasses fool me into thinking he was an arty, civilized guy. If that's how he thinks about women, he's worse than Mac Landis. At least Mac is honest about his primitive attitudes.

Obviously Tyler is the one living in a fantasy world. I assumed he was writing about me in his previous column, but this time he can't be. Not after I didn't return his call or e-mails, or track him down at school. His "lady" must be a figment of his imagination. Either that, or he's met someone new and they're moving incredibly fast. If the girl is real, I hope she discovers in time that there are great guys out there and she doesn't have to settle for Scoop.

As of today, however, I'm hoping there will be one less great guy on the market. Joey Carella is picking me up at noon. That means I have exactly five minutes to erase the evidence that I've been making far too much effort for a first date.

Flying around with armloads of clothing and makeup, I mutter a silent prayer of thanks to my friends. Rachel agreed to cover Dunfield's hot dog–eating contest for me, and Izzy did something even nicer: she took Keira for the afternoon, thereby freeing Grace to do whatever she does for fun, now that she's given up body art. The last thing I needed was my sister sitting here making me more nervous than I already am.

With Grace gone, I've been able to change outfits as many times as I like, which happens to be lucky thirteen. Not entire outfits, of course, but with various combinations, it amounts to thirteen looks. Joey probably won't care that much. There's nowhere to go but up from a spider costume covered in Jell-O, but I still want to look nice.

At one minute past noon, someone knocks at the door.

"Hey," Joey says as I open it. "Some lady with a poodle let me in downstairs."

Mrs. Ortiz from the third floor. She has a weakness for cute guys, and Joey is definitely that, in his dark jeans and bulky navy blue sweater.

"Have you got your hat?" Joey asks, leading me to the elevator.

I pat my purse, although there's no hat inside. I'd rather freeze than mess up my hair.

"So where are we going?"

"To the train station."

"Could you be more specific? My last mystery date didn't turn out that well."

"Trust me," he says.

Normally I wouldn't, but there's something about Joey's quiet confidence that makes me believe him. Besides, all the signs are positive. He's opening doors and working hard to keep the conversation going.

"So what do you think about Sparling?" he says. "Is he still going on about mythology being the greatest source of literary inspiration of all time?"

"Surpassed only by the Bible," I say. "But it's hard not to like him, isn't it?"

"Not so hard for me. He rides my ass."

"I didn't think he taught senior English."

"He doesn't. I'm doing some independent studies to atone for some, uh, transgressions last year."

"Attendance?"

He nods. "Also late assignments. And a missed test or two."

Maybe Joey is a risk after all. He has brains, but what good are they if he's not going to use them?

Reading my expression, he adds, "Could be worse. At least I didn't plagiarize, unlike a certain Dunfield athlete who got caught lifting ideas."

"Mac?" I ask, aghast. "I didn't think he was that stupid."

"He's not that stupid; he's that lazy. So he's doing penance too. We're both lucky that Sparling believes in second chances. I'm doing pretty well this year."

I breathe a sigh of relief. Any guy who's trying to turn his life around is worth thirteen wardrobe changes.

We get off at Madison/Wabash, the station closest to Millennium Park. I should have known that's what Joey had in mind, because he mentioned it last week and was surprised I'd never been there.

He seems happy to play tour guide, despite teasing me about my ignorance of my own city. Except for window shopping at the Loop and the Magnificent Mile, I haven't explored very much. Somehow there never seems to be enough time to wander. Joey probably makes the time because he's interested in architecture.

We check out "the Bean," a sculpture called *Cloud Gate* that's shaped like a kidney bean and is longer than a city bus. Joey points out how the sculpture reflects the sky and the surrounding buildings, and then leads me beneath the arch of the bean so that we can stare up at our reflections.

"What's our next stop?" I ask. "Sears Tower?"

"Better. But slippery."

"No Jell-O involved, I hope?"

"Relax," he says. "This'll be fun."

We're standing before an ice rink, and I am quite sure what he has in mind will not be fun at all. I haven't been on skates since . . . Well, it only happened once, and back then I didn't have far to fall. Putting skateboard wheels under my feet ended in disaster, and blades are sharper.

"I like to come as soon as they open for the season," Joey says, walking toward the rink. "It's sort of a tradition. My mom used to bring my sisters and me."

I abandon my plan to wait on the sidelines. When a guy brings his absentee mother into the equation, who could say no?

"I'm an excellent teacher," he assures me.

That's exactly what Russ said moments before I found myself flying toward a busy intersection. "But I'm a lousy student. I have gravitational challenges."

Joey ignores this and gets in the line for skate rentals. "In an hour, you're going to look as happy as she does," he says, pointing to a smiling blonde returning her skates.

The blonde in question turns out to be someone I know from my Spanish class: Ella Robinson. And she's standing beside none other than Tyler "Double Scoop" Milano.

Ella spies me first, and her wave causes Tyler to turn in my direction. He glances from Joey to me, and the expression on his face is nearly as chilling as the prospect of taking a face plant on the rink.

"Lu?" Joey says. "The lady needs to know your size."

I turn back to the clerk, and Joey collects our skates.

Trailing after him, I sneak another peek at Tyler. Now he has his arm coiled around Ella's shoulder. She must be Scoop's new lady. It's a shame because she seems nice and deserves better. Maybe I should drop an anonymous note in her locker to tip her off.

Tyler turns to stare after us, but Ella puts one hand on either side of Tyler's face and pulls him toward her. The kiss that follows proves she's a very willing victim, which takes away my guilt. I'm free to enjoy my afternoon with Joey, at least the part that comes after the skating.

Sitting on a bench, I unzip my boots and ask, "Can you get cooties from rental skates?"

"Cooties can't survive at this temperature," Joey says. "It's the fungus you have to worry about."

"Fungus?" I inspect the inside of the skate.

"You can't see the spores, but by this time next week your toenails will turn yellow and fall off."

I drop the skate. "Gross!"

"Oh, come on . . . Think about how much you'll save on pedicures."

I nudge the skates toward him with my boot. "Take them back."

"I'm kidding," he says. "No one gets fungus from skates."

"Especially if she doesn't put them on."

Kneeling before me, he takes my boot off and puts a skate on my right foot. I'm too stunned to resist.

In no time at all he has me laced up and ready to go. "There you go, Cinderella," he says, sitting beside me again. "A perfect fit."

I'd prefer the glass slipper, but every prince has his own style.

As soon as his skates are tied, Joey helps me to my feet, and I follow him reluctantly to the ice. Stepping on the smooth surface, he turns to face me.

"I don't think I can," I say, clinging to the rail.

"Take my hand."

It's an offer I can't refuse. No sooner do both blades hit the ice, however, than they shoot out from under me at perilous angles. Joey grabs me under my arms seconds before my butt connects with the ice. My scream startles him so much that he almost drops me.

After getting me balanced again, he lets go. This time I stay upright, if only because I refuse to budge.

A big guy brushes past me and says, "Get your girl-friend out of the doorway, buddy."

Joey glares after the guy. "Idiot."

I barely have time to wonder whether it's the guy's tone or the word "girlfriend" that irks Joey, before he turns around in front of me and takes both my hands in his. Skating backward slowly, he begins to pull me around the rink.

After the first lap I exclaim, "I'm skating!" and Joey has the decency not to point out that being towed doesn't quite qualify. Instead he takes me around again before letting go and suggesting that I try moving my feet.

"It's not like walking," he says, after my first flailing attempt. "Keep your blades in contact with the ice. Lean on your left foot and push off with the right."

I follow his instructions and move forward a few inches. Repeating the process with my other foot, I move forward a few inches more. Joey continues to skate backward in front of me, cheering me on. With my ankles turned in, my butt stuck out, and my arms outstretched, I'm far from hot, but at least I'm moving.

"You're working too hard," he says. "Just glide."

Some girls glide through life, but unfortunately Lu Perez is not one of them. I thrash and flail and flounder.

A group of guys whizzes past, and Joey turns to watch them with a look of longing.

"Why don't you do a few laps on your own?" I ask, releasing his hands.

Joey's eyes light up. "Are you sure?"

I nod, knowing that skating with me is like walking down the street with Keira. It takes twenty minutes to cover half a block, and by the time we're done, I'm exhausted.

Joey takes off, and I continue my awkward shuffle around the rink, ankles aching and toes going numb. Every time he passes, Joey gives me a cheery wave, and I wave back just as cheerily, all the while plotting my escape.

Before I can accomplish it, Joey skates up behind me, puts his hands on my hips, and starts pushing. At first I'm nervous, but as we pick up speed and the wind lifts my hair, I start to feel like Kate Winslet on the ship's prow in *Titanic*—only less cheesy.

As it turns out, with the right person behind her, sometimes a plodder gets to fly.

Joey's eyes widen as I wash down a chocolate-chip cookie with hot chocolate.

"Most girls I go out with don't eat," he says.

I wipe whipped cream off my lip with a napkin. "They're *alive*, right?"

"Usually. And obsessed with calories."

"Think about how many I burned on the ice today."

He snickers. "You barely moved."

"Are you saying I'm fat?" It's a dangerous question for a first date, but he had his hands on my hips earlier, so there's not much left to hide.

"I'm saying that it's nice you're comfortable enough with me to be yourself."

I watch as he picks up his own cookie, crams the entire thing into his mouth, and chews. "I guess I could say the same about you."

"What you see is what you get," he mumbles around the cookie.

That might be true of him, but it's not entirely true of me. If I were really being myself, I'd have put the kibosh on skating, tradition or no tradition. "So just how many non-eaters have you gone out with?"

He gives me a knowing glance. "I'm not as popular as *some* people. You've got guys hanging around all the time."

Even if I wanted to pretend I'm a hot commodity, someone already destroyed that notion. "Well, like Paz said, they're history."

Joey puts his elbows on the table and leans toward me. "Did I mention I love history?"

I put my own elbows on the table, flipping a saucer over with a clatter. "It's my favorite subject too. Well, tied with English."

He wrinkles his nose. "English? Really?"

"Sure. What's not to like about mythology? Everyone's running around in disguise doing whatever they want. Did you know that Athena turned Arachne into a spider because she bragged too much? I'd love to have that power." I scrape the last of the whipped cream from my mug before adding, "If I were Athena, Mariah would be in big trouble."

Laughing, Joey says, "Remind me not to cross you. You've got a vengeful streak."

I steer the conversation in a safer direction. "What are you going to do after graduation?"

Joey leans back in his chair. "Not sure yet. I don't want to work in a factory for the rest of my life, but I may have to for a couple of years to save for tuition. That buys me some time to figure out what I want to do."

"I thought you loved architecture."

"I do. But urban planning would be interesting too. Which reminds me . . ." He checks his watch. "Drink up, Athena, we have somewhere to be in an hour."

"Wow." That's the only word that comes to mind as I take in the view from the open-air observatory in the John Hancock Center, ninety-four floors above street level. Beneath us, the city stretches as far as the eye can see, and its buildings, lit by the setting sun, glow against a blue-black sky.

Joey leans close to my ear so that I can hear him over the wind that's whipping through the open skywalk and says, "See, I told you Chicago is beautiful." His cheek brushes lightly against mine as he adds, "You're freezing! Put your hat on."

"Actually, I didn't bring it," I confess. "I didn't want to mess up my hair."

Had I known we'd be scaling Mount Hancock I'd have made a different choice. My hair is not only whipping in my face, but Joey's as well. He plucks at a few strands that have circled his throat like tentacles.

"You mean you lied to me already?" he asks.

I didn't actually *say* I had my hat, but there's no point quibbling. "Well, I wanted to look good. You should be flattered."

"Believe me, I am," he says, pulling off his own hat and placing it on my head. Then he wraps his arm around me. "Better?"

Looking up at him I see the city reflected as pinpoints of light in his dark eyes. It's such a romantic ending to a perfect day that I'm inspired to rise up on tiptoe and kiss him. He kisses me back with cool lips that grow warmer instantly. There's an odd, hollow feeling in my chest that comes either from being so bold or from being ninety-four floors above civilization with oxygen in short supply.

Joey doesn't say a word when it's over. Instead he pulls me closer, and his hands find their way under my jacket and around my waist. Although he's wearing gloves, I can feel the heat of his hands through my T-shirt.

I close my eyes for a moment, and when I open them, Joey is pointing at the first star twinkling above us. "Make a wish," he says.

I try to think of one, but for the moment there's not a single request on my list.

THE WORD . . . FROM NEWSHOUND
Once Upon a Time at Dunfield . . .

. . . there was a misguided columnist who was so insecure about his own manhood that he had to demean someone who is, in fact, a prince among men. It's tempting to speculate about what Scoop is overcompensating for with his big theories and big accusations. But I don't have to go there. It's pretty obvious that Scoop's got a little something to hide.

Newshound's prince is definitely not gay, unless you're referring to the old-fashioned sense of the word. If you mean "happy," of course he is. He's won the affections of his queen, and so far he's satisfied with that.

Prince Newshound doesn't need sex to prove he's attractive and desirable. He knows that a meaningful relationship always transcends the merely physical. That's the difference between a real man and a boy who's still chasing tail around the school yard.

My co-columnist clearly feels threatened because Prince Newshound is everything he is not. I don't expect a small mind like yours to grasp this easily, Scoop, so I'll help you out here: you say you don't want a committed relationship and that you want to play the field. I say you wouldn't be so down on Prince Newshound if that were really true. If you were the prince of your lady's kingdom rather than the court jester, you'd be more positive.

Face it, you want a real relationship, but with a personality like yours you probably can't keep a girl around long enough to have one. I'm guessing you've been dumped so often that you've become scarred and cynical.

Don't waste your next column arguing that you've done all the dumping. A preemptive dump doesn't count. It just means that you sensed someone was going to offload you and beat her to the punch.

If you're wounded and suffering, I feel for you, Scoop. Newshound isn't wholly without compassion. But she wants you to understand that experiencing a real relationship requires being open to it. That means letting down your blustery, chauvinistic guard and being yourself.

Friends with benefits might be easier and more exciting, but too much of a bad thing doesn't work. Just ask Morgan McGee, who lost yesterday's hot dog contest after eating so many wieners that he threw up on a cheerleader's sneakers.

The moral of this story is don't be a wiener, Scoop. No girl worth having will ever choose empty calories over prime beef.

"God of Wieners?" Izzy asks, as we rush down the hall toward Mr. Sparling's classroom.

"Izzy!" We have a quiz today and we're supposed to be testing each other on Zeus and Hera's family tree.

"Okay, okay. God of War?"

"Ares," I answer. "Goddess of the Harvest?"

"Demeter," Izzy says. "Whose daughter was . . . ?"

"Aphrodite?"

"Wrong. But it's no surprise you've got the Goddess of Love on your mind."

Rachel laughs. "More like the Goddess of Lust."

"I think I'm the only one feeling it," I say. "Joey's walked me home almost every night this week, but he hasn't touched me since Saturday."

"What happened to meaningful relationships transcending the physical?" Izzy teases.

"Good in theory," I respond. "But the absence of *anything* physical is making me wonder if Joey is even interested."

Maybe you should make the first move," Rachel suggests.

"I did that, remember? It's his turn."

The uncertainty is driving me crazy. Although I profess to be the slow and steady type in my column, it turns out that I'm as impatient as anyone else, at least where Joey is concerned. I want to know how he feels, and I want to know now. After all, I put myself right out there on the ninety-fourth floor, and if he's not into me, it's going to be a *very* long drop.

"He kissed you back," Rachel persists.

"Yeah, but come on . . . He's a guy. What really matters is the follow-up."

"Give him a chance."

I sigh. "I shouldn't have been so aggressive."

"It was just a kiss. It's not like you proposed." Rachel turns to Izzy for support. "Right, Izzy?"

"I don't know what to think anymore," Izzy replies. "I made the first move with Carson, and where is he now?"

After leading Izzy on for a month, Carson showed up at last week's talent show fund-raiser with his ex-girlfriend. We watched in horror as the girl slid her hand into the back pocket of Carson's jeans during Mariah's perform- ance. Since Carson didn't object, that's where it stayed for the next half hour. Poor Izzy didn't say much, but she went home that night and dyed her hair back to its natural color. I wouldn't have believed *any* guy could reduce Izzy to mousy brown, but Carson managed it.

"You could ask one of the psychics at the mystic fair today," Rachel says. "Or you could give me the five bucks and trust me that Carson is in the cold, damp place all boyfriends go after turning back into frogs. Jason's there too, remember?"

Izzy and I are still laughing when a shout echoes through the hall. "Move or bleed, people, move or bleed!"

One of Mariah's Understudies charges around the cor- ner, clapping her hands. Behind her the corridor fills with light, and Mariah dances into view. The other Understudy follows with an old boom box while four guys train lights and video cameras on our resident star.

Izzy stops Understudy One. "What's going on?"

"We're making Mariah's promo video for YouTube," she replies. "That way Solana G. can see what a perverse—"

"*Diverse!*" Mariah corrects, advancing on us with her crew.

Understudy One squints at her glittery notepad. "Right. Solana can see what a diverse and accomplished dancer Mariah is before they meet at the literacy gala."

"At which point she will *beg* me to be in her next

video," Mariah concludes, now beside us. Striking a pose, she flings both arms wide and knocks my bag off my shoulder. Then she steps over my scattered belongings and continues on her way.

Stooping to collect my cell phone, I tell Izzy, "I just remembered Demeter's daughter: it's Persephone, Queen of the Underworld."

Joey and I near my apartment building, and I remind myself to be strong. He isn't holding my hand and he hasn't kissed me, and if that doesn't change within the next ninety seconds, he's going to find that this cold November day becomes positively arctic. Lu Perez is not desperate. She doesn't wait around forever for a guy to make up his mind. And she doesn't grope desperately for conversational topics trying to detain him so long that he cracks. Not this Lu Perez.

Granted, the Lu Perez of yesterday had less pride. *That* Lu came up with at least a dozen lame excuses to keep Joey from leaving. It was completely transparent, and since he's not stupid, he must have known. And if he did (know) and won't (act on it), then he obviously isn't (interested).

Today will be different. When we arrive at the door, I'll slow down just long enough to thank him for walking me home and then depart with a breezy good-bye.

"It was nice of you to walk me home," I say, which isn't as breezy as I hoped. I'm practically shouting "Kiss me, kiss me." Worse, my legs have stopped moving.

"Any excuse to hang out with you," Joey says.

That's pretty sweet. Maybe it wouldn't hurt to encourage him a little more. "I like hanging out with you too."

227

"Cool."

Cool? That's the best he can do?

"So I guess I'll see you tomorrow," he says.

I give up. "Sure. Bye."

Giving me a wave, he starts walking away. I let him take ten paces before calling after him, "It's supposed to snow tomorrow."

He stops and turns. "It is?"

"That's what I heard."

Joey walks ten paces back to me. "Well, you'd better take this then." He pulls off his hat and places it on my head. "Wouldn't want you to freeze."

"Thanks." He's still hanging on to the hat with both hands, so I add, "It'll be kind of hard to get around, though, with you attached like that."

Joey smiles. "I was just thinking about kissing you."

I smile back. "Any decisions?"

He uses the hat to pull me toward him, and this time when he kisses me, I get the same rush, as if I were ninety-four floors up with the wind howling underfoot. Maybe that's what love feels like, but it's not what I expected at all.

"I've wanted to do that for days," Joey says afterward.

"Well, I've waited for you to do that for days."

"Really?" He sounds surprised. "I wasn't sure I should. I mean, I didn't want you to think this was the only reason I spend time with you."

"If I thought that, I wouldn't have made the first move on the skywalk."

"Well, I've heard a beautiful sunset does strange things to a girl."

"You think I kissed you because I was moved by the view?"

"I hypothesized a causal relationship. It certainly looked like A caused B."

"You'd better head back to the lab, Dr. Carella. The sun's still up, yet I'm thinking about kissing you again."

"Hmmmm," Joey says, scratching his chin. "Then we could be dealing with a correlation instead. Which is to say, A and B are related, but . . . *how?*" He pulls me close a second time. "I guess the only way to find out is more research."

THE WORD . . . FROM SCOOP
No Happily Ever After

I owe our readers an apology. When I suggested Newshound write a romance novel someday, I had no idea she'd inflict it on 9,000 students across six schools so soon.

It would be sad if it weren't so embarrassing. With all her talk of princes and queens, Newshound has exposed herself as delusional in a way I never could. Take another look at your last column, Newshound, and tell me you don't want to take a big bite out of Snow White's proverbial poisoned apple. Scoop will be relieved to have this space to himself.

If you're still with us, understand that I'm not jealous of your supposedly meaningful relationship, but I am worried enough about your neutered prince to send some knights to the rescue. Is he still dancing around your throne in a golden loincloth?

Fairy tales aren't always pretty, and that's one reason Scoop prefers to live in the real world. Still, I dropped some coins into the hand of a psychic at the Dunfield Mystic Fair this week. I'm a skeptic, but I couldn't pass up the opportunity to get the "scoop" from beyond on my lady. The psychic took one look at me and said: "You've found someone very special. She'll take you to dizzying heights and terrible lows, but you'll never regret the ride."

If Scoop had a romantic bone in his body, he'd have become a believer on the spot. But I don't need fairy tales or spiritual guidance to confirm I'm on the right track with my favorite girl. Why? Because she can't keep her hands off me. That is the stuff that real fantasies are made of. And if she has any concerns about the size of my commitment, she hasn't said a word about it. It seems the lady is well satisfied.

I don't expect to be dumped anytime soon, Newshound, but if it happens, I'll know where to come for advice. By that time the Literacy Challenge will be over, and you can share some survival tips over coffee in the cafeteria. Something tells me you know all about getting off-loaded. Knowing that helps me understand where you're coming from with this fairy-tale crap. Your romantic delusions are probably the only thing keeping you going after so much rejection.

Wake up, Sleeping Beauty, and try using that bed for something more than escaping the real world. You'll be glad you did.

Chapter 15

Scientific Method: a body of techniques for investigating phenomena and acquiring new knowledge.

STEP 1: *Observe Phenomena and Define Questions*
There's probably a point at the beginning of any relationship where everything is absolutely perfect. It feels like being inside a bubble, all sparkle and rainbows.

That's what it's like for Joey and me right now. We spend every possible moment together, often in transit between school, work, and home. Sometimes I can't remember how we got from A to B, although I can recall every word of our conversation, what he wore, what I wore, what we ate, the music we heard, and how I felt when I saw him waiting beside my locker.

It's beautiful. And it can't last. Before long, something or someone will burst the bubble. The only reason we've escaped so far is that Paz is filling in for another shift lead on straight days, Grace is spending a few days at a friend's place, and Mariah is too caught up with being Mariah to notice us.

Meanwhile, each day is better than the last. It's as if neither of us can say or do the wrong thing. Every word Joey says is fascinating to me, and miraculously, he seems to feel the same. And somehow, impossibly, he gets cuter every time I see him. I love his eyes, his hair, and his smile—and especially his hands, with the two crooked fingers caused by an accident at the factory. Oddly, it's the tiny imperfections that make this feel more solid, as if it can last in the real world after the bubble bursts.

I know that time will tell if we're meant to be together, but like anyone else in this situation, I'm looking for an easy answer. Is there a sign? A test? How do you know when you've found *the one*?

STEP 2: *Gather Information and Resources*

I've read the books, I've seen the movies, and now I'm talking to people who've actually been there. Since my own life doesn't offer many examples of successful relationships, I've taken my search for answers to Dan's Diner, where people are usually willing to open up if I keep pouring the coffee. I put my question to a row of women sitting at the counter.

"Honey, you'll just know," says Mrs. Cortez, happily married to the owner of the tile store up the street for ten years. "It took me about a week with Leo."

"Was there a sign?" I press.

Her smile is half nostalgic, half embarrassed. "I had a strange feeling whenever he kissed me. Something I hadn't felt with anyone else."

"Exactly," says Mrs. Olivera, who works in human resources at Donner's. "That's how I knew. It's chemistry."

Mrs. Evans, married for twenty-six years, pushes her cup forward for another refill. "You'll know. Trust us."

"Dan?" I ask. "How did you know with your ex-wife?"

"Don't bring me into this," he says, escaping to the kitchen.

"But I want a guy's point of view," I call after him.

He sticks his head into the pass-through. "If you must know, it hit me like a lightning bolt to the boxer shorts."

STEP 3: *Formulate Hypothesis.*

I close Joey's textbook and slide it back to his side of the table as he arrives at our booth with a tray.

"You can do my homework while you're at it," he says, placing a plate of fries in front of me.

"Just curious," I say, pouring a pool of ketchup onto the plate. "I'm thinking of taking chemistry next year."

He sits down across from me and grins. "Good idea. I can teach you everything I know."

Dipping a fry into my ketchup, he feeds it to me. Then he leans across the table and kisses the ketchup from my mouth.

Even sitting in the middle of a busy diner, my stomach drops and the wind picks up in my head when Joey's lips touch mine. That has to mean *something*.

Hypothesis: A kiss can reveal your destiny.

STEP 4: *Experiment and Collect Data*

Joey wraps his arm around me as we walk out of the

second-run movie theater. It's a cold night, but I feel a rush of warmth as we stroll down the street analyzing our favorite scenes from *Almost Famous*. We agree on all of them. That happens a lot, but we're not exactly alike. Joey, for example, always puts his iPod on shuffle, whereas I prefer to play an album straight through. Similarly, he often mixes several foods on his fork, whereas I prefer to savor one thing at a time.

Still, it seems as if we have the important things in common. For example, we both worry about our parents and want to succeed in life so that we can make them proud. We both fight with our sisters a lot, and we generally lose.

Joey points to a copy of *Great Expectations* as we pass a bookstore window. "That's a great book. Has Sparling assigned it yet?"

"Still stuck on Mount Olympus." I tell him about Mr. Sparling's latest class assignment, in which we had to pretend that a god is retiring and write a letter to Zeus explaining why we'd be the perfect replacement.

Joey laughs. "We did that too. Let me guess . . . You chose Athena."

"Wrong." No need to explain that taking over the role of the virgin goddess has lost some appeal. Although Athena has many fine qualities, it's the gods who get around that seem to have the most fun. "I chose Hephaestus, God of—"

"Fire," he supplies. "I chose Hephaestus too. Something else we have in common."

"The list is getting longer every day," I say.

"Plus we share my new favorite pastime."

"Which is?"

He leans down to kiss me, and the street noise fades into the background, replaced by the sound of wind whipping through tall buildings.

STEP 5: *Perform Vigorous Field Tests*

Joey points to my head and asks, "Can I borrow that?"

He's referring to his hat, which has been in my possession for over a week. I've kept it not because the hat is particularly cool, but because every time I put it on, I get a muted hit of the same feeling I get when he kisses me. "It *is* yours."

He puts the hat on the little snowman we built from the first snow of the season and frowns. "He still needs a nose."

"We'll give him the gift of smell on the way home. Otherwise, we're going to be late for school."

"Check your backpack," Joey says. "I'll bet there's something we could use."

As it happens, I have a churro in my lunch bag that would make a perfect nose, but I love Izzy's mom's donuts too much to sacrifice it for a snowman. Clutching my backpack closer, I say, "There isn't."

Joey's eyes narrow. "Luisa's hiding something, isn't she? Open up. Or else."

I turn to run, and a snowball hits me between the shoulders. In seconds, Joey catches up and pushes me over into the snow.

"Who wins?" he asks, hovering over me.

"I do," I say, wrapping an arm around his neck and

pulling him closer. This time the wind in my head is warm and soothing.

STEP 6: *Repeat Experiment to Ensure Predictable Results*
"For the love of Pete, would you pay attention?"

Joey and I pull away from each other and look around the empty bus. "Huh?"

The driver peers over his shoulder at us. "Is the bus moving?"

As a matter of fact, it is not. It is idling at my stop.

"I don't get paid enough to babysit love-struck puppies," the driver grumbles as we scurry toward the door. "Any clothes come off and I'm charging you double."

STEP 7: *Analyze Data*
Staring at me through his zoom lens, Joey says, "That hat looks better on you."

I summon a stiff smile, discovering that it's much easier to be flattered when both feet are firmly on the ground. At the moment we're about 150 feet above it at the apex of the Ferris wheel's climb.

When Joey asked me to come to Navy Pier so that he could take some photographs for his urban development project, I expected to be an observer, not a participant.

He leans to one side to get a different angle, and the car rocks. I scream.

"Afraid of heights?" he asks, a grin appearing under his camera.

I nod silently, my lips too cold to form words.

Joey lowers his camera and slides closer to me—

slowly, so as not to rock the car. "I'm sorry," he says, wrapping an arm around me. "You seemed fine at the Hancock Center, so I thought you'd be cool with this. Why didn't you say something?"

I offer a slight shrug in response. Obviously I'm not going to tell him the truth, which is that I'd say yes to a ride in the space shuttle if he asked me.

"I want us to have the kind of relationship where we can tell each other anything," Joey says. "Don't you?"

Relationship? I love that word! Relationship means exclusive. It's just the two of us in our little red car, 150 feet above the ordinary citizens of Chicago—the desperate, lonely people who are *not* in a relationship with Joey Carella.

"Don't you?" Joey repeats. "Want to share everything, I mean?"

I nod. That's exactly what I want. I've told him so much about myself already, even some things I've never shared with Izzy and Rachel. For example, I told him about my one and only memory of my father, who swung me so high in our basement apartment that I cracked a Styrofoam ceiling tile with my head. Although it didn't hurt that much, I cried, and Grace made fun of me, and our father got mad at us both. It's not a story I'd feel comfortable telling my friends, because their families are normal; but Joey understands. He has worse memories about his family than I have, and he's told me about some of them.

Squeezing me tighter, Joey says, "Close your eyes and try to forget about where you are. The ride will be over in five minutes. In the meantime, I'll see if I can't do something about those blue lips of yours."

The moment I feel the warmth of his lips on mine, the fear retreats. The wind still rocks the Ferris wheel car, but it's familiar now, more exhilarating than terrifying.

STEP 8: *Draw Conclusions*

I follow Joey to the river, marveling over the size of the crowd. "I can't believe you come here every year."

"I can't believe you don't," he counters. "The Magnificent Mile Lights Festival is one of Chicago's great traditions."

"But it's so . . . touristy."

"Because it's so . . . *fun*," he says.

As the firework display begins, Joey pulls a thermos out of his backpack.

"What, no whip?" I joke as he hands me a steaming cup of hot chocolate.

"Patience, my lady." He gropes in his bag and produces a can of whipping cream. A few people turn and smile at the squelching sound as he fills my mug. He points the nozzle at the first explosion of color and light in the sky. "I figured this was a pretty good way to celebrate."

I stare at him, puzzled. "Celebrate what?"

"You forgot our three-week anniversary?" He pretends to be hurt.

"No, I thought we weren't counting because you ignored weeks one and two."

He shakes his head with mock sadness. "We're arguing already. What's going to happen when we're counting in years?"

He said *years*! I pull Joey to me and kiss him. I don't

238

even care if two dozen people are watching us instead of the sky.

We sip our drinks in silence for a few moments and then I ask, "Would you mind trying that again? I'm testing a theory."

Joey obligingly kisses me. "Did you get what you need?"

I nod happily. It turns out the answer was there all along, but I couldn't hear it until the wind subsided.

Conclusion: Luisa and Joey are meant to be together.

STEP 9: *Report Findings*

"He's my soul mate," I proclaim, leading my friends into Bebe.

Rachel smiles. "So you've said."

We've been shopping for several hours at Water Tower Place, and it's fair to say that I'm boring them with my tales of Joey.

"Well he is," I insist. "Don't you believe in soul mates?"

"Sure," Rachel says. "The Yiddish word for it is *beshert*."

"Well, Joey's my shirt. I'm telling you, there were fireworks."

"You were at the lights festival," Izzy says. "The fireworks were real."

I start to comb through the racks. "I put my theory through rigorous testing."

"Which explains why we've barely heard from you," Rachel says.

"I'm sorry," I say. "But now that I know where I stand with Joey, I can relax and get back to business as usual."

It isn't quite business as usual, though, because there's

a boyfriend in the equation now. Not a Future Boyfriend but a Current Boyfriend and hopefully a Forever Boyfriend. Still, I'm not the type to neglect my friends for a guy for long. Joey may be my soul mate, but he isn't going to help me shop for something to wear to the Literacy Gala. It's only two weeks away, and Mom gave me a hundred dollars last night to buy something special. I felt a little sick about taking it, knowing it amounts to almost a day's wages, but she insisted, and I succumbed. This is a big event, and if I choose wisely I'll be able to wear my new outfit again and again. Now that I am both a girlfriend and a columnist, there could be lots of events in my future.

Choosing wisely turns out to be the challenge. I'm trying to find an outfit that's hip and sexy, classy and professional—and a reasonable price. Everything we've seen so far has either been insanely expensive or skanky.

"What's your *beshert* wearing to the gala?" Rachel asks, heading to the discount rack.

"Actually, I haven't invited him," I say, holding up a flimsy dress. "I can bring only four guests, and that's my mom, Grace, and you two."

"I thought Buzzkill said you could bring Dan too," Izzy says.

"Okay, five. But I figure I've used up my favors."

Rachel stops picking over the sales rack to stare at me. "I'm sure she'd want you to bring your soul mate, Newshound. All you have to do is ask."

I drop the flimsy dress on the floor, but Rachel is still staring at me after I retrieve it.

"You haven't told him," she says.

"You haven't told him?" Izzy echoes. "But you've been welded to his side for weeks."

I throw out my only defense, knowing I'm going down. "It's a secret column."

Rachel turns away. "A secret that all your closest friends know about. Your soul mate might feel left out."

"You said Joey wants the kind of relationship where you tell each other everything," Izzy adds.

"I left it too long. Joey and I have already confided in each other about so many other things that it's going to be really awkward when I tell him. He might wonder what else I'm hiding."

"But, Lu, he's going to find out," Izzy says. "*Everyone* is going to find out."

"Yeah, but that's still a couple of weeks away, and by then Joey will like me even more, and he'll have to forgive me."

"Look how well that worked with Jason," Rachel says.

Izzy plucks a gray dress off the sales rack. "I don't see why you're so worried. Tyler's the one who's in trouble. When Ella finds out she's Lady Scoop, the easiest girl on campus, she's going to kill him."

Rachel takes the dress out of her hand and replaces it with a blue one. "Yeah, but Joey might not be too thrilled that Lu's been painting him as a prince."

Spinning another dress to figure out which plunging side is the front, Izzy says, "But a prince is good—isn't it?"

Again Rachel takes the dress and replaces it. "The prince is already catching flak from Scoop. How about when the rest of the school finds out Joey's the guy in the golden loincloth?"

Izzy seizes a third dress and holds it out of Rachel's reach. "That's just Scoop's take on it. He's an idiot, whereas Joey is a reasonable guy."

I inspect what appears to be a blouse but turns out to be a very short dress. "Aren't we overthinking this? Will anyone even remember what Scoop or Newshound said after the column ends?"

Rachel exchanges the dress I'm holding for a shirred number. "People have long memories for this type of thing."

"So I said he's sensitive and romantic. It's a compliment."

"Even good guys get stupid about their image, Lu. Think about what Paz will say."

My stomach sinks. Paz will definitely take Scoop's view, and Joey works with these guys thirty hours a week. "Oh, no. He'll be laughed out of Donner's."

Izzy offers me a black dress covered in metallic sequins. "It's not that bad."

I shake my head at the sequins and counter with a pink sheath. "It's pretty bad."

Rachel dismisses the sheath and passes me a white combo with wispy layers. "Like you always say, the column is the real you. If he doesn't like it, maybe he's not your soul mate after all."

The thought gives me a pang. Joey *is* my soul mate. I felt it, and I don't want anything to ruin that. Peering at Rachel through the transparent outfit, I say, "And like *you* always say, it's a persona. Hopefully Joey will understand a little poetic license."

"He'll try harder if he sees you in this," Izzy says. She

displays a purple satin halter dress. "The color is perfect, and exposure is minimal."

I perk up a little as I take the dress. "What if I minimize exposure by not writing about Joey in the December columns?"

Rachel nudges me into the change room. "That might help. But *can* you stop writing about him?"

"Of course I can stop writing about him," I say, slipping into the dress. "I can write about lots of other things. I'm practically a journalist."

Izzy gasps as I fling open the door. "You look beautiful!"

"That's definitely the one," Rachel confirms. "It's *beshert*."

I step in front of the three-way mirror and smile. The halter gives the illusion of a bigger chest but doesn't show too much skin. Best of all, it's fifty percent off. After tax I'll still have enough to buy us all lunch.

"You can borrow my black suede T-straps," Izzy offers, twisting my hair up and pinning it.

"And my crystal earrings," Rachel says.

My smile fades a little. I look like a million bucks, but strangely I don't feel half as good as I do when I'm wearing Joey's old hat.

"Do you think Joey's 'the one'?" Izzy asks later, over a pepperoni pizza.

Since we've already established that he's my soul mate, I have to assume she's moving on to less spiritual connections. "I guess so. Someday."

"But you're already thinking about it," Rachel says.

"Just thinking about it," I say. "Like I'm sure you thought about it with Jason. It's inevitable."

"What does that mean?" Izzy presses.

I grin at her. "It means I want him to be 'the one' when the time is right."

"When do you think that'll be?" she persists.

"Depends if he's still around after the gala," I tease.

Rachel and Izzy exchange a look, and I know what they're thinking: I was supposed to be the last to take that step. We all believed that Rachel, the most intrepid of our group, would be the first; Izzy, the most extroverted, would be second; and I, the most timid, would follow only when I got good and tired of sitting on the sidelines.

It's been that way since we met in kindergarten. Rachel and Izzy bonded almost instantly over hopscotch, while I sat nearby, admiring Rachel's natural skill and Izzy's determination. After a few days of this, Rachel called me over, but I was too shy to join them. Izzy had to march across the playground and drag me over to play with them.

Our trio never looked back, but our approach to life is pretty much the same. Rachel was the first to get her ears pierced, the first to buy a bra, the first to kiss a boy. Izzy followed shortly afterward. And I . . . got around to things in my own sweet time.

If their relationships with Jason and Carson had worked out, our lives would have unfolded as usual. In fact, they still may if Rachel and Izzy meet someone new before long.

Life is full of surprises. Who would have guessed that the Perfect FB was a guy I saw all the time and never noticed? And who would have guessed that I'd be courting trouble by writing about him in my very own newspaper column? So much has changed this year. I guess it would be nice to be a leader instead of a follower for a change.

THE WORD . . . FROM NEWSHOUND
The New Goldilocks Conundrum

In Newshound's opinion, there is no better hobby than shopping.

- First, it's social. Nothing cements a friendship more than bargain-hunting.
- It's creative. I seek inspiration on the Magnificent Mile and try to replicate those styles at the outlet mall.
- It's educational. I've learned to stick to my budget, or suffer the consequences when I can't afford fries at lunch.
- It's competitive. It takes smarts and agility to battle the crowds at the best sales.
- It's physical. A walk through the Loop gets anyone's blood pumping.
- It's enlightening. Some of my most treasured possessions came on the advice of my BFFs—items I would never have chosen on my own.

Shopping has always been the ideal escape from Dunfield life, so I was surprised to find myself stressed and grumpy during a recent trip to the Water Tower Mall. The purpose of the mission was to find an outfit worthy of the Literacy Gala.

When the veil of anonymity lifts, I want to be wearing

the right outfit—something that makes me look dignified and mature, even if that's not always how I come across on the page.

It was a tall order, especially with a modest budget. I wandered with my friends from store to store, all of us increasingly discouraged. Even my favorite shops let me down. I discarded one outfit after another, like a modern-day Goldilocks. Some were too tight, some were too short, some were too low, others too flimsy. None were just right.

Now, I'm fine with showing a little skin, but there's a huge difference between sexy and overexposed. Clothes tell the world about the person you are, and I, for one, don't want to tell the story all at once. I mean, who's going to sit through the whole movie if someone's already given away the ending?

So thank you, fashion world, but you can keep the microminis and transparent blouses.

If you ask me, a little mystery is where it's at.

"Luisa," Mr. Sparling says, directing me to the seat across from him. "What happened here?" He holds up the draft of my column.

I expected congratulations on my newfound restraint, not disapproval. After all, Scoop did suggest I poison myself in his last column. "What do you mean?"

"It's flat. You've danced around the issue instead of getting to the heart of it."

"But you and Mrs. Alvarez thought we were getting too personal, so I took a different approach."

"It's too late for that now. You've made a contract with your readers."

"A contract?"

"I mean, people like it, and they come back every week expecting the same thing. That's why we're running an extra edition of the *Bulletin* for the first two weeks in December. Your fans want all 'The Word' they can get before the big reveal. Plus, I'm putting it online."

"Online? That means it'll be around forever." And I'll *never* escape what I've said about Joey.

Mr. Sparling taps the column with his pencil. "What's really going on, Lu?"

I squirm uneasily in my seat. "Well, I've kind of started seeing someone."

He smothers a smile. "So I gathered."

"I realized he may not appreciate my . . . *interpretation* of events. He doesn't know about Newshound."

"Lu, any guy smart enough to hold your interest is going to recognize a literary persona when he sees one."

Mr. Sparling should not be giving me romantic advice. It's just wrong. And yet I really want to buy what he's selling right now. "His friends will tease him. Look at how Scoop reacts."

"Scoop is a persona too," he says.

"Yeah, most people would never guess it's Tyler Milano."

The pencil drops out of Mr. Sparling's hand. "Nice try, Newshound. I'm not revealing any secrets."

He doesn't have to; the pencil said it all. "I know it's Tyler."

He smirks. "Why so sure?"

I smirk back. "I'm not revealing any secrets."

"What I *can* tell you is that the person behind Scoop is a pretty decent guy."

"He's an idiot. His ideas about women are so backward he must be walking through the world butt-first."

Mr. Sparling laughs out loud. "*That's* the Newshound who keeps people reading. So I want you to revise this. Talk shopping if you must, but dig a little deeper. And dig fast. I need this back on my desk by morning if we're going to make the deadline for the new Wednesday edition."

If you ask me, a little mystery is where it's at.

It's the same with relationships. People like Scoop may want to cut straight to the reveal, but it's so much better to discover someone's personality layer by layer. By the time you've stripped to the core, you've built a solid relationship that may actually stand the test of time.

Scoop will mock this philosophy, but we all know that ridicule is a sign of discomfort. Maybe he's worried that if his lady gets a good look at what's under his exterior, she'll run screaming. Or maybe he's just afraid of connecting with anyone on an emotional level. There's a word for that, Scoop: immaturity.

You made your relationship sound as tacky as the clothes I saw at the mall the other day, which means you're no gentleman. I know the difference because I happen to be seeing a real gentleman. He knows how to take his time, and he realizes that intimacy and mutual respect are a major turn-on.

Best of all, he accepts that a slow burn is ten times hotter than a flash in the pan.

Chapter 16

"Someone grab a hose."

It's the sound of a bubble bursting. Joey and I are saying good-bye at the front door of my building. Not that we've done much talking. Standing on tiptoe, I look over his shoulder at Grace. "What do you want?"

"Are you done yet?"

"No." I don't plan to be done kissing Joey for a long time. Nor do I plan on letting my sister tell me who I can kiss anymore. Grace's reign is over.

Joey turns and gives Grace a sheepish wave, which she ignores. "I need you upstairs, Luisa."

"Unless something has happened to Mom or Keira, you don't need me upstairs."

"There's an important phone message. But if you want, I could tell you about it right here."

That gets my attention. Solana G. must have called. Grace is worried about her pulling out of the Literacy Gala. I guess she really wants to meet her.

I kiss Joey once more before following Grace inside. She starts in on me as the elevator doors close. "I can't believe Paz didn't tell me you actually hooked up with that loser."

I keep my cool because it's the only way to win any battle with Grace. "Joey isn't a loser. He's amazing, and I'm lucky to be with him. And Paz probably doesn't know. We haven't gone public yet."

Grace circles me like a shark trying to decide which limb to sever. "What do you call making out at the front door? No one should have to see that. Where's your class?"

I have to laugh at this. "You and Paz used to make out there all the time. You should try it again: it might bring the spark back."

"You're giving *me* relationship advice? You and Joey won't last a week."

The elevator door opens, and I saunter down the hall. "It's already been more than that. He's going to be around for a long time too, so you might as well get used to the idea."

"What do you know about guys?" she asks, following me inside the apartment.

"Enough not to listen to you." I sit down on the couch and start pulling things out of my backpack. "Now, if you don't mind, I have a column to write."

She glares at me. "What about Solana?"

That's it? The end of the attack on Joey? I expected so much worse. In fact, I developed mental scripts for several near-violent scenarios, and I'm almost disappointed I won't get to use them. "I'll listen to her message later."

"She wants you to call her."

I unfurl the new issue of the *Bulletin*. "Then I'll call her. Like I said, I have a column to write first."

Scoop's steaming pile of beauty came out today, and I want to read it and respond while my indignation is fresh.

THE WORD . . . FROM SCOOP
Born Too Late

How old are you, Newshound? Since our editor insists that you really are a Dunfield student, I can't help but wonder if your grandmother wrote your last column. Please tell me you don't believe that "slow burn" garbage. One day, when you live in a geriatric condo, a slow burn will be all you can handle. In the meantime, why don't you enjoy life while you've still got your original body parts?

Obviously you're only writing that drivel to disguise the fact that you're not getting any and I am. But whose fault is that? You're the one who decided to date a eunuch. Dunfield is full of red-blooded guys who'd show you a good time—especially if you managed to keep your antiquated ideas in your diary. Assuming you're at least marginally attractive, by my calculation you could be seeing one of hundreds of marginally attractive straight guys in our school. Instead, you chose someone who's either gay or simply not into you.

Wake up and smell the smoke, girlfriend, because there's a big difference between a slow burn and cold ashes.

Grace pushes the newspaper down to stare at me. "Solana wants you to come over to her place to look at the itinerary for the gala."

The gala is the last thing I want to think about at the moment. How can I attend now that Tyler has called Joey a eunuch? Maybe if I go to Mr. Sparling and beg, he'll let me remain anonymous forever. He was young once. If he can remember back that far, he might understand.

"Lu," Grace tries again. "Did you hear me?"

I raise the paper again. "Relax, I'll call her."

I hate to be the bearer of bad news, but someone has to be honest, and your friends are probably as misguided as you are. If you spent less time shopping and more time getting out in the real world, you wouldn't be in this position. You might have a closet full of clothes, but are you happy, Newshound? I am, and if that's immaturity, I'm all for it.

Lady Scoop seems happy too. In fact, so many sparks are flying that we have to keep a fire extinguisher handy at all times. Ignition has been achieved and liftoff is imminent.

You have no idea how freeing it is to have all the benefits of a romance without any of the drama. And I mean that. You clearly don't know what you're missing, Newshound. Lucky for you that ignorance appears to be bliss. Still, I urge you to not to write yourself off too soon. While your eunuch doesn't want to touch you with a ten-foot pole, someone else might, especially if you can fix your personality flaws.

None of us want to listen to you whine anymore, but there are plenty of support groups out there that do. So grab your cane and your bifocals and get on it before it's too late.

Grace hands me the phone as I lower the paper. "Call now."

I'm not going to call when Grace is eavesdropping. I pull out a yellow highlighter and start flagging items in the column that I need to refute. "I'll call later."

"But it's Solana. You shouldn't keep her waiting when she's doing you a favor."

Suddenly it strikes me how oddly Grace is behaving. First she dropped the whole Joey issue and now she's hovering over me as if I have something she wants. "What's up, Grace?"

She hesitates. "I want to come with you to Solana's."

"You're not exactly my biggest supporter. Why would I take you?"

"Because sisters do nice things for each other?"

"What's the last nice thing you did for me?"

"Hmmmm . . ." She pretends to think. "I didn't tell Paz about your stupid column, because you asked me not to."

Oh, right. That. I apply a little more yellow to Scoop's column. "I'll think about it."

Grace takes the newspaper out of my hand and scans it. "Think fast, because if you don't take me along, I may have to tell Joey who's behind his getting called a eunuch in a certain syndicated column."

Obviously Grace's reign isn't quite over yet.

Grace hangs her leather jacket on a hook and shakes Solana's hand.

"Great art," Solana says, examining Grace's rainbow-colored arms.

"Thanks," Grace says, offering a rare smile. "Kai at Cherry Bomb."

To me this is an unintelligible fragment, but Solana nods and points to a tattoo on her own forearm. "Kai."

Grace spots a framed concert poster on the wall over an old, upright piano. "I went to that one."

"That was years ago. You couldn't have been more than fifteen."

"Fourteen," Grace admits. "I knew the bouncers and they used to let me in if I promised not to drink. Our mom works nights, so it was easy."

"Mine too," Solana says. "That's how I got my start in the clubs. She didn't even know I was performing until someone showed her a review. But she did know I was having trouble at school."

"Ditching?" Grace asks, perching on the edge of the brown velvet couch. My sister has hijacked my meeting, but it's interesting, so I keep quiet.

"Ditching. Also taking creative license with report cards and letters from my guidance counselor."

My sister's face lights up. She had a talent for forgery herself. I witnessed her altering Dunfield notices many times, but she coerced me into silence with a variety of threats, some involving her body piercer.

"You can get away with murder in a school as big as

Dunfield," Solana says. "No one can keep track of you. If it weren't for music, I don't know how I'd have ended up."

"Probably pregnant and working in a diner," Grace says, her voice sounding a little wistful.

Solana studies Grace for a moment. "Well, we all do the best we can with what we've got, right? And it's never too late to try something new. I got help with my learning disability, and I'll be graduating soon."

Her phone rings, and she apologizes as she answers. "It hasn't stopped all day. I've a got a couple projects heating up."

After Solana hangs up, Grace asks, "Are you going to talk about your learning disability at the Literacy Gala?"

"No. Too personal."

"But your story would inspire a lot of people," Grace says. She pushes herself as far back in the couch as she can. "Like me."

Solana hesitates, switching the phone from one hand to the other and back. "I wouldn't know what to say."

"Luisa can help you. She's a great writer."

I stare over at my sister incredulously and then back to Solana. "I'd love to help you."

Solana ponders for a few more moments and finally says, "Okay. Maybe I should, if it will do some good."

The phone rings again. Before Solana can answer, Grace reaches over and takes it from her. "Why don't I handle your calls while you guys work?"

Solana sets Grace up in the dining room with her schedule and rejoins me. We listen in on a call, and she says, "Your sister is very persuasive."

By the time Solana and I have come up with an outline for the speech, Grace has rearranged about ten appointments and mapped them out on a grid. "Nothing starts before noon on the days after you've performed."

Solana is clearly more impressed with Grace's efforts than mine, which causes my constantly simmering sibling resentment to bubble up. I couldn't get Solana to speak about her problem, and Grace did. And then she upstages me even more by playing personal assistant. Why couldn't she let me have my moment without stealing my thunder?

At the elevator, Solana turns to hug Grace. I expect my sister to recoil because she barely tolerates displays of affection, even from Keira, but she actually throws her arms around Solana.

Hugging me next, Solana says, "Thanks for your help. I couldn't tell my story half as well without you."

As the elevator doors close, Grace says, "That was cool."

"Very."

Neither of us looks at the other, but I sense we're both smiling. As it turns out, there's plenty of thunder to go around.

The dart flies out of my hand and punctures the red balloon with a satisfying pop.

"Your girl's got quite the arm," the guy behind the counter tells Joey, who's standing beside me holding my purse and cotton candy.

We're at the Fun Fair, the last major fund-raising event in the Literacy Challenge. The guys' and the girls' teams actually came together to organize it, and the unseasonably warm day has drawn a huge crowd. Plus, since Tyler and I mentioned it in "The Word," students from other schools have at least doubled our usual crowd.

"The rest of her isn't bad, either," Joey says, stooping to kiss my cheek.

Rachel and Izzy beam at him. This is the first time they've hung out with us, and I can tell he's made a good impression. It shouldn't matter what other people think, but it makes me happy anyway.

I offer Joey a dart. "Two more red balloons and we get the teddy bear."

He slides the purse straps onto his shoulder before aiming and firing the dart with his right. It hits a blue balloon instead of a red one.

"Try it without your purse," someone says. "You might have better luck."

We turn to find Mac Landis standing behind us with Morgan the Moron and some of their crew. Mac hasn't acknowledged me in weeks, and I don't see why he's bothering now.

The guy running the game says, "Let the lady have the last dart. You could still win the plastic gecko."

"Yeah," Mac says, playing to the crowd. "Let the lady take her best shot. You've got your hands full."

"Shut up, Mac," I say, trying to take my purse back from Joey.

"Ignore him," Joey says, holding on to it. "He's an idiot."

Mac is enjoying himself too much to give up the stage.

"Let *me* give the lady a hand—I mean the little lady, not the big one." He holds out his hand for the dart. "I'll show you how it's done."

I turn away from him to take aim at one of the remaining red balloons. "I've seen the way you do things, Mac. I can handle this on my own."

"Ten bucks says she chokes," Mac says.

"Fifteen says I don't," I counter. I shouldn't be so cocky, but I'm determined not to let Mac get the better of me in front of Joey.

Raising the dart, I close my eyes and conjure up the memory of Mac rejecting me at the dance. Then I open my eyes and the dart demolishes its target. My friends cheer.

As the caller cuts down the gecko, I turn to Mac. "You owe me fifteen bucks."

He snorts. "Like that's going to happen."

"A bet's a bet, Landis," Joey says. "Unless you're a cheater. Are you?"

Mac scowls, and I remember what Joey said about his plagiarizing an assignment. Morgan takes a step toward Joey, but Mac stops him and pulls out his wallet. "Take the money," he says, handing it to me. "Buy your boyfriend a new handbag."

He disappears into the crowd, and I treat everyone to french fries with my winnings, knowing it's the best way to cleanse the tainted money.

Tyler and Ella are standing beside the food truck, feeding each other. They're so entranced that they barely notice us. Clearly Scoop wasn't exaggerating about his relationship reaching ignition point. I wait until Tyler looks up before standing on tiptoe to kiss Joey on the lips. He has no idea I'm Newshound, but I want Scoop to see that Luisa Perez's Forever Boyfriend is no eunuch.

"Holy PDA," Izzy says.

Joey grins. "What was that about?"

"Just thanking you for getting money out of the cheater."

"Hey, look, the circus just rolled into town," Rachel says, pointing to Mariah, who's approaching with her film crew. "Only, someone's had a make*under*."

Mariah's jeans are topped with a simple turtleneck sweater and a down coat that covers her butt. Her hair is twisted in a bun at the nape of her neck, and most shocking of all, she's wearing glasses.

When she sees us, she comes over. "Coconut, I liked it so much better when you stayed in the grease pit, where you belong."

"What's with the new look?" I ask. "Does Mac have a thing for librarians?"

"I just realized that with this body, I don't have to go around proving anything. A little mystery is where it's at."

"That's exactly what Newshound said. It's sweet the way you look up to her."

She stares down at me. "Mariah Mendes looks up to *no one*, at least not in this school. But if Newshound is hanging with Solana G., obviously she's almost as cool as I am. I might even give her my VIP phone number."

"Wow, that's quite an offer."

"It's incomprehensible."

"It sure is," I say.

"I think she means incomparable," Joey suggests.

Mariah notices him for the first time. "That's exactly what I meant."

Turning to Joey, I wordlessly remind him whose side he's on. Interpreting my look correctly, he hastily offers me his fries. I don't really like chili sauce, but I sample them anyway and offer mine in return.

Mariah observes this exchange, but before she gets to lob her next shot, Mr. Sparling joins us, marshaling two young Sparlings through the crowd.

"Well, well," he says. "If it isn't some of my favorite students." His eyes flit from our little circle over to Tyler and back. The same odd expression crosses his face that I saw in his office, only this time it's more pronounced.

"Hi, Mr. Sparling. Where's *Mrs.* Sparling today?" I ask.

"Happy to have some time to herself," he says. "Besides, she knew my students would be checking her out and wondering what she's doing with a guy like me."

I laugh. "She chose you for your sense of humor, sir."

"Sorry to break up the party," Mariah says, "but I have to do my time in the kissing booth." She points to a booth in which a cheerleader is paying lip service to a lineup of guys and tugs on Joey's arm. "Come on, cutie. I'll give you a two-for-one special."

Joey allows himself to be towed away, and Rachel, Izzy, and I stare after him. Waving a hasty good-bye to Mr. Sparling, we follow them.

By the time we reach the kissing booth, Mariah has taken off her glasses and pulled the pins out of her hair. She assists the cheerleader from the booth and takes the hot seat. The lineup doubles instantly, and Mariah holds up a hand. "Settle down, guys." She takes out a compact and pouts to apply lip gloss. Then she points to Joey and summons him. "You first."

Joey steps out of the line and walks to the booth. My tray of fries slips out of my hand. Surely my soul mate is not going to throw what we have away for a single kiss from Mariah Mendes?

"He can't," I moan, and Rachel squeezes my hand. The alarm on her face is surpassed only by the alarm on Izzy's.

"I can't," someone echoes. It's Joey's voice, and he's talking to Mariah. "I'm only interested in kissing Luisa. But I'd be happy to donate a couple of bucks to get you started. Since it's for a good cause."

I fiddle with the remote control for the DVD player, trying unsuccessfully to get the movie to start.

"Let me show you how it's done," Joey says, taking it from me.

I've used it a hundred times, but my fingers aren't working quite right tonight. I guess I'm nervous about being alone in the apartment with Joey. We were supposed to meet some of his friends, but Joey suggested hanging out here instead. I didn't want to say no, because A) I wanted to have him all to myself, and B) I didn't want to look like I was afraid to be alone with him.

Normally I'm *not* afraid to be alone with him; it's just that we're usually alone surrounded by people. I trust Joey, but things have been speeding up between us lately.

It's like someone pressed the FAST FORWARD button the minute I realized he was my soul mate.

Mom would be all over the PAUSE button if she were here. I finally told her about Joey a few days ago, and although she didn't say much, I can tell she's rattled. Well, she can relax. I have no intention of making the same mistakes she and Grace did. But I still want to be close to my boyfriend.

Last night at the bus stop we were a little *too* close for Dan's liking. He drove past us, slammed on the brakes, and hit reverse. Then he basically took us hostage, sticking Joey in the backseat alone. After dropping him off, Dan gave me a painfully awkward lecture about the birds and the bees. If I didn't already know the biology behind procreation, that discussion certainly wouldn't have enlightened me. Still, I appreciated that Dan cared enough about me to put himself through it.

Joey brings up the DVD's main menu and asks, "Are you free next Thursday?"

"I'm free after work."

He looks at me. "Actually, I meant in the afternoon. School lets out at noon because of the Literacy Gala."

"I know," I say. "But I've already made plans."

This is my chance to invite him, or at least tell him about Newshound, but I chicken out.

"Could you change your plans? There's something I'd really like to do."

I shake my head. "I made a commitment. Sorry."

I wait for him to press, hoping he'll force me to disclose my plans. Instead he turns silently to the television. Away from me.

Wanting everything to be right between us, I put my arms around his neck and pull him down onto the couch. If he's annoyed at me, he gets over it enough to slide a hand up my T-shirt.

It's still there when the overhead light flicks on. "Hey!"

We shoot apart like balls breaking on a pool table. Grace is standing at the door, balancing Keira on one hip. "What the hell is going on here?"

It's perfectly obvious what's going on here. "We're watching a movie."

"Couldn't you watch it with your shirt on? Joey, you'd better get going. It's late."

"It's 9:15," I protest, tucking in my T-shirt. "And you're not my mother."

Joey finds his voice. "We weren't doing anything wrong, Grace."

"No? Tell it to Paz. He's on his way over."

Joey scrambles to his feet and grabs his jacket.

"Don't go," I say, following him to the door. "I made popcorn."

"I'll call you later," he says, kissing my cheek. "Don't worry."

"Are you insane?" Grace asks as the door closes behind him. "Is my life so glamorous you want the same thing?"

"It wasn't like that," I say.

"I didn't think it was like that either. Then all of a sudden it was."

The fight drains out of me. "Grace, I'm not you."

"I know: you're smarter. Stay that way."

Chapter 17

THE WORD . . . FROM NEWSHOUND
Breaking Up Is Hard to Do

The Literacy Challenge is drawing to a close, and I think we're all amazed at how we pulled together to raise so much money. I'm not the only one who started this year with the usual Dunfield apathy, and I certainly never expected to be on a winning team. Okay, so we haven't quite won that vacation yet, but in other ways we're already victors. Our performance has impressed everyone from our parents to celebrities like Solana G. Even Principal Alvarez has been caught smiling lately. But no one should be happier about our achievement than we are. We proved our ability to achieve liftoff.

On the romantic front, it turns out that liftoff is more elusive. I started this term thinking that chemistry and good intentions were enough to get a relationship airborne. I've found out that it takes a lot more than that.

Communication is definitely key. If you can't—or won't—talk about problems and work through them, you're destined to crash and burn. Ironically, with all the mechanisms we have at our disposal to communicate 24/7—cell phone, text messages, instant message, e-mails—somehow it's easier than ever to avoid it. Anyone can hide behind technology to avoid hearing harsh words like, "I'm not into you," or "We're over."

Who knows, maybe Scoop was right about hookups being the way to go. It's definitely simpler. If you don't expect much, you won't be disappointed. And when you hit a rough patch, you can disappear without even going through the trouble of breaking up.

I'd like to continue to share my insights from the front line, but "The Word" is winding down. It's been quite an eye-opener for me. Thanks to Scoop, I've learned a lot about how the male mind works, and as a result I've been having nightmares for months. I think I speak for all Dunfield women in saying that I hope his personality is unique.

Newshound still stands by her view that mature, respectful guys are out there and worth waiting for, but concedes they're hard to find. I've decided to take a hiatus from romance and focus on friends, work, and study. One day, when I've shaken off the dust of this old dump, I'll give it another try.

Until then, dear readers, I wish you all the best in love and literacy.

THE WORD . . . FROM SCOOP
A Clean Break

Newshound, let me be the first to offer my condolences. It sounds like Mr. Dreamboat has already capsized. I hate to say I told you so, but I so called this one. Actually, anyone could have seen this coming. Your rose-colored glasses were six inches thick, girlfriend. Like I keep telling you, teenage guys and fairy-tale romance do not mix.

It's my last column, and I don't want to waste it gloating, so I'll get straight to the point: do not use your current disappointment as an excuse to become more bitter than ever. Get back in that saddle, only this time don't confuse a mule for a white charger. Enjoy the mule for what it offers—a good ride and a few laughs.

Since poor Newshound is howling the blues, I will toss her one bone: she's absolutely right about avoidance being the easiest way out of a relationship. Sure, there are a few guys out there brave enough to say, "Look, this is too much work." But it's so much easier to leave a voice mail when you know she's busy. To send the blasé text message promising to get together soon. To delete her from your friends list so that she can't tell if you're online.

Not that Scoop would do any of those things. He doesn't have to, because he's smart enough not to get involved. He keeps his relationships at arm's length. It isn't always as easy as it sounds. If you actually like the girl, you feel the weight of her expectations and you feel bad about yourself every time you let her down. Still, you have to know when you are not ready for a relationship. And anyone who likes violent video games as much as Scoop does is in no position to look out for someone else's feelings.

Maybe it will be different down the road. With so many great movies based on true love instead of casual hookups, there must be something to it. But this isn't the time to find out. Surviving Dunfield has to be my first priority, and it's been tough. This column has actually helped, even though apparently I had more rewrites than Newshound. I like to think that's because my ideas are more complex than hers.

Anyway, no hard feelings, Newshound. It's been a pleasure sparring with you, and I look forward to meeting you at the gala.

"What's up?" I ask, slumping into the seat across from Mr. Sparling.

"Just wanted to check in," he says. "Newshound seems a little down."

"I guess she's bummed that the column's ending."

"Well, 'The Word' might end, but there will be plenty of opportunities to write in the future—under your own byline."

"Really?"

"Sure. You've done very well, Luisa. I predict great things to come for you."

This should make me happy, but I'm incapable of happiness right now. "Thanks."

He watches me for a moment. "I gather things aren't going well with your boyfriend?"

I doodle an ax on my notepad, alongside the broken heart I drew earlier. "It didn't work out."

Sadly, this appears to be true. After Grace chased Joey out of our apartment last weekend, he vanished from my life. I exaggerate only slightly. He left a voice mail about an hour after he left, saying, "Sorry about what happened. We'll talk about it soon." But we didn't talk about it, because we didn't walk to school together, or meet in the halls, or walk home together. I'd have worried about foul play if he hadn't shown up at the diner. Three nights he came in with the crew. Three nights they sat in Shirley's section. Three nights he acknowledged me only with a wave as Paz glowered at him. Three nights he text messaged me afterward saying I looked great. I do not look great; I look like I haven't slept in ages. But I thanked him and said, "See you soon."

Grace obviously told Paz about the whole hand-up-the-shirt thing, and I assume Paz overreacted. Still, Joey has four inches and twenty pounds on Paz. If he really loved me, he'd fight for me. I guess the Perfect FB decided that Lu Perez comes with too much baggage.

After Scoop's final column ran in the *Bulletin*, it finally sunk in that that I was the victim of a cowardly, passive-aggressive offload. Joey didn't even have the decency to do it face-to-face. He's taking his cue from Scoop, and that somehow makes this more humiliating.

Well, if he can be this callous, he's not the guy for me. Soul mates don't bolt at the first sign of trouble. My hypothesis has been disproved. All a kiss can reveal is whether a guy has good oral hygiene.

"Relationships are never easy," Mr. Sparling says. "Are you doing all right?"

I nod. What else am I going to say? That I'm devastated? That I can't believe I've gone from no B to Forever B to Ex-B in the space of three months? I may admit this to Izzy and Rachel but not Mr. Sparling.

He looks relieved, in the way Dan always looks relieved when I refuse to talk about girl stuff. "There are plenty of fish in the sea, Luisa, and you're really too young to get serious anyway. When I met Mrs. Sparling, I—"

"Sir?"

"Yes?"

"That isn't going to help."

He smiles, rolling with it as always. The best teachers are pretty hard to offend, I've discovered. Dealing with people like me all day toughens them up.

Dan pulls up in front of the Harold Washington Library Center and cuts the engine on his SUV. "Last stop, ladies."

Solana continues to fumble through her purse, clearly in no hurry to go inside. I'm not sure whether she's really forgotten something or is just nervous.

"Did you bring your speech?" I ask. I printed a copy on note cards, and Grace delivered it to her two days ago. They went for coffee, and I wasn't even jealous. It helps that my brain has been so busy mulling over every detail of my failed romance.

She nods. "But I wish I were just singing today."

"You're going to knock 'em dead," I reassure her. She certainly looks the part of a VIP, in her funky suit and stiletto boots. "You were perfect in our run-through."

"But that wasn't in front of a crowd—a crowd that includes teachers who thought I was stupid."

"I bet they're ashamed of letting you fall through the cracks. Mr. Sparling feels bad about what happened with Grace. If he'd handled it differently, she might not have dropped out."

"I don't know," Solana says thoughtfully. "Maybe it's better to let things work out in their own time. I wouldn't be leaving on my first tour next week if I'd stayed in school."

"And we wouldn't have as good a chance to win the Literacy Challenge," I say.

Dunfield is still in second place behind Turnbull and ahead of Warwick, but the proceeds from the Fun Fair helped close the gap to five grand. Today, guests at the gala will be depositing checks in drop boxes at the door, and while bands from each school entertain the crowd, the teachers will tabulate the final results. Then the mayor of Chicago will announce a winner and invite Scoop and Newshound to say a few words and introduce the speakers and performers.

"So the dropout with the learning disability might win the literacy competition for the school that exiled her," Solana says. "It's ironic, isn't it?"

"It's not ironic," Dan says, turning in his seat. "It's downright poetic."

The rear door opens, and Grace slides in beside Solana. She's wearing a long-sleeved black sweater and black pants, and there's not a bit of ink showing. "Lu, you can't sit out here chatting," she says. "People might figure out that it's Newshound with her special guest."

She hands Solana a bag containing a compact, tissues, lip gloss, a pen, a small bottle of water, and a stack of promotional postcards for her CD.

"You've thought of everything," Solana says.

Grace beams as she climbs out of the truck. "It's easier to keep your cool when you're fully prepared. I even got the Center's piano tuned and billed it to Dunfield."

"Is she always this organized?" Solana asks when Grace is gone.

"Beats me," I say, realizing I don't know my sister as well as I thought.

Dan hops out, opens Solana's door, and offers her his arm.

Once he's escorted her into the Library Center, he returns for me. "You look very nice today," he says as we walk to the door. "I'm going to have to beat that Joey off with a stick."

"Actually, he won't be here."

"You did ask him." It's more a statement than a question.

"I haven't seen him. In case you haven't heard, Paz decided we should take a breather."

Dan isn't easily thrown off the trail. "Joey *does* know you're Newshound."

Another statement. "Not exactly."

"Luisa, I may not know much about romance, but I can say for sure that what you sweep under the rug tends to come back and bite you in the butt."

"If Joey can't handle some flak from Grace and Paz, he

definitely can't handle hearing about the column, Dan."

Dan's expression is shaded by his cowboy hat, but I can tell he's disappointed in me. "Joey's a nice guy," he says. "He'd have come around."

There it is: the past tense. Even Dan thinks we're history.

More than four hundred people are milling in the lobby, including teachers and student reps from all three schools, friends and families, business people and community members. Judging by all the cameras and notepads I see, the press has come out in full force. That has less to do with literacy than with the presence of high-profile guests. Turnbull and Warwick have recruited an artist, an entrepreneur, a football player, and a cellist from the Philharmonic. They're all good scores, but not as good as Solana.

I'm so glad the event is taking place here, and not in a grungy school auditorium. The organizers have created a makeshift stage beneath a mosaic mural that depicts the life of Harold Washington, the city's first African American mayor. Maroon velvet curtains hang from either side, creating two "backstage" areas. Midstage is a wide podium wired with two microphones, and behind that a grand piano.

Seeing those mikes makes me nervous, but not as nervous as I expected to be. Here again, a broken heart keeps you from getting caught up in the small stuff, such as stage fright.

Mrs. Alvarez looks fantastic in a black dress and high heels. Her hair, normally restrained in a bun, is blown out in a smooth shoulder-length bob that makes the gray slice all the more striking. As I watch, she walks away from a man in a wheelchair and joins my mother and sister. The expression on Grace's face is a combination of disgust and terror, but when Mrs. Alvarez rests her hand on Grace's shoulder, she doesn't shrug it off.

In one corner of the lobby, Turnbull's jazz band strikes up, the signal for teachers and the mayor's staff to disappear into an office with the drop boxes.

Rachel and Izzy emerge from the crowd to join Dan and me. Izzy's hair has turned a rich mahogany since I saw her yesterday. It's the first sign that she's getting over Carson; I can only hope I recover as quickly.

"We've been scouting the competition," Izzy says. "Tyler is hanging around that Chicago Bulls player along with Mac and the rest of the jocks.

"Nervous?" Rachel asks.

I nod. "I don't want to make a fool of myself in front of the media."

"You won't," Izzy assures me. "Besides, they've got all the fool footage they need."

She points to the three cameras currently trained on Mariah, who has managed to cut Solana off from the herd and is auditioning a new routine for her. Solana's eyes widen and she looks around for help.

I start to walk over, but I don't get far before Grace swoops down on Mariah. She gives her a glare that would be followed with a good slap if the cameras weren't rolling. Instead, she leads Solana away.

A few minutes later, Mr. Sparling arrives to take me to the wings. Solana and some other guests are already there. Beyond the curtain, the mayor is calling for silence.

"It's showtime," I say to Solana. "Do you still have your speech?"

She holds up her note cards. "Do you have yours?"

"I memorized it." My voice is higher than usual, betraying my nerves.

Mrs. Alvarez turns and shushes me before stepping out on the stage.

Over the microphone, the mayor is welcoming the guests and praising the city's public school system for raising nearly a million dollars in the Literacy Challenge. I squeeze Solana's hand and find it's just as sweaty as mine.

"The three schools we're honoring today have outshone all others," he says as the applause subsides. "I stand here with three very proud—and dare I say surprised?—principals." A laugh ripples through the audience. "Warwick Central, Colonel Dunfield High, and the Turnbull Academy each raised close to two hundred thousand dollars for this very special cause. For a while it looked like we might have a three-way tie, but thanks to some generous donations this afternoon, my staff informs me that one school has clearly taken the lead." There's a rustling as the mayor opens an envelope. "Ladies and gentlemen, it gives me great pleasure to announce that the winner of The Literacy Challenge is . . . *Colonel Dunfield High!*"

A good portion of the crowd erupts into cheers, but even more groan. There are boos and demands for a recount.

"Now, now," the mayor says. "Dunfield won the vaca-

274

tion fair and square. But I'm so proud of Warwick and Turnbull students that I'm going to give them a prize too." He waits for the murmur of excitement to abate and announces, "I'm sure you'll be proud to display this fine plaque at your schools."

Solana and I snicker as even more booing ensues.

The mayor moves on hastily. "It's now my privilege to introduce you to two spirited young columnists from Colonel Dunfield, whose friendly sparring helped put their school into the winner's circle. 'The Word' is now syndicated in five—"

"Six!" a familiar voice rings out, provoking another laugh.

"My apologies, Principal Alvarez," the mayor says with a chuckle. "The column appears in *six* school papers and online. Without further ado, I present today's hosts: Newshound and Scoop!"

As the crowd cheers, Solana gives me a gentle shove and wishes me luck.

I push through the curtains and step onto the stage, blinking in the bright spotlights. Before my eyes adjust I start walking toward the podium. I make out a guy approaching from the other side. He has a familiar gait, familiar hair, and broad shoulders. If I could focus I'd see two crooked fingers.

My feet stop of their own accord. What is Joey doing here? Did he come to surprise me? If so, why is he onstage? My mind races but doesn't come to any reasonable conclusions.

Mrs. Alvarez takes my arm. "Come and meet your

fellow columnist, Luisa." My shoes actually skid across the wooden floor as she pulls me toward the podium. "Joseph Carella, meet Luisa Perez."

Joey stares at me, and I notice his Adam's apple bobs as he swallows hard. I stare back at him, still trying to process what I'm seeing.

Finally Mariah's voice breaks the silence. "Oh my God! Coconut is the Newshound!"

A murmur travels through the audience. Mrs. Alvarez's head swivels from me to Joey and back, and then she initiates damage control. "I know you two have had your differences, but you wrote in the spirit of fun, right?"

"Fun," Joey echoes.

"Fun?" I repeat.

"Yes, fun," Mrs. Alvarez says firmly. "Now shake hands and let's move on with our program."

Neither Joey nor I make a move, so Mrs. Alvarez takes my hand. Then she grabs Joey's and pulls it toward mine. Each of us leans back, trying not to touch.

"Don't be silly," she whispers. "Hundreds of people are waiting. Do I need to remind you you're representing Dunfield now?"

The spotlight is making me hot and dizzy, and I look up at my principal desperately. "We were . . . together," I choke out. "He said I was easy."

Joey finds his voice too. "And she made me out to be a—"

"Eunuch," Mac Landis supplies. "With a small—"

"Mr. Landis," Mrs. Alvarez says. *"Keep your mouth closed."*

There's laughter throughout the lobby, and I realize that the microphones are broadcasting the entire drama. Still, I

276

speak to Joey directly. "I was trying to make you sound *nice*, whereas you told the world you got me into bed."

"You go, Coco-*slut*!" Mariah says, louder now. "Way to carry on the family tradition!"

I turn to see her pretending to rock a baby in her arms. Standing just behind Mariah is my mother, whose mouth drops open in shock.

"Mariah Mendes," Mrs. Alvarez begins, "I would like you to leave."

"But she lied to all of—"

The last word is cut off as a hand appears on Mariah's shoulder and yanks her backward. I see Grace's blond head, some thrashing, and suddenly Mariah is gone.

Tears sting my eyes as I glance from my mother's face back to Joey's. My stomach heaves, and I know if I don't leave now I am going to add to my humiliation by throwing up, fainting, or both.

"Luisa," Mrs. Alvarez calls after me as I hurry toward the wings on Joey's side of the stage. "Come back."

"I can't," I say, "I *hate* him!"

Seconds later I'm out the front door and running through the parking lot, the December wind freezing the tears on my cheeks.

I open the door quietly and creep into the darkened apartment.

The light switches on, and I stop, caught in the spotlight for the second time today.

My mother is sitting alone on the sofa, and she doesn't look happy. "Luisa, I was worried to death about you. I thought you were running around without a coat or dime on you, but I see you haven't frozen to death."

I'm wearing Dan's old plaid jacket over my halter dress. "Dan left his car unlocked. There was enough change in the ashtray for bus fare and coffee."

Mom sighs. "But not enough for a pay phone?"

"I'm sorry. I should have called, but I lost track of time."

"Well, Grace is covering your shift at Dan's."

I've never missed a single shift, not even for illness, but today I completely forgot. "Aren't you supposed to work tonight, too?"

"I couldn't go anywhere until I knew you were all right."

"I'm sorry, Mom," I repeat. "I'll make up the money by taking extra shifts."

"It's not about the money, Lu." She pats the sofa beside her, and I sit down. "Today's event wasn't my proudest parenting moment. I got all dressed up to watch my girl host a big gala, and instead I saw her run off the stage when the going got tough."

I'm shocked that she can be so cold. "Mom, in case you didn't pick this up, Scoop was Joey. *My boyfriend.* What else could I do?"

"Well, as Grace would say, you could suck it up. You had an anonymous column. You wrote some edgy things. He wrote some edgy things. But all masks come off eventually, and you have to face up to what you've said."

"I didn't say anything bad," I say, crossing my arms.

"You don't think so, but from where I stood, Joey had another take on it."

"Well, he told six schools he'd hooked up with me."

Her hand on my shoulder tightens. "Did he?"

"Hook up with me? No."

"Are you sure?"

I slide away from her on the couch. This is my time of need, and it's not fair to interrogate about something that can never happen now anyway. "I think I'd remember that."

"My point is, you don't want to get into that situation too soon—at least until you get to know the real person behind the column."

"Joey and I are through. And I'm not stupid, Mom."

"I know that, but I also know how easy it is to get carried away. I made that mistake with your father—as Mariah kindly pointed out today."

"I hate her almost as much as Joey."

"Well, she might think twice next time, thanks to Grace. At least no one got arrested."

I slide back toward her, and she puts her arm around me again. "I'm sorry I embarrassed you like that," I say.

"I just want you to have all the opportunities I never had, Lu. Don't throw your future away on a boy."

At the moment it's hardly a risk, but I am beginning to understand why my mother has never had a boyfriend and continues to avoid online dating. When I look at Paz, Joey, Carson, and Jason, it's difficult to believe guys are worth the trouble.

"What happened after I left?" I ask, hoping that Joey was so racked by remorse that he gave an impassioned speech about me.

"Joey left the stage, too. And when Mrs. Alvarez called on Solana to give her speech, she'd also disappeared."

"Oh, no!"

"Grace caught up with Solana, and she apparently said that if you weren't committed enough to stay, she wasn't going to put herself out there either."

"That's terrible. Solana could have done so much good with her speech. I've let everyone down."

The Chicago Bulls star Joey enlisted also left before speaking, but Mom isn't sure what happened after that, because she set off to look for me. "Rachel and Izzy will be able to fill you in, because I insisted that they stay."

We sit in silence for a while, and then I ask, "What time is your shift tomorrow?"

"Late enough for me to make sure you get to school."

"Since when do you worry about my attendance?"

"Since I have reason to worry."

Chapter 18

Chicago Tribune

R & B DIVA TURNS HER BACK ON LITERACY

Rising rhythm and blues singer Solana G. deserted hundreds of fans at the Harold Washington Library Center yesterday. Ms. G. was set to perform on behalf of Colonel Dunfield High, one of 120 schools competing in the citywide Literacy Challenge.

Ms. G. refused to comment, but some speculate that the move was a publicity stunt perfectly timed with the kickoff of the young singer's first national tour.

I drop the newspaper and let my head hit the table. "I can't read any more."

Izzy pats my shoulder. There's nothing she can say to make me feel better, and she has the sense not to try.

Eventually I find the strength to lift my head and stare at the photo beside the article. It shows Solana leaving the Library Center with Grace on her heels. As they both appear to be yelling at reporters, it's an unflattering shot.

"They've got the whole story wrong," I say.

Rachel pushes my caramel macchiato toward me, and I shake my head. This is a disaster even Starbucks cannot relieve, but at least I have my friends to help me through it. They suggested meeting here early so that we could walk into Dunfield as a united front, but that was before we knew about the article. Izzy's father discovered it as she was leaving the house.

"Solana had the best intentions, and they've tagged her as a diva," I groan. "Finding out that my soul mate's a loser and a liar was bad enough, but this is so much worse."

"Hold that thought," Izzy says, preparing to read the rest of the story aloud:

The Literacy Gala gave the three top schools a chance to add to their funds through donations from some of Chicago's most generous patrons. Colonel Dunfield had the strongest program, thanks to promised appearances by Ms. G. and Chicago Bulls point guard, Jordan Peters. This led to a surprise win for a school at which students traditionally miss more classes than they attend.

The event began unraveling when two Dunfield students who pen a popular syndicated column called "The Word" began bickering onstage. Their principal, Alicia Alvarez, tried to intervene, but heckling from the crowd prompted the female half of the duo, Luisa Perez, to flee.

Her male counterpart, Joey Carella, left shortly thereafter.

Mayor Grimsby attempted to get the show back on track by introducing the popular Ms. G., but by that time she had walked, too, taking most of the press with her. Mr. Peters also disappeared.

The show did go on eventually, with special guests of the Turnbull Academy and Warwick Central fulfilling their commitment.

Afterward, Dunfield donors complained that they had supported the wrong school. Mayor Grimsby responded by renouncing Colonel Dunfield's win and awarding the grand prize—an extended winter holiday—to the Turnbull Academy.

"I hope people will forget one misfire in what was a very successful campaign and remember that Chicago schools have raised nearly a million dollars for literacy this fall," Mayor Grimsby said.

"Oh, man, we lost the prize too," I say. "I can't show my face at school again."

"That's what your mother was afraid of," a male voice says.

Paz is standing over us, wearing a black leather jacket and combat boots. His hair is squished on one side as if he just rolled out of bed.

"What are you doing here?" I ask, injecting as much contempt into my tone as I can. Paz and I haven't really spoken since he scared Joey off, and while that turned out to be for the best, I still wish he'd stop meddling in my life.

"Your mom asked me to pick you up here and take

you to class," he says. "And don't give me attitude, because getting up early to visit Dumpfield isn't my idea of a good time."

"I do not need a bodyguard."

Paz crosses his arms. "You might, actually. This vacation was a big deal for a lot of miserable students. Some might want to show you how pissed off they are."

The attitude drains out of me pretty fast. "Well, maybe I should stay home for a couple of days."

"Not an option," he says. "Your mother's wish is my command, Shorty. So grab your things and let's get going."

"Wait," Izzy says, leaping to her feet. She digs a hairbrush and clips out of her bag and starts putting up my hair. "Rachel, get the rest of the stuff."

"Izzy, what are you doing?" I ask. "It doesn't matter how I look if I'm going to be torn limb from limb."

Rachel pulls out Izzy's mother's rabbit fur bomber jacket, a floppy hat, and sunglasses.

"Now, if you could just add a couple of inches to her legs," Paz says.

Izzy dangles a pair of steep platform shoes. "Done."

After Paz sends the girls on ahead, I ask, "Is it really going to be that bad?"

"Probably not," he says, pulling the hat over my face. "But if I have to take out a couple of Dunfield dweebs, I'm ready."

He reaches for my coffee, and I don't even complain as he chugs it. What's a four-dollar macchiato between in-laws?

* * *

"You look like a 'ho," Paz says amiably, as we turn the last corner and Dunfield comes into view.

"No risk of my *acting* like one, with you around."

He snorts. "I talked to Carella, that's all. If a guy on my crew has his mitts all over you, I feel responsible for making sure he isn't getting out of line. No one is going to disrespect my family."

"If Joey's mitts were on me—and that really isn't any of your business—it was just as much my doing as his. He was always a gentleman in person, Paz. He only dissed me in print."

"That was just showing off. Guys are idiots, remember?"

"Now you're taking his side?"

"I'm just saying that when the column started you weren't seeing each other, and by the time you were, the tone was already set."

What is wrong with the world when Paz starts to sound like the voice of reason? "He got a lot worse *after* we started seeing each other," I point out. "And he knew by then that his identity would be revealed, which would make the girl he was writing about a laughingstock."

"Whereas no one was going to laugh at Prince Newshound? I'd kill Grace for making me look like such a sap, and I'm a sensitive guy—practically a feminist."

I fight the urge to return his grin. "I don't want to talk about Joey. We're over."

"Give him a while to cool off, and I bet he'll accept your apology."

"*My* apology!" I look at him and find the grin has expanded. "That will *never* happen."

"'Over' doesn't always stay that way," Paz says. "I'll

have another talk with him."

"Don't you dare!"

He offers me his leather-clad arm as we approach the main staircase at Dunfield. As usual, the stairs are lined with students who can't bear to enter until the last possible moment. Some of them are smoking openly, although it's against the rules.

"Isn't that her?" someone mutters.

One guy steps forward and says, "Luisa Perez?"

Paz stops walking. He is several inches shorter than the thug, but there's no question, he has presence. "Who wants to know?"

And that's all it takes. The guy fades back into the crowd, and we continue up the stairs. Paz turns at the top to give everyone a last look and remind them that I have friends with muscle.

After he delivers me to homeroom, however, I'm on my own.

I never thought a summons to the principal's office could be a welcome reprieve, but today it is. I take my backpack with me in the hopes that I don't have to return to class. Being expelled would be a reprieve too.

Clattering toward the principal's office on Izzy's platforms, I replace my hat and shades, but the few students in the hall seem to have X-ray vision, because heads swivel as I pass. The Luisa Perez who wanted to be noticed was a fool.

"Good morning, Luisa," Mrs. Alvarez says, directing me to a seat. "Hat and glasses, please."

I sweep them off and get straight to the point. "I'm sorry about what happened, Mrs. Alvarez."

She gets straight to the point, too. "What are you going to do about it?"

"Wait it out?" I suggest. "People will forget what happened by next year."

"I mean about Solana. She's taken the brunt of this unfairly, Luisa. I'm sure you realize how difficult it was for her to agree to speak about her experiences."

I hang my head and stare at the gray carpet, worn thin by so many delinquent feet. "I already called her, but she didn't pick up."

"You'll have to be more creative," she says. "And I know how creative you can be." She allows her glasses to slide down her nose and looks over them. "Columnists have to take responsibility for any damage they cause. So I'll see you back here at the same time tomorrow with a progress report."

Great, I'm becoming a regular, just like my sister.

By 11 a.m. I'm exhausted, and Izzy's shoes are killing me. I walked over to Solana's building and got spurned by the doorman. I returned half an hour later with two expensive cigars for him, which won me the privilege of leaving a box of Donner chocolates and a card full of groveling for Solana. Then I walked to Dan's to catch Grace as she came in for the lunch shift.

"You're blowing off school," she says when she sees me. "Bad Luisa."

All things considered, she's being pretty decent. It must

be kind of nice for her to see *me* in trouble for a change.

"Mrs. Alvarez practically gave me permission," I say, telling her about our meeting. "I want to call Solana from your cell phone in case she'll pick up."

"I already tried," Grace says, sighing. "We're both blacklisted."

"What am I going to do? I have to make it up to her somehow."

Grace pours me a coffee and slides it across the counter. "You're creative. You'll think of something."

I wish people would stop saying that.

Rachel, Izzy, and I regroup just before 1:00. Since the hall monitor made me doff the hat and shades, I enter the cafeteria to glares and hisses.

"Holy hostile," Izzy says, glancing around. "Has it been this bad all day?"

"This is nothing," I reply. "My homeroom class *booed* when I walked in."

"Didn't the teacher stop them?"

"I think she started it."

I fill them in on the rest of my morning, but like everyone else, they're out of good ideas.

Someone walks by and deliberately knocks my water so that it spills into my lap. The ripple of laughter proves that everyone really is watching me.

"This is brutal," Rachel whispers.

It is, but I'm still glad I came back. If I want to graduate, I have no choice but to try to live this down. And as long as no one beats me senseless, I can take the hazing.

"Life was easier when no one except the other ten Luisa Perezes knew my name."

"Nine," Izzy corrects. "The one in my homeroom just announced she'll be using her middle name so as not to be confused with you."

"Ouch," I say. "Add that to my two prank calls last night."

We look up to see Jason Baca and Tyler Milano standing beside us.

"Well, I thought your column rocked," Jason says. "And I'm sorry it got ugly at the gala."

I smile up at him gratefully. "You're the first student to be nice to me today—other than these two."

"I'll be number four," Tyler says. "I enjoyed your column, too. When I designed the Web site for Mr. Sparling I read all of them."

So *that's* why he had copies of the column on his computer. "Thanks, Tyler. I'm sorry I blew it for everyone."

"We'd never have made the top three without 'The Word,'" Tyler says.

I stare at him, realizing that I should have stuck with Mr. Fantastic all along. Tyler might not be my soul mate, but he's a hell of a lot closer to fitting the glass sneaker than Joey is.

As if sensing my thoughts, Tyler adds, "My girlfriend loved your column. But Scoop's totally cracked me up."

Okay, so he's not my prince. But Jason might still be Rachel's. He keeps staring at her when he thinks she won't notice. "She still likes you, Jason," I say. Rachel gives me an indignant look. "Well, you do. And he likes you too. Believe me, there are worse things than parental trouble."

Rachel looks up at Jason and shrugs. "If he does, he can call me—on my cell phone—anytime."

They exchange a smile, and Tyler and Jason walk away.

"At least one of us gets a happy ending," Izzy says.

I point to Mariah approaching with Mac and the Understudies. "Mine is getting more tragic by the second."

"Well, if it isn't the famous Newshound, who left the party with her tail between her legs," Mariah says. "Mac and I worked hard to win that competition, and you ruined it."

I stand to face her. I deserve crap from some people, but not from her. "If it weren't for 'The Word' and my special guest, we wouldn't have raised nearly as much as we did, Mariah. And as for leaving the gala, it might not have happened if you'd kept your big mouth shut."

"I could still call the cops on your sister," she says, pointing out a bruise on her arm the approximate size and shape of Grace's hand.

"Go ahead. But Grace never forgets a grudge."

"The only reason anyone read 'The Turd' was to laugh at you and your loser boyfriend anyway."

At one time I'd have believed that, but not anymore. Somewhere along the line I had gained a little confidence. "Actually, you got a lot out of Newshound's advice. And I want you to know that I'm still here for you."

Behind her, Mac and the Understudies snicker.

She squints at them before jabbing me with a long nail.

I notice it's freshly stenciled and that she has reverted to her old uniform of skanky yoga wear. "I would never— *never*—take advice from you. Especially about relationships. I took another look at your columns last night—"

"I'm touched."

Mariah continues smoothly, "—and I couldn't help but laugh at how Mr. Sensitive played you to get between the sheets. But then, if I were you I'd probably be so grateful someone was willing to sleep with me that I'd have been that gullible too."

At this point Mac intervenes. "You've said your piece, Mariah. Let's go."

"I'll tell you when it's time to go," she says, backing away anyway. "Better stay out of my face, Coco-slut."

"Does this mean I don't get your VIP number?" I call after her.

She offers a string of Spanish expletives that generates a round of applause.

"Put a sock in the whining," Dan says as I plow through my second slice of coconut cream pie. "I pay you to serve, not complain, and there's a customer in your section."

Sighing, I head out front, only to discover there's a mutiny afoot. While Dan distracted me in the kitchen, someone set up foot-high chocolate lettering on table four that reads "SORRY." There's a white rose protruding from the O and dark eyes peering at me over the R's.

My first instinct is to return to the kitchen, but I realize it's better to go over there and explain in no uncertain terms who gets sole custody of the diner. If it were up to me, Joey Carella would never taste another Rodeo Burger.

"What do you want?" I ask.

"A large slice of humble pie?"

"We don't serve that here."

"Sure we do," Dan calls. "But you ate it all."

I glance over my shoulder at him. "Do you mind?"

"Give the boy a chance," he says.

"I don't think so." I turn back to Joey. "All the discount chocolate in the world can't fix what you did to my reputation."

"For the record, I paid full price for the S and the Y," he says. "But anyone with half a brain knows that column was pure entertainment. Have guys come around today looking for a good time?"

"Right now, no one would touch me with the ten-foot pole Scoop mentioned. I'm not ready to *saddle up* the next mule anyway."

"You made me out to be a spineless—"

"Eunuch. Your word, not mine, by the way. Maybe the guys thought so, but I guarantee you the girls didn't. Do you really think making me look easy is the same thing as making you look sensitive?"

He opens his mouth to reply and closes it again.

"You knew it was bad. That's why you avoided me the whole week before the gala, isn't it?"

"At least I tried to ask you to come with me. You can't say that."

"Maybe not, but at least I portrayed you as a decent, caring guy. You, on the other hand, portrayed me as a slut."

Joey leans forward. "You're exaggerating. If I hinted that things were a little hotter between us than they were, it was to get a rise out of Newshound. That's the dynamic that made our column so popular." He slumps back into his chair. "And maybe I was overcompensating a little for feeling outclassed."

It's a red herring designed to throw me off the trail. "What are you talking about?"

"You didn't notice me for the first two months I came in here because you assumed I was a dumb dropout. Meanwhile, all these guys you thought were so much better than me were welcome to hang around. Maybe I talked big in my column to make up for that."

"So you're saying this is my fault because I'm a big fat snob."

"No, I'm just trying to explain." He pushes the chair out for me to sit down, but I ignore it. "In a weird way, I thought the column might even impress you—and make you laugh. I mean, once you got over the spin."

I roll my eyes. "You've got a lot to learn about girls."

"Haven't we all?" Dan calls, elbows propped on the ledge of the pass-through.

"I was planning to ask Mr. Sparling to run a retraction," Joey says.

I perch on the edge of the seat for a moment. "This isn't about my feelings anymore, Joey. It's about Solana. I made her look bad in the press. She's just starting out, and it could hurt her career."

"I know," he says. "But I've got a plan. Get your coat."

I highly doubt he has a good idea. It's probably just

an excuse so we can pick up where we left off. But I'm not forgiving him. Ever. "I can't leave. My shift goes till eleven."

"You're off in ten minutes. I already asked," he says. "Can you really afford not to trust me? What are you going to tell Buzzkill tomorrow?"

Looks like I'm not the only one who got the summons today. "Fine. I'll come with you, but don't think it means anything."

"Should I return the chocolate?"

I turn to Shirley. "Can you wrap this up? Big fat snobs like me need all the calories we can get."

Dan shakes his head. "You sure you want her back, Joe?"

We hover in the alley until a guy in a white uniform beckons us into the back door of Mama Zeta's Jazz Crib. The guy looks familiar, but I can't quite place him.

"You're Paz's sister-in-law, right?" he asks. "I'm his cousin, Ricky. We met at the christening."

I nod. It was pretty clever of Joey to take advantage of this connection, but I only hate him about five percent less for it. If it works, that could drop another twenty, but still nowhere near reunion range.

"I could get fired for this," Ricky says, leading us into the cavernous room and pointing out a table, where we grab a seat. "So don't order any booze, and don't cause any trouble."

"We won't." I hop up to give Ricky a hug.

He pushes me back into the chair. "And don't draw

attention to yourself."

"Quiet as mice," I say.

Joey shushes me as Solana steps into the spotlight.

Joey is already outside when the bouncer pushes me out of the club.

"You're lucky Solana wouldn't let me call the cops," the bouncer says, giving me one last shove.

"What happened?" Joey asks as we walk to the train station. "You were gone so long I came to look for you, and then I got the boot."

I snuck backstage and into Solana's tiny dressing room before intermission, just as Joey had planned. But Solana didn't even let me apologize before laying into me about everything that's happened. Mrs. Alvarez told her that a reporter was trying to dig up some dirt about her years at Dunfield, and apparently there is dirt to find.

"She *cried*," I tell Joey. "So then I cried. It was awful. She said she wished she'd never trusted me and her reputation is ruined."

"That's a little harsh. Your running off the stage didn't ruin her rep—*her* running off the stage did that."

"Yeah, but Grace and I talked her into sharing the story of her learning disability. She got rattled when I took off."

"We'll think of something to fix this." Joey walks in silence for a while before adding, "I understand what you mean about your reputation, and I want to apologize again for what Scoop said."

I look up at him and he self-corrects. "I mean what *I* said as Scoop. I take full responsibility, and I'll write that retraction tomorrow."

"Don't bother," I say wearily. "It seems stupid to get so worked up about what people think of me, given Solana's situation."

If a few Dunfield losers think I have a more exciting life than I do, it's not the end of the world. Until recently I was so average I was practically invisible.

"Does this mean we still have a chance to make things right between us?" he asks.

"I don't even want to think about it until I've figured how to make things right for Solana."

It's not an absolute no, so he wraps his arm around me tentatively. I don't shrug it off. Someone who feels as horrible as I do right now deserves a little comfort.

"So how do you want to do this?" Joey asks. "Should we warm up first or just get straight to it?"

I roll over on his bed and stare up at the ceiling. "I'm not sure. I haven't done it before."

"Neither have I. But how hard can it be? We should just follow our instincts."

"If you want my opinion, you should talk less and write more," a third voice says. Joey's father wheels up behind him and looks at the computer screen. "You haven't even started yet. I put a roast in the oven when you asked if Luisa could stay for dinner, and I'd like to serve it today."

"It won't take that long, Mr. Carella," I say, sitting up. "We've got some good ideas. We just need to get them down."

"So get them down already," he says, shaking his head. "You two had plenty to say when you were writing *at* each other instead of *with* each other."

"This has to be just right," Joey says. "We're trying to grab the attention of the *Tribune*'s city editor."

"Trying too hard to get noticed is what got you into trouble before," his father says. "Tell the truth simply and well, and you'll grab all the attention you need."

We have a good story to tell, thanks in part to Grace, who learned a few things about Solana when she worked on her schedule. The problem is figuring out how to tell it together.

"I think it would work better if I typed," I say, getting off the bed.

Mr. Carella intervenes on my behalf. "Let the lady drive, son. It usually works better that way."

Once my fingers touch the keyboard, ideas really start to flow. Joey leans over me and makes suggestions.

"Now that's more like it," Mr. Carella says, reversing his wheelchair toward the door. "Dinner's at six, but don't worry if you're a few minutes late. Pot roast only gets better with age."

Chapter 19

$\mathfrak{Chicago}$ $\mathfrak{Tribune}$

FULL OF SOUL

By Joey Carella and Luisa Perez

Recent articles about the Chicago High School Literary Challenge billed Solana G.'s untimely departure from the final gala as a cheap publicity stunt. This is absolutely untrue, and it's time to set the record straight.

At the request of Colonel Dunfield High student, Luisa Perez, Ms. G. kindly agreed to perform a song from her first album, "Exiled," at the gala. The song describes her unhappiness at Dunfield, where Ms. G. faced academic challenges. Yielding to pressure, she finally agreed to talk about her personal experience, in the hope of helping others.

It should have been an amazing event, but it was

virtually ruined by two genuine divas, neither of them Ms. G. A battle of the sexes that began in a Dunfield column spilled onto the stage and turned the gala into a farce.

When the tone changed, Ms G. felt uncomfortable putting herself on the line by sharing her story. No one should blame her for that. It takes a huge amount of courage even in the best circumstances to talk about personal challenges in public.

As the columnists in question, we take full responsibility for what happened. We're apologizing privately to many of the people we let down, but Ms. G. deserves a public apology.

Far from being a diva, at the age of only 22, Ms. G. is already a role model for youth. Six months ago she established the Maria Gomez Drop-in Center (MGDC) in memory of her mother. The MGDC offers children of low-income families a chance to learn about music. Open after school and on weekends, the center has a full range of musical instruments and volunteer instructors to guide hands-on training.

Launched with the proceeds of Ms G.'s first album, the center has already earned high praise from the community.

"The MGDC is proving how quickly a child's life can change when he finds something to care about," says Ms. Betty Willis, a social worker with the city for 35 years.

Eleven-year-old James Furlong agrees. His fascination with the guitar has kept him out of the gangs that some youths his age have already joined. "I'd rather practice," he says simply.

Ms. G. drops by as often as she can to teach piano or simply jam with the young visitors.

"I love Solana," says Jasmine Jacks, a budding singer at age 10. "She sounds like an angel."

"She is an angel," her grandmother adds. "And no one had better say otherwise."

If you want to argue with Grandma Jacks, do it after you check out the MGDC. It will push the word "diva" right out of your mind and make you reach for your wallet to donate.

The *Tribune* article is mounted on the wall at Mama Zeta's, where we've gathered for the all-ages benefit concert Solana and Grace scrambled to organize after our article came out four days ago. Solana and several other local acts will perform, with proceeds to be split between the drop-in center and the Literacy Challenge Fund in Colonel Dunfield's name. Judging from the turnout, the event will be a huge success. It's too late to win the contest, unfortunately, but I'm happy to be part of something so positive. The past week has taught me a thing or two about priorities.

Joey and I are drinking virgin Cosmopolitans sent over by "the Dispatcher," the nickname of the bouncer who threw us out last week.

"Half of Dunfield is here," Rachel says, joining us with Jason. I notice they are holding hands.

"Turnbull and Warwick students are still lined up

outside," Izzy says. "It's nice to be on the VIP list."

Rachel looks over my shoulder. "Lu, your mother's chatting with the mayor. Anything we should know?"

I turn and see that Joey's father is also involved in the conversation. "They're probably apologizing for us in case we didn't do it thoroughly enough. Grace caused a lot of trouble in her day, but she never caught the attention of the mayor."

"That's a competition you didn't need to win," Mr. Sparling says, joining us. He introduces us to Mrs. Sparling, a math teacher at Warwick. She's surprisingly normal-looking, with a blond bob and cool jeans. "Could I talk to my columnists for a second?"

Izzy and Rachel start quizzing Mrs. Sparling, leaving us with Mr. Sparling.

"I'm not going to dwell on how disappointed I was over your behavior at the gala," he says, although that's exactly what he's done for the past week. "It certainly didn't help that you skipped my final classes, Luisa."

"I only missed a couple," I protest. "I had a note." It was actually written by Grace. What good is having an expert forger in the family if you don't take advantage of it? My hope is that by the time we come back from the holiday the worst of this will have blown over. "Hey," I say, turning to Joey. "Your remedial work for Mr. Sparling . . . was that the column?"

"Among other assignments," Mr. Sparling answers for him. "But I'm glad Joey has turned his act around this year. Unlike some people." He squints in Mac Landis's direction. "Anyway, I've been thinking about 'The Word,' and while you two messed up, I don't see why the students who enjoy it should have to pay. So I've decided to run it again in the new year."

"Really?" Joey asks, sounding excited.

"Really," I say, noticeably less excited.

"Obviously it won't be anonymous anymore, and if you say the wrong thing, well, it won't be pretty," Mr. Sparling says, smirking.

"Keith," Mrs. Sparling admonishes, "don't pick on the kids."

"You should try picking on *your* students," he says. "Mine came in first place. For a while, anyway." He frowns at us and continues, "Now, I don't have the time to study every column for the nuance that could get your butts kicked—either by each other or by your classmates. So I propose that you both officially join the *Bulletin* staff where you'll review and edit each other's columns pre-publication."

"How will it represent my point of view if he's edited it?" I ask.

"Figure it out," he says. "You'll both have to learn how to be more objective and to take criticism. It's a good exercise for anyone thinking of becoming a columnist."

"Well, *I'm* not," I mutter.

"You might change your mind when you finish sulking," Mr. Sparling says.

"Keith."

"Yes, dear, I'll stop picking on the kids. Luisa and Joey, you talk about it. I think you could have fun and you obviously wouldn't mind spending the extra time together."

Mrs. Sparling takes her husband by the arm and drags him off to their seats.

"What do you think?" I ask Joey.

"I think we should do it," he says. "What have we got to lose?"

How about each other? We're barely back together, and working as a team puts pressure on any relationship. Still, this will probably be a far better test of whether Joey and I are meant for each other than my first experiment. "Let's give it a try."

"Whatever you two are trying, it had better be G-rated," Paz says, joining us with Grace, Dan, and my mother.

"Didn't you promise not to interfere anymore, Paz?" I ask.

"That doesn't sound like a promise I'd make," he says. "But I'll give you a break tonight because we're celebrating: Gracie got a new job." He kisses her cheek and she doesn't object. "Tell them about it."

Grace waits a moment for the group to quiet down and announces: "I'm going to be Solana's assistant. Just part-time, to start. I'll be holding down the fort while she's traveling."

"It's because she did a great job helping to organize this gig," Paz adds.

Mom is beaming from ear to ear. "I'm so proud, Grace. Now, tell your sister about your other plan."

This time, Grace is less exuberant. "I'm going back to school."

"Dunfield?" I ask, trying to keep the horror out of my voice. That would mean we'd be doing junior year together, and as vast as the school is, it's not big enough for both of us.

"Yeah," Grace says. "I asked Buzzkill to put us in the same class."

I swallow hard. "That's great."

Paz squeezes Grace's shoulder. "I'm thinking of joining you. It sounds like fun."

They watch me squirm for another five seconds before cracking up. "Gotcha!" Grace says. "I'll never cross Dumpfield's threshold until Keira's parent-teacher night."

"Grace is going to work with Solana's tutor and take correspondence courses," my mother explains.

I reach out to hug Grace, and she holds up her hands. "No sibling PDA's."

"Now, Gracie," Paz says. "Let's try to get along with Lu. We're all going to be living together soon."

This time I don't get taken in as readily. "There is no way Mom would crowd another adult into that apartment." I turn to her anxiously. "Would you?"

Grace answers for her. "There's plenty of space in the living room even if we have another kid."

If my mom is in on this joke she's doing a good job of acting stunned. "I think we'd better talk about this at home."

"Gotcha!" Grace repeats. "Keira and I are actually moving in with Paz again. You get your room back, Lu."

I heave a sigh of relief. "So the groveling finally worked, Spaz."

"I think it was my promotion that sealed the deal. I'll be working days, which means I can look after Keira at night while Grace studies."

"Congratulations," my mother says, sounding a little hesitant.

Paz drops his act and reassures her. "We're going to make it work this time. I promise."

Mom hugs Paz, looking happier than I've seen her in a long time. After nearly four years in production, it looks like the Spaz Show has finally earned decent ratings.

The spotlight dances off Solana's copper-colored camisole and black satin pants as she stands at the microphone. "Good evening and welcome. I'm Solana G., and anyone who attended the Literacy Challenge gala will understand why I wanted to make my own introductions tonight." She looks down at me in the front row and winks. Joey and I sink a little lower, and there are a few jeers behind us.

"We've raised a lot of money tonight, and half of it will go to the Literacy Challenge on behalf of Colonel Dunfield," Solana continues. "It's a cause that's near and dear to my heart."

She takes a deep breath and launches into the speech we wrote together a few weeks ago. When she's done, the audience springs to its feet, applauding. Solana smiles, tears shining in her eyes.

"I had some help with the speech," she says, directing the spotlight onto me. "That's Luisa Perez, a Dunfield student who has a real way with words. She and the guy beside her, Joey Carella, attracted a lot of attention to the Literacy Challenge with their syndicated column—a fact people forgot after the gala." She waits until the next round of applause subsides before adding, "I have a surprise for Joey and Lu that's going to do wonders for *their* reputations."

Mayor Grimsby joins Solana on the stage. He begins by acknowledging the great work Solana and Grace did in organizing tonight's fund-raiser and says that proceeds have given a huge boost to the Literacy Challenge Fund—even though the drive has officially ended. Looking down at Joey and me, he says, "You found a creative way to fix the damage you caused, and I tip my hat to you both. I also tip my hat to a school that's turned its rep around this year. Since Dunfield has surpassed Turnbull's tally by nearly ten thousand dollars, I feel I have no choice but to let your school take a month-long holiday as well."

This takes a few moments to sink in, but then Dunfield students leap to their feet to cheer, whistle, and stomp. The mayor covers his ears and flees.

When the commotion dies down, the first band takes the stage and performs its single, a song I've heard often lately. It's called "Fated." From what I can tell, it's about two people destined to be together in spite of everything.

"Remember how you showed up on my bus that day?" I whisper to Joey. "Maybe it was fate."

He laughs. "Actually, it was careful planning. I figured out your work schedule and guessed which bus you'd be on. It took me three tries till I got it right."

I think about all the times I "saved" the seat beside me for my FB at school assemblies. He found me on the bus.

"I persisted even when you weren't that friendly," he reminds me. "I think you make your own fate."

A thump on the back of my chair prevents further discussion.

"Some of us are trying to hear the band," Mrs. Alvarez says. "Do I have to separate you two?"

During intermission, Mariah approaches, surrounded by Mac, the Understudies, and a handful of basketball players. She hasn't made a move on her own since she got here and saw Grace circulating. Grace can't do much because she's on duty, but she makes idle lunges at Mariah now and then just to see her jump.

"Great news about the vacation," Mac says, shaking Joey's hand. "No hard feelings?"

Of course there are hard feelings, but before I can elaborate, Joey says, "It's cool." It's so not cool. Scoop and Newshound are never going to agree on that one.

"I really liked Scoop's column," Mac says. "Show me a guy who doesn't boost his image when he has a chance."

Mac and Joey laugh, causing me to roll my eyes at Rachel and Izzy. "Witness the bonding of the North American male. Here's a subject for my next column."

Mac turns to me. "Newshound was kind of weak, but you pulled it together with the *Tribune* article."

Mariah steps forward, unable to contain herself another second. "Excuse me, but this waste of oxygen was only fixing what she screwed up in the first place."

"Excuse me," another voice echoes. "I don't like your tone, Maria. Or your attire."

It's Principal Alvarez, and she's giving Mariah's micromini, fishnets, and skimpy tank top a disapproving once-over.

"We're not on school property," Mariah says.

"Quite right," Mrs. Alvarez concedes. "If you want to look like that on your own time, I suppose it's your right."

"Exactly," Mariah says. "Since you're here, Mrs. A., I want to say that I feel my leadership in the fund-raising hasn't gotten the attention it deserves."

Mrs. Alvarez plays along. "No?"

"Dunfield students would never have supported the idiot challenge without me."

"The idiot challenge?"

Mariah shrugs. "Idiot, illiterate . . . it's the same thing."

Mrs. Alvarez purses her lips. "I see. Well, I didn't actually see you doing much to promote the cause, Maria. As far as I could tell, you mainly promoted yourself. That's not my idea of what leadership is all about." She turns to Mac. "Mr. Landis, on the other hand, did offer leadership to the male students, and that's why I've decided to give the boys an extra three days off at spring break."

Mariah puts her hand on her bare hip. "You can't be serious."

"I generally am, Maria. I promised to reward the team that impressed me, and the gentlemen did. The same can't be said for the ladies." Mrs. Alvarez's lip curls over the last word, and she eyes Mariah's belly ring. "Now, if you'll excuse me."

Mariah gives the one-fingered salute to Mrs. A.'s back as she leaves. "See if I thank Buzzkill when I win the YouTube award. My video was top-rated this week."

"I haven't seen it," I say. "But I heard it was killing in the comedy category. Are you branching out, Mariah?"

"Comedy?" She gives me a sharp look. "You're lying, Coconut."

Joey looks at his new buddy. "Landis, could you ask your girl not to call my girl 'Coconut' anymore?"

Mac shakes his head and pulls Joey away to join the basketball team. "We were over a long time ago, Carella."

Mariah screeches after Mac, "Excuse me? *I* decide when we're over." He doesn't respond, so she adds, "We're over. Do you hear me?" Still no response. She turns to the Understudies and says, "Let's go. I saw some reporters earlier."

Understudy One shakes her head. "We'll catch up with you later."

Mariah snaps her fingers and gestures to them to heel. "Now."

"Sorry, we're hanging with Lu," Understudy Two says.

Mariah's eyes jump from one Understudy to the other. Beneath the sparkly bronzer, her face is blotching. "You're choosing the Coconut over *me*?"

Understudy One shrugs. "She knows Solana G."

Glancing at Mariah's leg warmers, Understudy Two titters. "Besides, the dancing thing is getting old."

Mariah draws back her arm to swing, but the Dispatcher materializes and restrains her. He looks at me and says, "Is she bothering you?"

"Only for the past ten years," I say.

He yanks her backward. "It sounds like someone needs etiquette lessons."

Mariah puts up a fight, so the Dispatcher picks her up and carries her to the door. "Do you know who I am?" she screams. "I was on *The Right Moves.*"

"And thus Persephone returned to rule the under-world," Izzy says gleefully.

I smile, remembering the class in which I imagined staging a revolt against Mariah and Mac. What seemed so farfetched in September has nearly come to pass.

> *The battle raged for days, and when the dust finally cleared, the Dancers and the Jocks surrendered to the Mighty Trio. Peace descended on the newly christened Newshound High, and an era of serenity began, as the Goddess of Uniqueness, Luisa, ruled the heavens alongside Joey, God of the Good Guys, and Izzy and Rachel, whose goddess powers continued to grow daily.*
>
> *With Mariah and her followers banished, Luisa freed Mac and his boys from perpetual basketball and allowed them to wander freely, trusting them to remember their loyalties.*
>
> *And so it is that everyone lives in perfect harmony at Newshound High.*
>
> *Meanwhile, demons and spirits revolt in the underworld over Hades' decision to welcome Mariah into their realm. The bounty on her head is so high that—*

Rachel snaps her fingers in front of my face. "Wake up. Solana's on in five minutes."

I head back to my seat, only to find Mac Landis loitering beside it.

"Do you mind if I sit down?" he asks, motioning to Joey's empty seat.

"Yeah, I do," I say. "That seat's taken."

"Don't be like that, Lu. I'm willing to let bygones be bygones if you are. We should go back to the planetarium sometime."

I stare up at him in disbelief. "You *can't* be asking me out. You just shook my boyfriend's hand."

"Carella's a good guy," Mac says. "But all's fair in love and war, right?"

Joey slides around Mac and into his seat. "Nice try, Landis. But the seat beside Lu Perez is going to be taken for a long time."

They grin at each other, and I watch them, baffled. Something tells me Joey and I will also have plenty to write about for a long time.

As Solana takes the stage, Mac disappears and Joey's arm settles around me. Resting my head on his shoulder, I smile. I may not understand guys, but I intend to enjoy trying.